Demon War

Book 4 of the Demon Cursed Series

SADIE HOBBES

Also by Sadie Hobbes

The Demon Cursed Series
Demon Cursed

Demon Revealed

Demon Heir

Demon War

The Four Kingdoms Series
Order of the Goddess

BOOKS BY R.D. BRADY:

Hominid

The Belial Series (in order)
The Belial Stone

The Belial Library

The Belial Ring

Recruit: A Belial Series Novella

The Belial Children

The Belial Origins

The Belial Search

The Belial Guard

The Belial Warrior

The Belial Plan

The Belial Witches

The Belial War

The Belial Fall

The Belial Sacrifice

The Belial Rebirth Series

The Belial Rebirth

The Belial Spear

The Belial Restored

The Belial Blood

The Belial Angel

The Belial Templar

The A.L.I.V.E. Series

B.E.G.I.N.

A.L.I.V.E.

D.E.A.D.

R.I.S.E.

S.A.V.E.

The H.A.L.T. Series

Into the Cage

Into the Dark

The Steve Kane Series

Runs Deep

Runs Deeper

The Unwelcome Series

Protect

Seek

Proxy

The Nola James Series

Surrender the Fear

Escape the Fear

Tackle the Fear

Return the Fear

The Gates of Artemis Series

The Key of Apollo

The Curse of Hecate

The Return of the Gods

Be sure to sign up for R.D.'s mailing list to be the first to hear when she has a new release!

CHAPTER 1

ADDIE

It's only a matter of weeks before the demon invasion begins. It will be a war between humankind and the demons bent on ruling us. It's the war we'd hoped to avoid, the war that will change everything.

The war we have to win.

According to Vera, we have at best two months. I'd hoped for more time but in my gut, I know she's right. I can feel the threat drawing closer.

But right now, there's a slight reprieve from all the running and the fighting of the last few weeks. So much has happened, it almost seems surreal. I stopped the archangel Michael from killing Vera and my father. He's now resting in a cell underneath the Seraph Force Academy.

And he's slowly becoming human.

That, though, terrifying wasn't the biggest revelation. No, the biggest revelation was that the angels have been working with the demons. They were the reason that the demons had been attacking the humans in ever increasing numbers. And now, as we prepare, we don't know if we'll be fighting only the demons or if the angels will join the fight with them.

It had only been two hours since the fight at the training yard. It felt like it had been years. I'd overseen Michael's transport, reported everything I know to a group of Majors from the Seraph Force, and helped put out what felt like a million fires.

Finally making it back to Graham's, I couldn't resist taking a small moment to sit in the quiet on the side porch.

When I opened my eyes, I saw that Vera had joined me. She, too, had turned her face to the wind, a small smile on her face. The archangel looked like a woman in her seventies, but I'd seen how easy it was for her to transform into her true self: a warrior angel. But she seemed to like the more experienced look she had developed over her years on Earth. She had been living on Earth for the last 100 years or so. She wanted to experience life, to understand what humans were all about.

Her long white hair was pulled back into a braid. Her clothes were still disheveled from her treatment at the hands of her archangel brothers. And now she'd been cut off from most of her family because she'd chosen to side with the humans.

She'd chosen to side with me.

"Where have you been?" I asked, realizing I hadn't seen her since the training yard.

"Thought I'd do a sweep of the surrounding area. See if any angels or demons were hanging about."

"And?"

"All quiet," she said as she settled back against the chair, closing her eyes once more.

I was tempted to let her rest, but I didn't know if I'd get a chance to speak with her again. "What are you going to do now?"

Looking over, Vera raised an eyebrow at me. "What do you mean?"

"There's a war coming. And I don't know where you stand in all of this. I mean, you don't have to be a part of it. You could just—"

Raising one of her hands, Vera stopped me mid-sentence. "Do you actually think I'm going to sit on the sidelines when the demons pour out of one of those portals?"

Smiling, I shrugged. "No, but I figured I should at least give you an out."

Vera gave off one of her cackling laughs. "Well, you did. Now I am going to go and see if I can find me a shower and a change of clothes in this monstrosity of a house. But first, I'm going to go and check on Lucifer. I haven't talked to my brother in a while, and I find myself looking forward to the conversation."

"Can you tell him I'll be down in a minute?" I asked as I stood as well. "I need to go check on Noel, Micah, and Torr."

Vera nodded. "I will. You go on and see those kids of yours. Give them a hug for me."

"I will." The two of us stepped into Graham's home and headed toward the kitchen. As we walked, I felt torn. I wanted to go see my father and make sure he was all right.

But I also needed to make sure that Noel and Micah were okay. They'd been through a lot. D'Angelo's forces had grabbed them and taken them hostage to get me to face Michael. From the glimpse I'd had of them at the training yard, they looked physically okay. But those weren't the wounds I was worried about. I needed to make sure that emotionally they were sound.

I still couldn't believe that D'Angelo had been so underhanded. Actually, I guess I could believe it, but I couldn't believe that the archangel Michael had been so underhanded. He was supposed to be the greatest of the angels. He was supposed to be this beacon of, I don't know, purity and goodness. Instead, he was a jealous, smug jerk who tried to kill me just because I existed.

Losing his grace seemed the least that should happen to the guy, although I knew for an angel, it was a big deal. Part of me wondered how he'd be able to deal with that, and the other part of me really didn't care. The man didn't deserve any of my sympathy, not after what he'd done.

I detoured toward the back of the house and the well-used kitchen. While Graham's parents had liked the pomp and circumstance of the massive dining room, Graham didn't. So when they weren't here, that room went unused. Graham, Franklin, and Mary Elise ate their meals in the kitchen with whoever happened to be around.

In Graham's home, the kitchen was most definitely the heart of the home. The room had large windows overlooking the back of the estate. There was a massive stove flanked by long counters. In the center of the room was a long worktable. And in front of the windows was a wooden table with upholstered chairs.

Fresh flowers softened up the space. These weren't the perfectly designed floral arrangements that most homes in Sterling Peak had. No, these were the flowers Franklin picked from the garden for his wife every day. And to me, those bouquets were worth much more than the elaborate displays.

There was also always something on the stove or in the oven. The kitchen was a warm spot, not just in terms of temperature.

Stepping in, I expected to see Mary or Franklin. They would know what room Lucifer had been taken to. But the room was empty. No scent of fresh bread or anything else. Then I remembered that Franklin and Mary had been in hiding over in Blue Forks.

Footsteps approached the kitchen, and Dr. Jade stepped in from the opposite hall.

Dr. Jade was a short woman whose dark hair was always

pulled back into a bun at the nape of her neck. She had to be close to sixty, but there was no gray in her hair and only a few lines around her eyes to indicate her advanced years.

Appearing lost in thought, she looked up, her eyes widening for a moment as they landed on Vera and me. Then a small smile appeared as she read the question in my eyes. "He's fine. He's resting comfortably. I removed all of the arrows, but it'll take him a little time to recover. Although he assures me it won't take him nearly as long as humans."

Vera shuddered. "Hell stones, a nasty business. It weakens us quickly. It weakened me pretty bad, and I was only exposed to it through my skin. But to have it actually inside of you. Yeah, that'll weaken you for a while, all right."

"I gave him something to help him sleep. But if you'd like to see him . . ." Dr. Jade gestured back down the hall.

"I would," Vera said before I could answer. "I won't disturb him. I'd just like to look in on him, and maybe I'll see if I can stay in there tonight. Let you get some sleep." Vera said looking over at me.

It was on the tip of my tongue to argue with her that I didn't need any sleep. But the mere mention of the word had me fighting back a yawn.

Vera gave me a knowing look and pushed me gently toward the main stairs. "Go find your kids before you fall over. I'll keep an eye on your dad. And he'll sleep through the night, right?" Vera asked, looking at the doctor.

Dr. Jade nodded. "Through the night and hopefully most of the morning."

"Okay. I'll just go see the kids, and then I'll come down and check on him," I said.

"Sure you will," Vera said with a smile.

Casting an eye around for Graham, I headed for the stairs. I didn't see him anywhere.

The front door opened as I was crossing the main floor. Franklin and Mary stepped in. The two of them smiled when they caught sight of me and hurried over to hug me. Then they stepped back, Mary wiping at tears at the edges of her eyes. "You're all right?" she asked.

I nodded. "I'm fine."

"And the kids?" Franklin asked.

"They're good too. I was just going to look for them."

"Have you seen Graham?" Mary asked.

"I think he's still up the academy. He said he'll probably be there for a while." I knew that he had a lot to deal with. D'Angelo was under arrest, or at least would be soon. I wasn't sure if they had actually found him yet.

Plus there were hundreds of soldiers in town and a rather abrupt change in leadership. He would need to take charge and see what kind of a mess D'Angelo had left him.

"I'm going to go make some soup for everybody. It's going to be a long couple of days," Mary said, heading toward the kitchen.

I watched her go with a sense of gratitude. I'd gotten used to there being food in the house from staying with Graham. But I knew what it was like not to have any nearby.

Looking uncertain in front of me, Franklin's gaze shifted around the hall, looking behind me.

"Is something wrong?" I asked.

He shook his head. "No, no, nothing, I just . . . Graham's all right, isn't he?"

The last time Franklin had seen Graham, he'd been under the orders of the archangel. It was as if all of his emotions had been locked away.

Reaching out, I squeezed Franklin's hand. "Yes. He's Graham again."

His shoulders sagged with relief. "Thank goodness."

"And we've got a little time before things get crazy again. At least I think."

He patted my arm. "I'm sure you're right. After all, Michael's locked away, and D'Angelo's on the run. What else could be out there?"

I gave Franklin a nod as I turned for the stairs, but his words sent a chill through me. There couldn't be anything else out there, right?

CHAPTER 2

ABADDON

The cries of the human faded away as the man's head fell forward. His chest heaving, Abaddon stepped back and glared at the pitiful sight. He'd had his people grab a human from Blue Forks. Michael and Uriel had gone quiet, and Abaddon had questions.

He hadn't liked the answers.

With a wave of his hands, two of his guards hurried over from where they'd been standing along the wall. Quickly, they untied the unconscious man and dragged him from the room. A blood trail followed their exit.

He'd gotten a little carried away with his response. He should have held back, if only to get more answers.

"What do you want us to do with him?"

Abaddon grunted. "If he survives, take him to the camps."

"And if he doesn't?"

The question brought a smile to Abaddon's lips. "Then take him to the camps."

Even death wasn't an escape from Hell.

But it would take time for the man to heal, and Abaddon didn't have that kind of time. He needed every possible soldier to be within his ranks, and every soul down in Hell played a role in that.

The man who was dragged from the room wasn't much right now, but with Abaddon's aid, he could turn into a soldier, or at the very least be the reason someone else turned.

He walked over to the small table on the side of the room. Rounded archways lined the room, providing an unobstructed view of Hell. A dark hazy sky above a barren, dry landscape. This had not been the plan when he fell. He barely remembered those days, but he did remember how it had felt the first time he'd stepped on Earth.

That had truly been heaven.

And after that one taste, he'd needed more. Nothing else mattered, certainly not his duties. Hell, in many ways, wasn't that different from Heaven. He was still stuck.

Pouring himself a long drink, he stared out over the city of Jabal. Michael had been defeated. His ticket out of this cruel existence was gone.

He crushed the glass in his hand. Shards dropped to the ground, some cutting into his skin. He ignored the pain. It was small compared to the pain of his everyday existence.

Uriel was supposed to keep Michael in line. But that was the problem with angels. They all thought they knew everything. *Much like I did, so long ago.*

The moment he'd seen her, Abaddon had known that Addie was going to be a problem. The angels were focused on Lucifer as the issue, but Abaddon had known that Lucifer's power had weakened during his years in Hell. He had softened.

But his daughter, she was a different story. Strength radiated off her. She was lit with a glorious purpose from within. There was a core that burned bright within that one. It was a power, a purpose he had not felt for a very long time, not even from the angels. No, between father and daughter, it was the daughter he needed to worry about.

And that daughter had eluded his assassins on more than one occasion. She'd also eluded the assassination attempts of the angels themselves.

Abaddon's gaze stared out over the stark landscape. He watched a herd of the Damned in the distance. Aimless, hopeless, mindless, they would ravage whatever living creature they came across. They had no purpose, no direction.

He did not like to think about how easy it would be to slip into that mindset.

For eons, this had been his home. He'd once enjoyed everything that Heaven had to offer. Heaven was a landscape of unending food, drink, and light.

Abaddon missed the light most of all.

But he'd wanted the freedom. That freedom, though, had come at a cost. Even now, he knew the cost had not been worth it. This was not true freedom. This was a different type of jail cell.

This hellscape, while it allowed him to tap into his violent tendencies, did not offer him a chance to truly live. For that, he needed to go back to the real world.

And that's where the angels had come in.

They were sick of the humans and the favoritism that they had been shown. They were more than happy to help Abaddon bring them to heel.

With Michael now out of the fight, though, Abaddon was worried that the angels might take a step back. But at the same time, the demons' forces had grown so much in such a short time. Perhaps they didn't need the angels for this fight after all.

They *were*, however, going to need a new way in. They were

going to need a way to gather information. And they couldn't simply grab humans every day to get a regular report.

They needed a spy.

"You sent for me?"

Abaddon turned from his rumination and saw one of his newest recruits. It normally took a year to make the transformation from human to demon. Humans had to fight through their conscience and the morals that had been instilled within them to bring out their true violent nature.

This one in front of him had not taken nearly as long. His violent tendencies had been so close to the surface. And his moral compass had long ago disappeared.

He was called Ruth by the other demons because of his ruthless nature whenever he went on a mission. He was a rising star among Abaddon's ranks.

But Abaddon also saw the glimmer of ambition in his eyes.

He was a rising star, it was true. But he was also one that Abaddon would keep a tight leash on to make sure that he didn't find himself stabbed in the back.

"Ruth, come in."

The man stepped inside. He was about six and a half feet tall, and like all of the demons, heavily muscled. He had a faint green tint to his skin indicative of his newer nature.

"I have a situation that I think you would be well suited for. I need a spy within Sterling Peak. Someone who can keep me up to date on their moves and can identify those who will be easily swayed to our side. Someone who can see what we're doing, or at least see what the benefit could be to them."

Although the plan was to rule the humans, there would be a select few who would have elevated positions to help in that endeavor. Ruling an entire world was a daunting undertaking. He'd need someone to help keep the humans in line. And after being in Hell this long, he knew there were humans that would easily turn their back on their fellow man to make a few coins for themselves.

Ruth smiled. "I know someone who can help us."

CHAPTER 3

ADDIE

Reaching the bottom of the stairs, I stopped and stared up. Had they added some stairs while I was away? I trekked my way up to the second floor, my thighs protesting more activity. Vera was right. I really needed some sleep.

As I reached the landing, I realized I wasn't sure where exactly the kids were. But I was hoping they were in the room that we'd shared when we had stayed with Graham after the demon attack in Blue Forks.

I shook my head, realizing that had been so long ago. I'd had to go on the run after the archangel had changed Graham. God, it had been months since I'd been in this house. It felt like it had been forever, and somehow, at the same time, it felt like I'd been here yesterday.

By the time I reached the hallway that led to the guest rooms, my legs felt heavy. *Please let them be here.* If they weren't, I might need a power nap before I had the energy to go searching for them. A door opened at the end of the hall. A slim man with light brown skin bustled out, his eyes downcast as he mumbled to himself.

"Marcus?" I asked.

Looking up, Marcus Jeffries's light-brown eyes widened. He hurried over to me. "Addie. How are you?"

"Good. I was coming to check on the kids."

Marcus nodded. "Yes, yes. Of course."

"Where are you heading?"

"Well, I tried going to go see if I could talk to your father, but Dr. Jade explained that he needed his rest. So I thought I'd head up to the academy and see if I could get Michael to speak. I wanted to stop in my office and check my notes before I spoke with him, though." Marcus waved vaguely down the hall.

I arched an eyebrow at the statement. "You think Michael's going to talk to you?"

Marcus shrugged. "Well, he's pretty arrogant. And I've found that arrogant people like having people listen to them, so I thought I'd see if he wanted to explain what his plans were or what the demon's plans were. Who knows? Maybe he'll let something slip."

It was information that we needed. I felt bad that I wasn't doing more. I straightened my shoulders with a nod. "Let me go and check on the kids, and then I'll go with you."

Marcus shook his head. "Oh, absolutely not," he said, his tone firm.

I frowned. "What? Why not?"

"Addie, you've done the heavy lifting. Let me do a little bit. Take a moment, enjoy the time with the kids. You've been on the run for months now. It's okay to take a short break. And besides you look like you need a good night's sleep."

Apparently, everybody thought that. Part of me shuddered at the idea of looking in a mirror.

Marcus continued. "Besides, you might elicit an emotional response from Michael that would get in the way of him answering questions."

I couldn't deny that was true. Michael and I weren't exactly on the best of terms being I defeated him in battle and I was part of the reason why he probably lost his grace.

I really wasn't sure how all of that worked. But nevertheless, Marcus was right—Michael was not one of my biggest fans. And the feeling was most definitely mutual.

"Okay. But even though he's not fully an archangel anymore, he's still dangerous."

"Oh, I have no plans on getting near the man. I will make sure that he is in a cell and that there are Rangers within yelling distance."

"Good."

Marcus headed down the stairs, and I watched him go, wondering at the professor. He was the reason that I'd gotten to know Graham and all of the others. What if he hadn't decided to walk from the ship that day? Would everything else that followed have actually happened? Would the kids and I have been on our own when the demons came looking for us?

The idea of it made me shudder, and I quickly shoved the thought away. The world of what-ifs was not a good place to live.

I turned back down the hall and continued on my way to the kids' room. The door was slightly ajar, and I gently pushed it open. Then I stopped, leaning against the door frame for a moment.

Noel and Micah lay on the bed inside, their eyes closed. My guess was they'd been waiting for me and had fallen asleep. They probably hadn't gotten much last night after they'd been grabbed.

They weren't alone, though. Their guardian, a creature that

looked like a pale-blue lion with wings, lay on the ground next to the bed, snoring away.

Contentment rolled through me. They were safe. The fact that they had fallen asleep confirmed it.

My heart filled at the sight of them. Meeting them had been the best part of this world. They had grounded me in a way that made me feel like I belonged.

We'd met when the three of us were in the same place: alone and looking for a place to belong. And we had found it in each other.

Sliding off my boots, I walked into the room. Careful not to disturb either of them, I crawled into the bed between them. Reaching down toward the end of the bed, I pulled a blanket over the three of us. Snuggling under the blankets I let out a sigh, my whole body sinking into the mattress.

It was almost perfect. All that was missing was Torr, who was no doubt still downstairs with Lucifer. But that was all right. I knew he'd find us. He was part of this family too.

I took Noel's hand as Micah curled into my side. Then I closed my eyes and let sleep take me.

CHAPTER 4

GRAHAM

Graham trudged down the hill toward his home. His head ached from all of the conversations he'd had over the last few hours. The Seraph Force was in disarray after the spectacle on the training field.

D'Angelo's duplicitous actions had only further fractured the troops. He'd warped their brains with his distorted views, and Graham knew that some of the Rangers remained loyal to him.

They believed in the changes he was attempting to make: the exile or diminishment of the Demon Cursed within society. Luckily that was only a small portion of the Seraph Force, but it was going to take a while to weed them out.

But with a war coming, Graham didn't have a lot of extra resources to direct to doing the weeding. He was going to have to make the time, however. He couldn't risk a rebellion at a critical moment. He hated to think that his own people might work against them during war, but the thought was there.

Right now, what he needed more than anything was information. He needed to know what D'Angelo promised them. He wasn't even sure if D'Angelo had even told them about his arrangement with Michael.

God, what a little weasel.

He'd never liked D'Angelo. The man had been too smooth, too fake in all of his interactions. The rest of the Angel Blessed seemed to eat it up and look at him like a favored son.

But then, of course, a lot of them held the same views about the Demon Cursed.

And yet it was a Demon Cursed who'd saved them all from the demon invasion just months earlier. And a Demon Cursed who'd taken on and defeated Michael.

He smiled, picturing Addie as she fought the archangel. She'd been a sight to behold. More than a few of his Rangers had asked about her.

Graham still wasn't sure how to explain her. Not to himself and not to them.

How did he explain that she was the daughter of Lucifer and yet also a force of good? How did he explain that the archangel Michael wanted her dead because she would be the only one who would be able to help the humans in the war to come?

He'd tried, but he wasn't sure if he'd done a good enough job. The prejudice against the Demon Cursed went so deep. His words alone weren't going to be enough to sway some.

But some who'd seen what Addie had done and who knew who D'Angelo was, believed what he was saying. For others, seeing what Addie had done only confirmed that she was a danger to them.

And Graham really wasn't sure how to counter that kind of thought process.

He could also tell more than a few understood that Addie meant more to him than just a resource in war. But he didn't care if they saw that. She *was* more than important to him.

She was everything to him.

When she had come into his world, everything had shifted. Even before he'd known who she was, there was something about her that had pulled at him, that had always caught his gaze whenever she appeared in his orbit.

And now he knew that he would risk his life to keep her safe.

He smiled at the idea. She didn't need a lot of help in that department, but he'd be damned if he wasn't the one who was going to provide it when she did.

Making his way around to the kitchen entrance, he reached for the door handle, but the door was pulled open before he could grasp the knob.

For a moment, Franklin seemed like he was frozen in place before rushing out and hugging him tight. Graham smiled, feeling the tremor run through his true father, the one who'd raised him even though there was no biological link between the two.

Pulling back, Franklin stared at him, looking him over. "You're all right? You're not hurt?"

"I'm fine. How about you?"

Waving away the words, Franklin said, "We were completely safe. We weren't near anything. You and Addie, you were the ones in the thick of it."

"How is she? Have you seen her?" Graham asked.

Franklin led him down the hall. "Yes. She headed up to check on the kids a while ago. I went to go check on them, to see if they wanted anything to eat, and the three of them were sound asleep."

Graham nodded. He'd had Rangers stationed around the house to let him know if there were any problems. They would have told him if there had been an incursion of any kind.

Although Graham wasn't sure what exactly kind of incursion

he was worried about: angel or demon. At the moment, they seemed to have a problem with both. "I should go—"

Franklin latched onto his arm and pulled him toward the kitchen. "You should come and have something to eat."

Graham let Franklin pull him into the kitchen. Mary let out a happy cry as she caught sight of him. Hurrying across the room, she wrapped her arms around him.

Hugging her back, Graham rested his head on her shoulder. As a kid, he remembered when he'd been so happy that his head had reached her shoulder. He felt like it had taken forever to reach that point. And now he towered over her.

Leaning back but keeping her arms around him, Mary looked up at him. She didn't ask any questions, just looked into his face. She always had that ability. She could look at him and know how he was feeling. She placed a hand on his cheek. "It's going to be all right." Then she nodded to the table. "Now sit. You need to eat."

Graham shook his head. "No, I need to—"

"You need to eat. You can sit for a few minutes," Mary insisted.

The list of everything that Graham still needed to do rolled through his mind. But instead of rushing off, he found himself heading to the table and sinking into one of the chairs.

Mary walked over to the stove and grabbed a bowl. She ladled soup into it while Franklin grabbed a few rolls and placed them on a plate with some butter.

The two of them arrived at the table at the same time, setting the food down in front of Graham. And while he hadn't been hungry before, the smell of Mary's vegetable soup made his mouth water. He dug in, finishing the bowl and using the bread to sop up the little he couldn't manage with the spoon.

Then he sat back and nodded, patting his stomach. "Thank you. I needed that."

Mary and Franklin had taken seats across from him while he'd eaten. And now the two of them exchanged a glance before they looked over at him.

"What is it?" he asked.

Franklin answered for the two of them. "When we were in Blue Forks, people were wondering what was happening. We need to tell them something. You need to tell us something. What is going on, Graham?"

Graham sat back with sigh. "I'm not entirely sure. It appears that the archangel Michael was somehow working with the demons to allow them through to our world."

Mary let out a gasp. "He betrayed humanity?"

"Michael is not who we were told he was," Graham said, simply not up for the long explanation, although he knew that he would have to give it soon.

He reached over and squeezed Mary's hand. "But we are safe for now. It's going to be a difficult time in the not-too-distant future, though. And you're right, the people of Blue Forks deserve to know. As soon as I have a handle on exactly what's going on and what's coming, I'll make sure that I make an announcement to them to warn them about what's in store for all of us."

"So that they can prepare?" Franklin asked.

The weight of the fight to come pressed down on him. "No. So they can hide."

CHAPTER 5

ADDIE

Light streamed in around the edge of the drapes as I finally opened up my eyes the next morning. The brightness of the light made it clear that it was not early morning but well into the day.

A rustle of material to my left had me turning my head, expecting to see Torr. But instead it was Graham in the chair next to the bed.

The bed itself was empty. I sat up quickly, looking around. Graham, whose eyes were closed, jolted up. "What's wrong? What's the matter?"

"Noel. Micah."

He slunk back into the chair. "It's all right. They just went downstairs to get some breakfast. They slipped out with Torr about an hour ago. I was coming down the hall at the same time and told them I'd wait until you woke up."

I sat back, feeling relieved, even as my body longed to go back to sleep.

I'd been fine for the last few days as long as I kept moving. But apparently stopping was not something I should have done. It was like the need for sleep had been waiting for me to tap into it and now couldn't quite be sated.

Blinking hard and pushing the blankets away, I fought through it. "My father?"

"Jade's already been in to see him this morning. She said he's healing well. Vera stayed with him last night."

I nodded. "That's good. I should—"

"Do nothing. I'm having a meeting with the Seven after lunch. There's nothing to do until then. Why don't you sleep for a little bit longer?"

I narrowed my eyes, studying him. His face was drawn, and there were dark circles under his eyes. "What about you? Have you gotten any sleep?"

He shrugged. "A little," he said before stifling a yawn.

I crossed my arms over my chest. "If you're not sleeping, I'm not sleeping."

Graham sighed and then stood up. He walked over to the bed and sat down on the edge of it. Toeing off his boots, he swung his legs onto the bed and leaned back against the pillows. "Honestly, I could use with a little more, and I'm not needed until the meeting with the Seven as well."

He stretched out next to me, and I could feel his warmth. Part of me thought I should take advantage of the fact that he was finally lying next to me in a real bed.

But the other part of me yearned to go back to sleep.

And Graham looked so exhausted. He wrapped an arm around me, and I snuggled in tight to him. "Sleep, Addie. We have time."

My eyelids closed at his suggestion, and I wrapped my arm around his and let sleep take me again.

CHAPTER 6

When I awoke again, the room was quiet. Graham was gone, but his side of the bed was still warm, which meant I had just missed him.

I sat up, feeling much better than I had earlier in the day. There was no one else in the room with me, but I wasn't worried. Graham would have woken me if something was wrong.

Taking advantage of the solitude, I made my way over to the bathroom and took a shower, washing away the last vestiges of sleep. By the time I was dressed, I was feeling more energized and more like myself.

And more hungry.

As I made my way down to the kitchen, I only had room in my mind to think of food. I was really hungry. From the hall, I could hear the voices of my gang. I stepped in, and Micah caught sight of me first.

He sprinted over to me, a smile bursting across his face, and hugged me tight. "Addie."

Hugging him back, I rested my chin on the top of his head

and breathed in deep. Noel made her way over, and I wrapped an arm around her as well. "Are you guys okay?" I asked.

Noel broke away from me first with a nod. "Yeah, we're good."

"The soldiers didn't hurt you?"

Noel shook her head. "No. In fact, I got the feeling that most of them didn't really like what they were having to do."

As she talked, I looked Noel over for any bruises or injuries. The action didn't go unnoticed. "We're okay, Addie. I promise. And luckily, Mary's been stuffing us to make up for the months that we weren't here."

Mary laughed. "You've all lost too much weight. I intend to put it back on you."

I smiled at the motherly inclination of Mary. And I was glad that the kids were exposed to someone like her. None of us had really had much of a mother figure in our lives.

The thought brought me up short because actually I had. I just didn't remember her.

Over at the kitchen island, Mary was putting a tray together. "Who's that for?" I asked.

"Lucifer," Noel said.

"I'll take it into him. I need to speak with him."

Mary nodded, and I could see that she was relieved not to have to take the tray in. I had to bite back a sigh. Lucifer's reputation preceded him, and it was going to take a long time to get people to realize he was not the devil they'd made him out to be.

Finishing up the tray, Mary pointed at the table. "You can take the tray, but you need to eat first."

Scooting away from me, Micah grabbed me some eggs and cheese and bread and brought it back to the table along with some fruit.

Although I was tempted to put up a fight, my growling stomach dictated otherwise. Besides, I could see the concern on both Noel's and Micah's faces when Mary mentioned Lucifer. So I smiled as I took a seat. "Thanks."

Micah took the seat next to me while Noel sat across from me. "Is your father really the devil?" Micah asked.

Biting into my eggs, I nodded. "Yes. But he's not who people think he is."

Franklin, who'd just walked into the kitchen, overheard the comment. "What do you mean?"

"Well, it turns out him being in Hell was part of a mission."

I explained to them about how the angels had been stirring rebellion in Heaven. And that Lucifer had been put in charge of keeping them in order in Hell so that at the very least, they didn't make their way into the human world.

By the time I was done, Franklin had taken a seat at the table as well. "So, what happened? How did the demons start entering our world?"

It was a struggle to keep in the growl. "Michael. Apparently, he wasn't very happy with humanity. So, whereas before, the demons kept their violence within the boundaries of Hell, Michael gave them a way into our world."

Mary shook her head. "How could he betray us like that?"

"Because the angels aren't beneficent beings. They're soldiers, and kindness is not an attribute that many of them have," I said.

Franklin's eyes widened. I winced, realizing I probably should have softened how I said that. It was a lot of information to take in. And there was a lot more to discuss to make it clear that Lucifer was not the bad guy in all this.

I eyed the tray that Mary had made up for my father. That conversation would have to wait. I didn't want it to get cold. I stood up. "I'm going to go talk to him and see how he's doing." I looked at Noel and Micah. "Do you guys want to come?"

Micah looked nervous, but Noel nodded. "Yes. I'd like to meet him."

She was nervous too, but she was doing a better job at hiding it. Standing up, I grabbed the tray, and the three of us made our way down the hall.

Frowning, I looked at the row of closed doors. I wasn't sure which room Lucifer was in, but apparently Noel knew. She nodded to a door next to Graham's study. "He's in there."

The door opened before we reached it, and Dr. Jade stepped out. Alarm flashed through me. "I thought you came this morning. Is something wrong?"

Dr. Jade smiled. "No, not at all. I just thought I'd come back and see how much he's healed. It really is quite remarkable."

"How long do you think before he's fully healed?" I asked.

"At this rate, he should be fully healed by the end of the day."

I knew that was supposed to be good news, but that meant that he would be going back, and selfishly, I wanted him to stay. "Okay. Thank you for everything."

Dr. Jade flicked a glance over her shoulder and shook her head. "I can't believe I've been tending to Lucifer. He's really not what we've been told, is he?"

"No, he's not," I said, glad that the doctor could see him for who he really was.

She stepped out of the way and waved the three of us in. "Don't visit for too long. He's healing, but he's not fully healed yet, and I don't want anything interfering with that, all right?"

"We won't stay long," Noel promised. But she hesitated, looking at me.

It was clear she wasn't comfortable stepping into the room first, so I went in with the two of them following me.

Vera was nowhere to be seen, but Grunt lay curled up in the corner of the room. He must have been invisible because Dr. Jade had not looked terrified when she'd stepped out. Grunt was a ganta and had come back from Hell with me. He was massive, standing at least five feet tall at the shoulder and looked like a gigantic pale-blue lion with wings.

Grunt wasn't the only visitor Lucifer had. Torr sat in the chair next to the bed. His gaze met mine when I stepped into the room, and he gave me a tentative smile.

I smiled broadly back at him. "Hey there, brother."

"Hey, sis," Torr said softly.

"You didn't know we were related?" I asked.

Torr shook his head. "No. I mean, I knew you were the daughter of Lucifer, but I didn't know I was his son."

"And I'm sorry for that. I should have found you in that camp. I should have made sure that your mother—" Lucifer cut off, shaking his head.

Torr leaned toward him. "You didn't know. They made it look like she had died. It's okay."

Apparently, the two of them had been having some deep conversations this morning. My heart filled at the thought of it.

Lucifer looked over at his son with pride and then over at me. "But I'm glad to hear that the two you found each other. That you became a family."

I placed the tray on the side table next to the bed. "And speaking of family, I'd like to introduce you to Noel and Micah."

Looking at the two of them, Lucifer grinned. "I've heard a great deal about the two of you from everyone."

Inching forward, Micah gave Lucifer a tentative smile. "Are you really the devil?"

Looking Micah straight in the eyes, Lucifer nodded. "Yes. I have been the ruler of Hell for eons."

Micah frowned. "How come you don't have any horns?"

Lucifer's mouth dropped open before his head fell back, and he laughed. "Horns?" he choked out.

"You're always depicted as having horns and a tail and a pitchfork," Micah explained.

Composing himself, Lucifer grinned broadly. "I see. Well, I'm afraid I don't have a tail or horn. I do, however, have a pitchfork, but I only use it for farming."

Micah's smile dropped. "Farming?"

"I have a community over in Hell, and we do a lot of farming," Lucifer explained.

"As a punishment?" Micah asked.

Lucifer chuckled. "No, as a way to make food."

"Oh," Micah said, looking confused.

I wrapped an arm around him. "There are some people in Hell who don't deserve to be there. My father's created a camp for them, and they have to make their own food. There are no stores."

"Oh," Micah said again, but he still looked a little confused.

A glance at Noel showed that she wasn't nearly as intrigued or at least as willing to look intrigued as Micah was. She stood with her arms crossed over her chest.

My father picked up on her reticence as well. "I hear that you are the one who has helped protect Torr and my daughter."

Noel gave an abrupt nod of her chin.

"I'd like to thank you for that. I've heard how strong you are, and I'm glad they found you."

I could see Noel softening a little at his words.

Apparently everything they said about Lucifer wasn't entirely inaccurate. He did seem to know how to read people and to say the things they needed to hear.

But I needed to have a conversation with my father, and that wasn't something that I wanted everyone here for. "All right, why don't you go and see if Mary needs any help with anything? I need to speak with my father."

Torr shook his head. "I'd prefer if I could—"

"Dr. Jade said we shouldn't tire him out. I'll explain everything that you guys need to know as soon as I know it, okay?" I gave Torr a pointed look.

He sighed, standing up. Noel was already stepping toward the door, obviously a little relieved at being out of Lucifer's presence. It was going to take him a while to win her over.

"Okay," Micah said, looking disappointed as he slid off the bed. "But we can come visit later, right?"

"I'd like that," Lucifer said with a twinkle in his eyes.

Micah grinned him.

"And maybe you could bring a chessboard," Lucifer suggested.

"I'll do that," Micah said, slipping out of the room.

As Torr started to step out the door, I nodded toward the other two. "Do me a favor and stay close to them, okay?"

Torr frowned. "Is there a threat I need to know about?"

I shook my head. "No, nothing specific. But until we know exactly when the demons are coming through, I'd just prefer if all of you kept your guard up."

"All right," Torr said.

"You'll come back later, though, right?" Lucifer asked.

Torr turned and gave him a nod. "Yeah, I'll be back," he said softly before he slipped through the door, following Noel.

With a large yawn, Grunt cracked open an eye. I nodded to the door. "Can you go keep an eye on them as well?"

Grunt stretched, his front paws extended, his long nails scraping along the floor. Standing, he headed to the bed and leaned into it. Lucifer patted him on the head. Content with his greeting, Grunt headed to me for the same treatment. "Keep an eye on them and stay invisible. I still have to explain you," I said as I rubbed his side.

He turned his giant head and licked my hand before he padded out the door.

There was a wistful look on my father's face as he looked at the empty doorway. "He's been through so much. I should have been there for him."

I knew it wasn't Grunt he was talking about. "You didn't know he existed. Neither of us did."

"Maybe, but I should have done more."

Taking a seat on the bed, I held his hand. "You can't blame yourself for that. You thought she was dead. Apparently, we both did. And that's because Abaddon made it that way."

Lucifer's eyes narrowed. "I owe him a great deal of pain."

"We both do, and there are some things you need to know. Some things about what's coming."

Titling his head, he studied her for a moment before he spoke. "The angels are working with them."

Surprised floated through me. "You know."

"I guessed after the events in the training yard."

"I saw Uriel down in Hell. He was giving them the stones that allow them to go through the portals."

Lucifer lay back in the bed, shaking his head. "I could never figure out how they got through the portals. I'd heard rumors that they were coming over here, but I couldn't even get over here without my medallion, so I couldn't imagine how they could do it. I knew the heaven stones were the key, but it never occurred to me that angels would actually be helping them, not until I saw Michael in the training yard."

"Well, they are, and we need to figure out a way to stop them."

He was quiet for a moment. "I don't think we're going to be able to."

Fear and uncertainty were in my father's eyes. But there was none in me. In me, there was a cold ball of steeled focus. "We have to. Because if we don't, humanity won't survive this war."

CHAPTER 7

D'ANGELO

D'Angelo paced along the confines of his bedroom. The room was massive, extending thirty feet by fifteen.

And yet D'Angelo felt like the walls were pressing in on him.

Hunter, that idiot, had been caught. And he'd sung like a canary, claiming that D'Angelo had been the one behind the whole debacle in the training yard.

Running a hand through his hair, D'Angelo pictured strangling the man.

While he'd been the one who'd provided the instructions to Hunter, he hadn't actually been the one behind them. That had been Michael. He was simply doing the archangel's bidding. There was nothing wrong with that, was there?

But that wasn't how his actions were being viewed, and now he was under house arrest. Somehow, in one day, he'd gone from being the leader of the Seraph Force to being a prisoner in his own home.

He growled as he pictured Graham's smug face as he escorted him back to his home. He'd known that Graham had wanted to throw him into one of the cells over at the Seraph Academy. Perhaps a cell near Michael.

But the Council had interceded and argued that he should be placed under home confinement until all of the evidence could be gathered.

It was a small blessing. But the Council *should* have been able to get him out of this entirely. They were as much against Graham's rule as he was. They knew that the Demon Cursed needed to be wiped from this world, or at the very least, put in their place.

And Michael was after the same thing.

D'Angelo's stomach growled. He placed a hand on it and cast a glance toward the door. He wanted to go downstairs and get a bite to eat, or better yet, have them bring something up to him.

But his staff had been sent home. Graham didn't trust any of his people around him. And so, if D'Angelo wanted to eat, he'd have to make something for himself. And he had absolutely no idea how to do that.

It was insulting, the idea that D'Angelo would be able to do the work of a Demon Cursed. It was not his place to sully his hands in a kitchen. That was what the Demon Cursed were for.

It wouldn't come to that, though. His mother would arrive in a short while with food. And he didn't care who the Ranger was on duty. They would not be able to say no to her. But evening was upon them, and he wished she would hurry up.

A noise sounded from his balcony. D'Angelo whirled around, his heart racing. The sound came again. Someone was out there. He was on the third floor. His balcony was not easily scaled.

Heart rate ticking up, he took a step toward it, but all grew quiet. Grasping the handle of the door, he squinted into the darkness. Nothing. He let out a breath as he moved to the edge of the balcony and turned his attention back to the source of his anger: Graham Michael.

He'd overheard the Rangers talking about how Graham had sent letters out to all the Seraph Force Academies across the nation, demoting D'Angelo and reinstating Donovan. He wasn't even waiting for the trial.

All his careful plans ruined. He was the one who should have been in charge of this Seraph Force. He was the one who had vision.

Years ago, when Brock had been in charge, the two of them had made plans. They had been good plans. He'd known it was only a matter of time before their plans all came to fruition. The only problem then had been that Brock had been the one in charge and not D'Angelo.

But now things had been placed in the correct order. D'Angelo had been in charge of the Seraph Force. He'd been almost unable to believe that Graham had willingly handed that power over. But then, Graham hadn't exactly been acting like himself.

The angel had done something to him. Whatever it was, it had been to D'Angelo's benefit. And he'd made great use of the short time he had in power. He'd curtailed the abuses of the system by the Demon Cursed. They'd coasted by for far too long. If he'd had just a little more time, he would have cemented his reign and the place of the Demon Cursed in society.

But Graham had ruined all of that.

He pulled his glass back up and put it to his lips, growling when he realized there was nothing left. He turned back to the house.

"You always drank too fast."

Stumbling, D'Angelo stared into the darkness.

The man stood in the shadows. He was huge. D'Angelo hadn't heard him arrive and hadn't seen him when he stepped out onto the balcony. He reached for the sword at his waist.

"There's no need for that. We're old friends, you and I."

D'Angelo didn't know what the man was talking about. He didn't recognize the voice, although there was something familiar in it. But his friends certainly didn't wait for him on balconies. The only one who would even think he was close enough to D'Angelo to take such liberties was Hunter Uriel, and he was too scared of his own shadow to wait in the dark.

"Who are you?" D'Angelo demanded.

The man gave a deep full-throated laugh, although there wasn't much humor in it. "Has it been so long that you've forgotten me? I'm hurt. Really, I am. And here I was looking forward to our reunion."

The man stepped forward. His green skin became clear.

D'Angelo stumbled back. The demon was between him and the door, and the balcony was three stories up. He glanced toward the railing anyway.

As if reading his mind, the demon said, "Oh, I wouldn't do that if I were you. You'd never survive the fall."

Although D'Angelo yanked his sword from its scabbard, he made no move toward the demon. He'd fought a few demons in this time but never on his own, and in those cases, he often let the people he was with do most of the fighting.

The demon smiled. "You always did like to let other people do your fighting, didn't you?"

Staring at the creature, D'Angelo frowned. Something about that smile... "Brock?"

CHAPTER 8

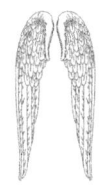

ADDIE

Graham was just coming down the hall as I stepped out of Lucifer's room. My father and I had talked for another ten minutes after the others left, but I could tell that he was tiring. There was so much I wanted to ask him about Michael, about Hell and what was coming, but it seemed like he needed his rest.

A ripple of excitement soared through my chest as Graham's eyes lit up when he caught sight of me. Seeing him striding down the hall toward me made it clear that we had made it through all of the trials of the last few days. We had survived.

Unable to pull my gaze from his, I walked toward him quickly. He opened up his arms. With a last burst of speed, I slipped into them. Warmth, contentment, and a feeling of rightness rolled through me as he wrapped his arms around me, holding me tight.

Breathing in deep, I closed my eyes. We had made it. I looked up into his eyes and saw exactly what I was looking for. Graham lowered his head to mine. My lips tingled in anticipation.

Franklin appeared at the end of the hall. "Oh, excuse me."

Graham and I jumped apart like we'd been caught by a schoolteacher. With a hasty retreat, Franklin disappeared back the way he'd come. Graham gave a nervous laugh, running a hand though his hair. "So, how are you?"

"You just saw me a few hours ago."

"True, but you were sleeping. So how are you?"

"Everyone seems to be asking me that."

Stepping forward, he traced the edge of my cheek with his thumb. "Because everyone's worried. You've been through a lot."

"We all have." I wanted to stay there forever, staring up into his beautiful face, but his words brought reality crashing back down. We had been through a great deal, and we weren't done yet. I took a step back. "And unfortunately, there's still a lot that's coming."

Nodding his head toward his study, he said, "Let's go in here."

After stepping inside, Graham started to close the door when a hand reached out to stop him. Donovan grinned as he slipped into the room. "You two weren't looking for some privacy, were you?"

Graham rolled his eyes. "Of course not. Why on earth would we be looking for that?"

"Good, good," Donovan said as he made his way into the room and took a spot on the couch.

Despite Donovan's easygoing words, I could see the limp in his step and the bruises that still dotted his face.

It was on the tip of my tongue to ask how he was doing, but being I was getting a little sick of everyone asking me, I had the feeling that he probably felt the same. So I gave him a nod. "Good to see you up and about."

"Right back at you. That was some serious airborne acrobatics you managed. I'm guessing all of our training sessions really paid off. You've learned well, young student."

A chuckle burst out of me. "Yes, I wouldn't have been able to do any of it without you."

Donovan puffed out his chest. "As I've been telling everyone."

Walking over, Graham leaned against the edge of the desk. I was too nervous to take a seat, so I just stood over by the windows, casting a glance out them every few seconds. When I realized that I was actually checking the sky to make sure that there were no angels arriving, I forced myself to walk over and sit next to Donovan.

"So catch me up," Donovan said, stretching out his long legs. "What have I missed?"

"Not much," Graham said. "The Seraph Force is a mess. We have a civil war brewing."

"That bad?" I asked.

Graham nodded, his jaw tight. "I'm afraid so. On one side are those individuals happy with D'Angelo's approach and perfectly willing, if not eager, to crack down on the Demon Cursed. On the other side are those that were dead set against it."

"Which side is bigger?" Donovan asked.

"Still getting a read on that. In fact, I was hoping you could use some of your connections to ferret that out for me."

"You mean my charm." Donavan grinned for a moment before it faded. "And yes, I'll look into it immediately. This is no time for our forces to be divided."

"No, it definitely isn't," Graham replied.

The idea of the Seraph Force fighting amongst itself was terrifying. We needed a unified front if we were going to take on the demons. Even with us all standing in solidarity, it was going to be a tough road.

"What about D'Angelo? Any sighting of him?" I asked.

Graham nodded. "Yes. He was staying at his butler's home down along the water's edge. He was brought back. The plan was to lock him in a cell but the Council interceded and had him placed under house arrest instead. He's back at his home."

Not exactly the rough treatment he deserved, but at least he was under guard. Although if the Seraph Force was as divided as Graham said, that could be a serious problem. As if reading my thoughts, Donavan asked. "Who's guarding him?"

"I had Mitch handpick the team," Graham said, mentioning a member of the Seven. "They will not be D'Angelo supporters."

"So what's the next step?" Donovan asked. "From the looks on your faces, I'm guessing that Michael being locked away isn't the end of everything?"

"Not even close." I took a deep breath and told Donovan what I'd heard overheard between Uriel and Abaddon.

In front of my eyes, the easygoing Donovan slipped away, the warrior taking his place. I could see the calculations already happening behind his eyes. "So we have a war coming."

"I'm afraid so. And we're going to need to prepare," Graham said.

"Can we even prepare for something like that?" Donavan asked. "How many demons are we talking about?"

"I don't know," I said, his question making me realize how truly in the dark we were. We knew they were coming, but we didn't know how many or where they would attack first. I needed to talk to my father as soon as possible and lock down some answers.

After flicking a glance at the hallway, Donovan raised his eyebrows. "But there's someone in this house who does."

"Yes. He's sleeping right now, but as soon as he wakes I'm going to need to ask him some questions," Graham said.

"Do we have time to wait for him to take a nap? Don't we need these answers now?" Donavan asked.

Graham snorted. "Do you want to go wake Lucifer up from his nap and then demand he answer your questions?"

Donavan winced. "Yeah, maybe waiting just a little bit is a better call. But there have to be other sources that we can tap before then."

He was right. There were. "Where's Cornelius?" I asked, glancing between the two of them.

"Who's Cornelius?" Donovan asked, and I realized that he'd been grabbed by the time we returned from Hell. He didn't know about our guest.

Graham ignored Donovan's question, looking at me. "He's staying down at Tess's place. But you're right, he would be a good source."

"All right, then, let's go have a conversation with him," I said, standing up.

"Wait," Donavan said. "Who is Cornelius?"

I looked at Graham, who shrugged back at me. I turned to Donovan. "He's a three-hundred-year-old dead guy I brought back from Hell."

CHAPTER 9

D'ANGELO

The demon smiled. "I was wondering how long it would take you to recognize me."

As his mouth fell open, D'Angelo stared at his former best friend, who he'd assumed was deceased. The man was easily a foot taller than the last time D'Angelo had seen him. He was wider too, and not just in the body. His face had somehow widened by a good few inches. "What happened?"

Brock raised an eyebrow. "Well, I'd say that's pretty apparent, but you never were the sharpest tool in the shed. I was taken rather than killed." He spread his arms wide, his muscles rippling across his chest. "And they made me into this."

With horror, D'Angelo pictured how his friend had once looked, strong, confident, handsome. But now... He and Brock had grown up together. They had been close. As close as D'Angelo had been to anyone, and to see him like this... "I'm sorry."

Brock laughed. "Sorry? This is the best thing that ever happened to me."

"What?"

"Do you realize how much power I hold in my hand? We used to work on building our bodies to be strong enough to fight. Demons don't have to do any of that. I am naturally strong. I fear nothing and no one, not even that little sword of yours. If you use that sword, it'll be the last thing you do."

D'Angelo stared at his old friend. It was Brock. He was sure of that. And yet at the same time, it wasn't. This creature wasn't the Brock he knew. Yet the arrogance, the complete confidence in his superiority: that was Brock. It was a trait they both shared. He crossed his arms over his chest. "Sorry. It's a bit of shock. But what do you want?"

Brock threw back his head and laughed. "See? I knew you would adjust quickly. I knew you wouldn't engage in a useless fight that would only serve to get you killed." Taking a seat, the metal chair creaked under his weight. He gestured to the other chair.

Hesitating for only a moment, D'Angelo finally took a seat as well. After all, if Brock wanted him dead, he'd be dead already.

And he and Brock *had* been friends. There'd always been a competition between the two of them, of course. And with Brock now a demon, he could rule out the possibility that he'd come here just to kill him as a way of finally ending the competition once and for all. So he sat carefully in the chair, ready to spring up in a moment's notice if he needed to.

"I have a proposition for you," Brock said before he grabbed the decanter of brandy from the table and took a long swig. He smiled. "Now that, I have missed."

"There's no alcohol in Hell?"

Curling his lip, Brock grimaced. "It is not what we were told. All debauchery and sin, it is not."

"So what's it like?" D'Angelo asked.

Brock's smile faded. "It's a grayer version of this world.

Haven't you ever wondered why the demons wanted to come into this world? It's not just humans we want. Your world, my former world, is so much better in every possible way. The demons don't just want your people, they, we, want your world. Humans are a small obstacle in our way."

"So that's the plan? To rid the world of humans?"

Brock shrugged. "Not all of them, of course. Some will remain as servants and slaves. And there could be a place for you amongst us."

"You want my help?" D'Angelo asked.

"Look at your face. You look horrified." He laughed. "Don't worry, I'm not asking for your help out of the goodness of your heart or even your sense of self-preservation. No, I have an opportunity for you."

The gears were turning in D'Angelo's head. If the demons were going to invade, perhaps they had a better chance of winning this time around. With the archangels' recent actions, that meant humans were a low priority on their list. "What kind of opportunity?"

Leaning forward, Brock turned his intense focus on D'Angelo. And he couldn't tell if it was a trick of the light, but his eyes seemed to glow a bright yellow. "Make no mistake, we will be taking over this world. And when we do, those that oppose us will die without mercy, although it'll mean a little fun on our part, perhaps. But that doesn't have to be your fate."

"Demons have tried that before, tried to take over this world. But they were stopped."

Brock smiled, his teeth bright against the dark night. "That is true. But humans didn't defeat them on their own. In fact, without the archangels' intervention, it's safe to say the humans would have most definitely been defeated."

"But the archangels will help humanity again," D'Angelo said. "In fact, Archangel Michael was just on Earth not that long ago. The angels will intercede again, and demons will be defeated again."

Brock smiled. "Are you so sure about that? Because I have it on good authority that they will not be coming to your aid again. You humans have angered them by disobeying their rule. You have failed to hand over the human who goes by the name of Addison Baker. Some of you have actively tried to hide her. And the one Michael entrusted to kill her has failed. He even went so far as to refuse the angel's instructions. From what I understand, angels don't like when people do that."

That was new information. He knew that Graham had been corrupted by Archangel Michael, but he hadn't known he'd rebelled. But Graham had stood with Addie against Michael, so Brock could be telling the truth. In fact, he most likely was.

D'Angelo's mind whirled. And if he was telling the truth and the demons were going to invade, without the archangels' help, he was right. They would never survive. The archangels had turned the tide in the last war. Without it, humanity would have been rolled over.

All these thoughts ran through D'Angelo's mind in seconds. He studied his old friend, who sat confidently and without fear in front of him. Brock had always been an excellent strategist. D'Angelo could admit that Brock was a better strategist than he was. Brock seemed to see all the angles before D'Angelo even realized they were there. "Are you sure?"

"I made sure of it. The demons are smart, though strategy is not their forte. It's why I have done so well. Even Abaddon recognizes the need for greater input in that area. It's one of his few weaknesses. And one that I have been able to exploit."

"Abaddon?"

"The leader of the demons."

D'Angelo frowned. "Isn't that Lucifer?"

Brock's teeth glinted in the moonlight. "Like I said, Hell's not what we've been taught. But I am sure that the archangels will not be interceding this time. I am sure that humanity will fall. Now the only question is: Are you going to fall with them?"

Staring at the demon in front of him who'd once been a friend, he weighed the pros and cons of the options laid before him. He decided Brock was still being a friend, keeping him safe from what was to come. He nodded. "What do you need me to do?"

CHAPTER 10

ADDIE

Major Tess Uriel was one of the wealthiest Angel Blessed in all of Sterling Peak. The wealthy in Sterling Peak all had monstrous mansions up on the main hill. That wasn't Tess's style. For years, she had simply lived in the Seraph Force Academy apartments provided for Rangers. Now, though, she had small place just down the street from Sheila.

With Graham and Donovan by my side, I walked up to the front door. "When did she get this place?"

"Turns out she's had it for the longest time. She just preferred staying up at the academy. But she figured with Cornelius, it would be better if he wasn't around quite so many people yet, until he becomes a little more acclimated," Graham said before he knocked on the front door.

They waited only a few moments before it pulled open. There was a familiar face standing in the doorway.

"Nigel," I said in shock before I smiled.

His smile was just as wide. "Addie. I'm so glad to see you." He stepped forward as if to hug me, then seemed to remember his position. The glance at Graham and Donovan probably reminded him. He cleared his throat as he pulled the door wide. "I'm sure Miss Tess will be as well."

I shot a confused look at Graham.

"I suggested to Tess that Nigel would be a good addition to his home, and she agreed," Graham said with a shrug.

When I had last worked at the Uriels with Nigel, I had worried about him slowing with age. My plan had been to help take on some of his tasks to ease his burden. And to hopefully hide his diminishing skills from the Uriels. But with everything happening, it had slipped my mind. I hadn't been back to the Uriels since the demon attack in my apartment.

But Graham hadn't forgotten. He'd looked out for Nigel. If I hadn't been falling for Graham before, that definitely would have pushed me over the edge. He knew that Nigel was struggling with the duties at the Uriel home, and he'd taken it upon himself to find him another place of employment.

"Beth is here as well. She's in the kitchens," Nigel said.

My jaw dropped. Beth had been with the Uriels since she was a girl. "She left the Uriels?"

"As Miss Tess is also a Uriel, technically she just shifted over. But both of us are very happy with our current accommodations."

I had no doubt that was true. The Uriels were difficult task masters, and always very demanding. Tess was the exact opposite. She was as easygoing as they came regarding her living space.

"And the Seven are very happy that Beth is here. No offense, Nigel," Donovan said as he rubbed his stomach.

Nigel laughed, something that I had rarely seen in my time at the Uriels. "Oh, no offense taken. I'm quite thrilled she's here too."

"We're actually looking for Cornelius," I said as I glanced down the hall.

"Ah, yes. He was just in the yard. He said he wanted some sun. It looks as if he's been quite ill. I couldn't blame him for wanting to be out there. Beth has been fussing over him all morning, making sure he's been eating."

It was good to hear that Cornelius was being spoiled a little bit. The man deserved it. Nigel showed us through the house and to the backyard. With a little bow, he left us at the door. Out in the yard, Cornelius sat in a chair, his head tilted back, his eyes closed.

He looked so peaceful that I hated to disturb him. After all he'd been through, it seemed like the least he deserved was a little peace and quiet. But unfortunately, his quiet was going to have to wait a little bit longer.

As we stepped outside, Cornelius's head jerked up. He turned, his eyes widening. Even with the distance, I could see his chest pounding before his shoulders slumped. "Addie. Graham." He started to stand.

Moving forward quickly, I waved him back down to his seat. "Don't get up. We'll come sit with you."

We each grabbed a chair and pulled them over to where Cornelius sat. By the time we'd had them arranged, Beth had bustled out of the back door with a tray.

She placed it on the table next to Cornelius before hurrying over to me with a hug. "I'm so glad to see you, girl. I heard about everything that you've been through. And I saw you fly over the city. You've been keeping some things from me."

"It was actually a rather new development at the time," I said, returning the hug.

"Well, I'm glad to see you in one piece."

Beth and I spoke for a bit more, me asking about her family and her asking about the kids before she slipped back inside. Cornelius, Graham, and Donovan took the opportunity to dive into the scones that Beth had brought out.

Donovan sighed contentedly. "Beth really is the best baker in all of Sterling Peak."

Taking a scone for myself, I had to agree. As I took a bite, I studied Cornelius. Even the short time he'd been back in the world seemed to have done him some good. There was more color in his cheeks, and I was surprised to see that his hair was blonde. I suppose years of not washing it had made it dark and grimy, but now I could see the lightness in his locks.

"You look good, Cornelius."

He ran a hand down his shirt with a smile. "I haven't seen a white shirt in forever. This almost seems unreal. I have to keep pinching myself to make sure that I'm not dreaming."

I couldn't blame him for that. Cornelius had died centuries ago and been banished to Hell. He should have transitioned to Heaven at some point after his time had been served, but somehow Abaddon had been blocking the movement of souls out of Hell. I knew in the back of my mind that he was doing that to build a big enough army to take over our world.

"I'm hoping you're up for a couple of questions."

Cornelius's eyes turned to me. Gratitude shone through them. "Anything. I owe you so much, Addie. Anything I can do to help."

I was a little uncomfortable with the adulation in his tone, but I did understand it. It was only because I had been holding him that he managed to come through the portal. Somehow, even though he had died centuries ago, I was able to bring him back to the land of the living. How I did it was another question in the long list that surrounded my abilities. I was going to have to ask my father about that one as well.

Graham leaned forward. "We were wondering what you know about Abbadon's forces down in Hell. We're trying to get an idea of what we'll be facing."

Cornelius blew out a shaky breath, and even his hands started to tremble. "He's got legions of soldiers. There are dozens of training camps that are spread throughout Hell."

"Do you have a number?" Graham asked.

With a glance at each of us, Cornelius's lips became a thin line. He looked like he very much didn't want to answer that question. But finally, he spoke. "We're talking tens of thousands."

Donovan sucked in a breath. "That many?"

"Souls haven't been able to leave Hell. They've been trapped down there for I don't know how long. Abaddon and his forces round up absolutely everyone they can find to turn them. And once they've turned, they're his. And then he sends out his demons to pull humans into Hell as well. And those ones, he turns too. Each demon in turn brings back five humans."

"How do you know that?" I asked.

"Because that's how they get promoted. And each one wants to be promoted. Being promoted means more food, more responsibility, more freedom."

"It also makes them more loyal to Abaddon," Donovan murmured. "Because once you've taken five souls, taking five more probably isn't that big a deal."

Cornelius nodded. "True."

"What about the children?" I asked, picturing the young ones in my father's camp and the stories of children who'd disappeared. "Why take them?"

Cornelius was quiet for a long moment. "Because they can

train them from early on. The children who are grabbed eventually become the most brutal of Abaddon's forces."

His words fell heavily upon us all. It was horrifying to think about. How had this been allowed to go on for so long? How hadn't the angels interceded to stop this? But I knew the answer to that: Michael had stopped them. He didn't want humans to be part of this world, and the sooner they were wiped out, the better as far as he was concerned.

"How did you avoid being taken?" Donovan asked.

Cornelius shook his head. "I didn't. I was grabbed almost as soon as I arrived. And I spent time in one of the camps."

"You mentioned camps before. What are they?" Graham asked.

Taking a deep breath, Cornelius turned his head slightly toward the sun, as if seeking its strength. "It's where they take souls before they're turned. You can't just turn someone immediately. It's a process. It takes a long time. And then individuals have to take the last step themselves."

"That's why Torr is the way he is. He never took that last step," Donovan said, looking to me for confirmation.

"Yes. The last step is killing an innocent," I said. I would like to think I would stand up to that kind of pressure. Torture, even. But everyone had a breaking point. The strength in Torr amazed me.

"Yes," Cornelius said. "It's another reason why they bring people over from this world. They need the innocents for the demons to kill. They're the initiation sacrifices, at least the ones that don't have that killer edge."

I shuddered at the idea but then had a thought. "But they're already in Hell. Aren't they already dead?"

Cornelius shook his head. "No. The ones that are brought over haven't died yet. That happens once the demons kill them.

And then they're trapped in Hell too. And they begin the process of turning into a demon."

Donovan shook his head. "I still don't understand how you escaped that."

"Not easily. They wanted me to be turned. After all, I was a soldier. That made me extra valuable in their eyes."

"Yet you managed to avoid that fate," Graham said.

"Not without difficulty," Cornelius said softly. "And it's not something I want to talk about." Taking a breath, Cornelius sat back. "Those camps are still there. There are at least six that I know of. But I've heard rumors of more."

"If we could empty those camps, we could at least cut off their supply of new soldiers," Donovan said.

Graham nodded. "True. But that's a huge risk."

It was. An image of Torr flashed through my mind. And there was something I still didn't understand. "How exactly do they change someone into a demon?"

Shifting in his chair, Cornelius said, "I only saw the process from afar. There's a stone that they use. After repeated exposure to it, it shifts them over the course of a year into the appearance of a demon. But then they still have to take that last step."

I nodded, my mind racing. "Is there any way that process can be reversed?"

"I don't know," Cornelius said.

"We need to free those people from those camps," Donovan said.

Graham frowned. "Yes, but I don't see how that helps us in the war ahead."

I knew he was focusing on the war and calculating each step we had to take in relation to that effort. "It probably doesn't. But we're not leaving those people down there. We need to find a way to get them out. They don't deserve to be there."

"But how will we know who was taken there and who was killed and ended up there?" Cornelius asked.

I shook my head. "At this point, that doesn't matter. The human should be able to go through the portal with the bracelets. The others, I can take them back through."

Donovan raised his eyebrows. "You're going to, what, resurrect hundreds of people?"

With more than a little worry at what I was getting myself into, I nodded. "I guess I am."

CHAPTER 11

D'ANGELO

Although D'Angelo knew it was Brock in front of him, it was still a little difficult to accept. But the more he talked and explained what he wanted, the more Brock shone through, despite how he currently looked.

They had been talking now for thirty minutes, and D'Angelo was growing anxious. What if the Rangers stopped by to check in on him? And his mother was supposed to be stopping by with his food. "You should get going. I'll get to work on learning everything I can about Graham's plans."

Brock put up a claw. "In a minute. There's one more piece of information I need, and now you prove your worth to Abaddon."

It took everything in D'Angelo to ask him to just spit it out. He flicked a glance at the door, waiting for a knock at any moment. "Yes, what is it?"

"I need to know Addie's weaknesses."

"Weaknesses?"

Brock nodded, his eyes pinning D'Angelo in place. "Yes. What is it that we can use to get to her?"

D'Angelo slumped in his seat, his mind racing. He didn't truly know much about her. She'd been a Demon Cursed, not someone that he would pay attention to.

And then Graham had taken off after her. D'Angelo had been happy to let him do so. It allowed him to get to the business of being the head of the Seraph Force. His policies had been the focus of his time, not Graham's search for Addison Baker.

"Well?" Brock demanded.

D'Angelo stood up and paced. "I'm thinking, I'm thinking. Give me a minute."

Impatience radiated off his old friend. Even before Brock had turned, he had not been a patient man. And D'Angelo had the feeling that that character trait hadn't changed.

An image of Addison's two wards popped into D'Angelo's mind. He pictured her taking flight in Graham's training room when he'd ordered the two of them to be arrested. "She has two wards," D'Angelo said. "She's very protective of them."

Brock nodded. "Will you be able to find where they are?"

Puffing out his chest, D'Angelo stood. "I may be imprisoned for now, but yes, there are people still loyal to me. People who know where the Demon Cursed belong in our society."

"Find out where these wards are being held."

"I will. It might take some time, though. What are you going to do?"

Brock smiled, and the sight of those teeth made a shiver run through D'Angelo. "Make Lucifer's daughter come to heel."

CHAPTER 12

NOEL

Even though it had been a week since the events in the training yard, so much had happened in that time, that Noel was having trouble wrapping her mind around all of it. Addie's father was Lucifer, the ruler of Hell and the literal Devil. But he was actually a nice guy. D'Angelo, the leader of the Seraph Force and protector of humans, who was supposed to be a good guy, had been in cahoots with Michael to kill Lucifer.

And Michael, the vaunted archangel, turned out to be the villain in all of this. Noel was probably less surprised by that last revelation than others. She could have told everyone that one from the first time she saw him.

People would try and deny it, but removing someone's free will like Michael did with Graham wasn't the action of a good guy. Michael wanted the humans gone. Another revelation that wasn't a shock to Noel. She'd never put much stock in the idea that angels were the protectors of humankind. After all, the

Angel Blessed certainly didn't think protecting the Demon Cursed was a priority.

Now Michael was residing in the cells beneath the Seraph Force Academy, and if what Noel had heard was accurate, he was turning human. Noel didn't even think that was possible. She itched to sneak into the academy to see it for herself.

And to get a little payback.

He'd caused her family so much strife. He'd caused Addie so much pain. He deserved a little payback.

But she knew that wouldn't go over well when Addie found out about it. And she had no doubt that Addie would.

"Do you want to play cards?" Micah asked as he lay on the bed in the guest room of Graham's home, throwing a ball up and down.

Shaking her head, Noel turned back to the window. "Not right now," she said.

Through the glass, she stared at the expansive lawn that spread for two hundred yards before it touched the edge of the woods. Beyond it was the peak of the mountain. Once again, they were staying at Graham's mansion.

Although she would never admit it out loud, she'd missed this place. She liked having a comfortable bed and food whenever she wanted. It had been such a rarity in her life that she hadn't yet been able to take it for granted.

But it wasn't just that. Being here, she, Micah, Addie, and Torr had been surrounded by people, good people. There had been laughter and smiles. And she'd spent more time with Addie here than she ever had at their apartment. There, Addie was always running off to work or going out to patrol. Here, she'd seen Addie relax for the first time since she'd met her.

And Noel wanted that for her. She wanted Addie to have some peace in her life. But even though no one had said anything, Noel knew that everything wasn't over. They might have locked Michael up, but the rest of the angels were still out there. D'Angelo also wasn't locked up yet, at least not in a cell. He was stuck in his home, which was the same existence that Noel and Micah had right now.

But D'Angelo, Michael, and the angels weren't her greatest worries. No, her worries were more immediate: demons. They were still ready to ride into this world and destroy it.

Shifting her position at the window so she could get a better view of the front of the house, she watched as two guards walked up the path to the front door. Apparently, they were changing shifts.

Graham, or maybe Addie, or maybe both, had made sure that there was a Ranger nearby at all times, keeping an eye on Noel and Micah. Another sign that peace was not at hand.

They were there for their protection and not to keep them locked up, but the end results were the same: They were stuck once again in Graham's house. She sighed, wishing she had Torr's ability to be invisible. He could walk around with impunity.

Right now, he was down visiting with Lucifer.

Noel knew Torr was struggling with the idea that Lucifer was his dad. But at the same time, she could see the hope in his face at the idea of having a family. Of course, she, Micah, and Addie were his family too.

But if Lucifer was going to be hanging around, Noel wanted to speak to him a little more to make sure that he wasn't going to hurt Torr. She felt very protective of him, the same way she did of Addie and Micah. He was her and Micah's own personal guardian angel. But it didn't mean he didn't need someone to look after him too.

A loud snore erupted from over by the fireplace. Noel looked over with a smile as Grunt rolled onto his back, all four paws up in the air. Grunt was a creature from Hell. In appearance, he looked ferocious, but he behaved like a giant dog. He was an absolute cuddle monster with those he liked. Yet in a fight, he was fierce with those who tried to do others harm. Noel smiled, feeling a kinship with the beast. He kind of reminded her of herself.

But right now, the ferocious beast looked like a giant teddy bear. He was another addition to their group. Noel really hoped that Grunt wouldn't have to go back to Hell anytime soon. She liked having him around.

The sound of footsteps approaching the room caused her to turn to the door. She frowned as two Rangers appeared in the doorway. She didn't know either of them.

The men looked around for a moment, their gazes glancing right over Grunt. Apparently, Grunt had slipped into his invisible mode. But Noel and Micah could still see him. Once again, she really wished she had that ability.

"Commander Graham sent us for the two of you. He needs you up at the Seraph Academy."

Noel's interest perked up at that. She was dying to get out of the building. She grabbed a seat as she pulled on her boots. "What for?"

"He didn't explain. He just told us that he needed you."

Micah rolled off the bed with a grin. He pulled on his boots as well. His movement caused Grunt to shake himself awake. Careful not to stare at Grunt, Noel flicked a glance at the Rangers. They didn't look anywhere near Grunt. He was still cloaked.

Tilting his head, Grunt looked at the two Rangers and then at Noel. Standing, she patted the back of her leg as she walked toward the two Rangers. Grunt got to his feet and happily trailed after her.

Once again, she watched the Rangers closely, but they gave no indication that they realized he was coming with them as well.

She had to bite back her smile. Most people reacted with terror when they caught sight of Grunt. That was, of course, until they realized that he was just a big softy.

But Noel figured he could use some fresh air as well. They'd taken him out back of Graham's estate to stretch his legs a few times each day, but he probably needed a longer walk than that. And it was at least a mile up to the Seraph Academy.

Her legs felt stiff from lack of movement and wanted to stretch out. She practically tingled from the anticipation of getting outside. Maybe at the academy, she'd even get a chance to sneak in and see Michael.

She stepped onto the first floor and caught sight of Torr stepping out of Lucifer's room. A shimmer rolled over him, and she knew that he had just cloaked himself.

He frowned as he looked at them. Noel subtly inclined her head, indicating they were heading out. Torr moved toward them to join their little group.

She smiled in part because the two Rangers had absolutely no idea two others had joined their little party. And because she anticipated something exciting happening at headquarters. She smiled, looking up at the hill, wondering what the day would bring.

CHAPTER 13

ADDIE

A report came in from the academies across the nation, and Addie wasn't sure how to respond to it. Apparently, new developments in the demon attacks had appeared while Graham had been under Michael's sway: demons had begun to appear during the day across the nation.

There hadn't been any so far in Blue Forks, but it did seem as if they were starting to lose citizens. No one was sure if it was demon related or if people were just reading the tea leaves and getting out of town.

Nevertheless, Graham made sure that Rangers were patrolling in double the usual numbers, both day and night. Addie knew that was stretching their ranks to a breaking point. Adding in the duplicitous nature of D'Angelo and trying to weed out his followers as well as knowing there was a war on the horizon, to say things were stressed was an understatement.

Graham's approach was a good one and necessary. But Addie worried that it was going to cause people to burn out before they ever got to the big fight. And these kinds of patrols were happening everywhere right now.

And although Addie would rather be spending time with the kids and making sure they were all right, she needed to do her part as well. So now, she walked along the streets of Blue Forks with Laura Raguel, one of the members of the Seven.

Laura was strong, capable, and always seemed to be ready to laugh despite the warrior mentality. Or maybe because of it. Maybe it was because Laura knew that life was tenuous, that she looked for the fun in it as much as possible.

Addie wasn't sure how much longer even Laura could hold onto that happy outlook, though. War had unofficially been declared. There was a heightened state of awareness that all of the Rangers were currently feeling. And it was trickling out to all of the citizens. People weren't talking on the streets. They seem to be rushing to get from point A to point B, casting nervous glances over the shoulders the whole way.

But there was nothing that could be done about that. Until the demons attacked or until they were stopped, this was just how life was going to be.

And Addie still wasn't sure how stopping it was going to work.

"Hello, ladies."

Addie's head jolted up, and she smiled as she caught sight of Lucifer. He'd healed fully days ago. Instead of heading right back to Hell, he'd decided to spend a little time here. Time worked differently between Hell and here, so he wouldn't be gone for that long. He'd gone back yesterday just to check in. And she'd worried that he would have to stay there to deal with whatever was happening.

But seeing him back here made her heart lift. She didn't remember him, but she knew that she felt safe when he was around. And she was going to go with that gut impression.

Next to her, Laura stumbled. For anyone else, it wouldn't have been noticeable, but Laura was always so sure-footed that it was like a blazing sign to Addie. She flicked a glance at her friend and saw the awe on her face.

After the events at the training yard, Lucifer's presence among the Rangers was unfortunately known. The reaction was mixed. For some, he was the subject of hot glares and angry glances, not to mention a few fearful looks.

But for others who got to know him, there was an awe on their faces when they saw him. Once you got to know Lu, it was hard not to like him. And the Seven had gotten to know him very well over the last week. He'd explained in detail the nature of Hell, along with drawing a map of Jabal City.

He was knowledgeable. He was efficient in his explanations but detailed enough that they could practically picture it in their minds. He was even a good artist and had drawn out some of the geographic locations that would be critical if they had to go over, which Addie knew was going to have to happen soon. They needed to at least check out those camps and get a better handle on the numbers.

Lu fell in step with them. "I just got back in, and Franklin told me you were here. I thought I'd patrol with you if that's all right."

"That'd be great," I said, looking at Laura, who couldn't seem to quite find her words yet.

Looking over at Laura, Lu smiled. "It's lovely to see you again, Laura."

"You as well, sir."

"I told you to call me Lu."

Laura's cheeks flamed. "Right, Lu. How was your trip?"

His face clouded for a moment. "Good. Everyone's all right, although it does seem as if something is going on. There seemed a tension in the air, although there was no identifiable cause. And I noticed more demons around Jabal City."

I grabbed his arm, pulling him to a stop. "You went to the city? You could have been seen."

He patted her arm with a smile. "I have missed your concern for me. And I was careful. I was not seen. But there was something in the air. The humans looked even more nervous than usual." Lucifer shook his head. "Maybe I'm just bringing some of my worries back with me."

"But the camp is all right?" I asked as we started to walk again.

Lu nodded. "Yes. Ian's got it locked down. They're not going to be going on any hunting trips until we get this situation resolved."

That was good. The hunting trips involved getting supplies and sometimes people for the camp.

The camp was self-sufficient in terms of food and water, so they didn't need to go hunting for anything along those lines. Their last hunting trip was before Lu arrived, and that was to get the last pieces of the amulet that he used to cross through the portals.

I still didn't understand why I could cross through them without any sort of device while everybody else seemed to need one. The fact that my father also didn't know why I could go through without one was a bit of a curiosity.

But then, there was a lot about my life that I didn't understand. I was starting to get used to it.

Lu joined us when we had just reached the edge of Main Street and had turned toward back toward the bridge. We were cutting down the alley along the back of my old apartment building.

Flicking a glance over at it, I remembered all of the times I'd had there with Noel and Micah. It was amazing how distant those times felt now. I had stopped by a few days ago, but the apartment had felt so empty, despite the fact that everything was essentially still there. But the spark of life was gone. It was so sad, I hadn't returned since.

"Did you stop by and see the kids?" I asked.

"I tried, but they weren't there."

Stopping still, I turned to face him with a frown. "What do you mean they weren't there? They should be there. In fact, they're not allowed to go anywhere."

Lu shook his head slowly. "Addie, they weren't there. Torr and Grunt weren't there either. I thought you knew."

I exchanged a glance with Laura. She nodded at me. "Go. I'll take care of— Look out!"

From the corner of my eye, I saw the movement and shoved Laura out of the way as my father leaped back.

The demon's sword cut through the air, slicing through the space where I'd just been standing.

CHAPTER 14

NOEL

It was good to be out of the mansion. The sky was cloudy, but the sun was peeking through. Noel lifted her face toward it, enjoying the feel of it on her skin.

It was weird. When she'd lived in Blue Forks, she'd dreamed about what it must be like to live across the bridge in Sterling Peak. And now that she essentially did, she found that she didn't like being locked up. Graham's house was nice and all, but it wasn't her home. She realized that the apartment back in Blue Forks didn't feel like their home either.

Right now, she supposed she was technically homeless.

No, that wasn't true. She didn't have a building that she currently viewed as a home, but she had Micah, Torr, Grunt, and Addie. Wherever they were, that was home.

She dropped down as if she was adjusting her boot and flicked a glance back at Torr. He looked at her, raising an eyebrow, and she just shook her head.

"We need to get going," one of the Rangers said as he stepped near her. Another two Rangers had joined them a few houses back, so now there were four accompanying them.

"I'm coming. My boot just got a little twisted." She stood up, shrugging her shoulders at Torr. She didn't understand why they were heading up to the academy either.

But she did like being out. Without conscious thought, her shoulders seemed to relax, and she seemed to be able to breathe a little deeper.

She'd only been in this part of Sterling Peak twice. And one of those times she'd been under guard, and the other times she'd been rushing back to Sheila's after the events at the training yard.

A frown crossed her face at the memory of the training yard. It had been really hard seeing Vera like that and knowing there was nothing she could do to help her. She hated feeling powerless like that.

It had turned out all right in the end, but Noel didn't like the fact that she had been used as bait. She needed to be able to help. She needed to be able to do more.

The Ranger in front turned off the road to a small path that cut through the trees on the left.

Micah stopped, frowning. "I thought we were going to the academy?"

"We are. This is a shortcut," the Ranger said. "Come on. Graham's waiting." He started forward again.

Before Noel could say anything, Micah followed him. Flicking a gaze around, concern rose up inside of Noel as she started forward, her steps a little slower. She didn't like this. She might not have been around here much, but it didn't seem like the path would take them to the academy. If anything, it seemed like it was taking them away.

Two more Rangers waited for them inside the path. They fell in step next to them. Now there were two Rangers in front of them, one on either side of them, and two behind them.

They still didn't know that Torr and Grunt were following close behind. The hair rose on the back of Noel's neck. She kept waiting for the path to circle back toward the academy, but it kept going straight. Something was wrong. And it wasn't just the path. There was no way they would spare six Rangers right now just to escort the two of them up to the academy.

She picked up her pace until she was next to Micah. Bumping into him just a little bit, she nudged his arm. She looked down at him and read the worry in his eyes. Flicking a glance at the Rangers in front of them, she gave him a nod to indicate that he needed to be ready.

He met her gaze for a long moment and then nodded slowly, straightening his back.

Noel took a deep breath. "So, what exactly are we doing at the academy?"

"I told you: Commander Graham wanted to meet with you."

"Why are we meeting at the academy and not back at the mansion?" Noel asked.

The Ranger didn't even look back as he answered. "He's a busy man. He can't be running back to the mansion just to speak with you."

It was entirely possible that was true but also unlikely. Graham took their safety seriously. He wouldn't risk them just because he was a little busy. Noel was kicking yourself for not asking more questions before they even began this little trek.

Vera was up at the Academy with Graham, so she'd thought that it was possible they wanted them to join them.

But her gut was rolling right now, and she had learned to trust it. Something was seriously off. And she had a sickening feeling that she'd made a mistake. A horrible, horrible mistake.

CHAPTER 15

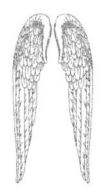

ADDIE

Laura and I crashed into a couple of garbage cans and rolled over them. We scrambled back to our feet. Lu had been a little more graceful in his dive out of the way and had already engaged with the demon.

But three others charged at Laura and me. My eyes narrowed, and my wings flamed bright as they unfurled. One charged, and I slammed my foot into his chest, sending him flying. Pulling the sword from the scabbard strapped along my back, it was immediately engulfed in flames as another demon reached out for me.

I swung quickly, swiping through his arm at the elbow. He cried out as the flaming sword cut right through like butter.

A second swipe cut him from waist to shoulder. Not completely through but enough to do the deed.

He fell forward as I stepped out of the way.

From the corner of my eye, I saw Laura engage the other one, but she was holding her own. Two residents of Blue Forks had tried to join the fight. They managed to stop one of the demons from charging, but he backhanded them and sent them flying.

The one who I'd kicked back had regained his feet. He and his friend both moved toward me, but neither of them made a quick move. Obviously they were smarter than their friends.

But I didn't have time for them to decide who was going to attack who. I needed to find out what had happened to the kids. They should be at Graham's house. They weren't allowed to leave Graham's house. It was possible that Graham had taken them up to the academy, but I couldn't figure out why on earth he would.

No, something was wrong.

But I couldn't just fly off and leave these guys here to wreak havoc on the citizens of Blue Forks. I needed to take them out as quickly as possible.

Casting a glance at the kid who'd dropped, I realized that I recognized him. It was the tall blond kid who'd been friends with Cecilia. He'd been arrogant and full of himself on the beach that night, but he'd also tried to stand with me against the demons, so I gave him points for bravery.

But right now, he was unconscious.

I saw my father engaging with a second demon after dispatching the first. He was keeping the fight away from the kid.

Returning my attention to the two in front of me, I didn't have time to wait. This time I was the one who darted forward.

Aiming for the demon's chest, I raised my sword. But at the last second, I used my wings to leap into the air.

Shifting my shoulder back, I landed a kick to the side of his face.

"Addie!" Laura yelled out just before I felt a tug on my wings. One of the demon's had darted up and grabbed ahold of my lower wings. Pain roared through them and into my back.

Gritting my teeth, I forced the flames in my wings higher.

The demon behind me cried out as his hand burned. He quickly let go.

Turning, I sliced my sword across his throat. He dropped to his knees, his hands scrambling for his neck.

I turned back to deal with the first one, but he was already disappearing. Lucifer took out his last one. Laura was still fighting with hers.

As Lucifer ran toward her, he met my gaze. "I've got this. Go."

That was all the encouragement I needed. I burst into the air, praying that I was just overreacting.

CHAPTER 16

NOEL

The forest had quieted as they walked. Noel's mind raced, trying to figure out what she could do to change the course of what was happening. But the farther they walked into the forest, the more nervous she became.

There were six of them. Even with Grunt and Torr, she didn't like those odds, especially since she didn't have a weapon. But she needed to do something, and she needed to do it before they were too far from the house.

Leaning down to Micah, she whispered, "When I say so, you need to run. Get to the street and just start yelling. There's got to be some real Rangers around that you can attract the attention of, okay?"

Micah looked up at her and shook his head. "I'm not leaving you," he whispered.

"No, you're not. You're going for help," Noel responded.

One of the Rangers looked over at them and then flicked his gaze to the Ranger across from them.

Noel's gut clenched. The Ranger started to pull his sword from his scabbard. Noel shoved Micah out of the way and slammed her boot into the man's groin. He dropped with a cry.

The Ranger closest to her turned, but Noel was already moving. She slammed a side kick into his stomach, followed by a round kick to the side of his knee. Before he could recover, she shot a kick to the side of his other knee.

The two Rangers behind them didn't even have a chance to move before Torr and Grunt dropped their invisibility. The two men cried out, especially the one who Grunt landed on. His cry was high and terrified, and then it was no more.

"Micah, run!" Noel yelled as she grabbed the sword from the scabbard of one of the downed Rangers and turned to face the two who'd been farther ahead.

One already had his sword drawn and charged at Noel. Her sword clashed with his, the vibration rolling down her arms. She gritted her teeth and ignored it. They'd done weapons training with Addie, but this was the first time she'd had to use it.

And she had no intention of failing. She parried each of the Ranger's moves, her arm vibrating with the strength of his blows. The second one charged past her, aiming for Micah.

"Torr!" Noel yelled, not taking her gaze off the man in front of her.

"I've got him!" Torr yelled back.

Ducking a slice of the man's sword, Noel popped up just to his side, slamming the hilt of her sword into the man's face. Blood burst from his nose as it broke. He cried out, taking a stumbling step back in shock.

Noel didn't hesitate. She stepped forward, her sword already moving. She whipped the sword across his chest, cutting through his tunic. More blood bloomed there. Part of Noel recoiled at the sight, but another part cheered that her training had paid off.

The Ranger staggered back. Noel turned as the other two that she had taken down stumbled to their feet.

Breathing hard, she turned to face them when a deep voice chuckled behind her. "Well, isn't this entertaining."

Shooting a glance over her shoulder, she saw three demons as they stepped out onto the path.

CHAPTER 17

ADDIE

Sterling Peak was quiet as I soared across the bridge and up its hill. Scanning the area, I looked for any disturbances, but there was nothing.

And yet that fact did not quiet my nerves. If anything, I was more worried. As I made my way closer to Graham's mansion, I didn't see any sign of trouble.

Maybe I was overreacting. Maybe there was a perfectly logical explanation for why the kids weren't at the mansion. Maybe—

"Help! Help!" The cry came from farther up the hill. Heart pounding, I soared toward it. Up head, Micah burst out of the trees. He called out again. "Help!"

Two Rangers who'd been on patrol darted toward him. I tensed until I recognized one of them was Mitch, another member of the Seven.

Putting on a burst of speed, I dropped down quickly in front of Micah. Both he and the Rangers jolted at the suddenness of my appearance.

Micah's words came out between pants. "Noel... trouble... that way." He pointed down the path.

That was all the explanation I needed.

Retracting my wings, I tore down the path on foot. The trees were too close, and I'd have trouble flying. And even if I managed it, I'd probably set the whole forest on fire. My control was thin at best right now.

Someone had come after the kids.

Up ahead, I could hear the sounds of a fight.

Behind me, Mitch yelled at the other Ranger to call for reinforcements and get Micah to safety. Then he bolted after me.

I outpaced him quickly and heard Grunt's roar as I came around a bend in the path. My heart nearly stopped at the sight in front of me.

Two demons were fighting with Torr, Grunt, and Noel. A third massive one stood in the back, watching with his arms crossed over his chest.

Grunt was taking on one of them, but even he was struggling to get a hold of the guy. Frowning, it took me a second to spot the long dark wound in his side. A few feet from him, Torr and Noel tag-teamed the other demon.

But a Ranger jumped forward and tackled Torr to the ground. The demon fighting Noel smiled and feinted a punch high before dropping low to tackle her at the waist.

A roar burst from my chest as my wings unfurled and burst into flame, forest be damned.

I leapt across the space and landed with both feet on the back of the man who'd tackled Noel. He cried out at the force exerted against him as he stumbled forward.

Noel managed to scramble out from in front of him.

Grabbing the demon by the shoulder, I yanked him back. My

hand latched onto his hair, and I pulled him closer to me. Without a second's hesitation, I pulled my knife from its sheath and slid it along his throat.

Torr managed to kick off the Ranger who had tackled him. The Ranger looked at me as I turned to face him, his eyes widening. He went still for a second and then sprinted away. Another Ranger who was with him followed.

Mitch, who'd just joined the fight, stopped at the edge, sending three arrows into the demon that had been fighting Grunt.

The arrows brought the demon up short. He stopped for a split second. That was all Grunt needed. With a deep growl, Grunt's head darted forward, his jaws wrapped around the demon's throat. With an angry snarl, he shook the demon and then flung him to the side of the path. Blood sprayed across the area, the demon's throat practically gone.

Not letting myself stop, I whirled around to face the last demon, the one who'd stood and watched.

There was something so familiar about him. He smiled as he watched me. "Not yet, Addie," he said before fading away.

CHAPTER 18

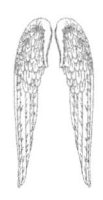

For the first time, I noticed the other wounded Rangers. Two of them were trying to crawl away. My eyes narrowed, but then they latched on to the demon that I'd taken down. He was starting to dissolve.

"The bracelets!" I yelled as I dove toward the nearest one. I managed to rip the bracelet from his arm just before he disappeared.

With a curse, I glanced over at Mitch, who shook his head. He'd been too late to get the bracelet off the one near him.

But that was a different issue and not my priority at the moment. Anger dogging my steps, I stormed for the soldier who was trying to crawl away. Grabbing ahold of him, I yanked him up, bending his arm behind his back to hold him in place. "What were you doing? What was your plan?"

Squirming under my hold, the Ranger looked over at Mitch. "We were under Graham's orders."

"He's lying," Mitch said. "There's no way Graham would have done this."

I knew that was true. But I also knew that it would take a

little time to get these guys to give us the truth. And I intended to get exactly that.

Mitch handed me some rope. I quickly tied the man's hands behind his back as Mitch went and tied one of the other ones. Torr had another one held down. The other three were too injured to crawl anywhere.

Two more Rangers hurried down the path toward us, stopping short. I flicked a glance at Mitch as I jumped to my feet.

He held up a hand. "I know them. They're good."

My shoulders lowered, but only a little. "Something's wrong here, Mitch."

"I know. You take those guys back to the academy. It's closer. We need to figure out what's going on. I'll arrange to get these guys back. We'll lock them in the cells and get some answers."

I looked over at where Noel stood with Torr and Grunt. Blood seeped through the shirt that Noel and Torr held to the creature's side. Torr had given his up in order to use it as a bandage for Grunt. Grunt lay on the ground, his head in Noel's lap.

If Grunt and Torr hadn't been with them . . . My mouth went dry at the thought.

Micah came running down the path. "Grunt!" he cried.

Grunt wagged his tail heavily in response as Micah dropped to his knees in front of him. Tears were in Micah's voice as he ran a hand over Grunt's fur. "It's okay, boy. You're going to be okay. I promise you're going to be okay."

The worry I heard in Micah's voice made my blood boil. My kids had been through enough. They did not need this. They did not deserve this.

And whoever had set these demons upon my family was going to pay.

CHAPTER 19

Mitch urged me to take the kids to the academy, but I didn't want to leave until there were enough Rangers there to safely get the others back. I wasn't going to take the chance of these Rangers escaping. Besides, I thought Grunt needed a moment.

Once the reinforcements arrived, I headed back down the path to the street with Micah, Noel, Torr, Mitch, and Grunt. Mitch left the removal of the other Rangers to the reinforcements.

Now that a little time had passed, I knew that these Rangers had to somehow be connected to D'Angelo. That guy was not someone who was going to take defeat easily. And he was cowardly enough to use kids to do it. What did he think he was going to accomplish? That I would simply bow out if something happened to the kids?

The appearance of the demons, however, suggested an even darker possibility. Was it possible that he was actually working with the demons? D'Angelo was power hungry, but to actually turn against his own species? That seemed like a stretch, even for him.

And yet according to Noel and Torr, it looked like the demons and the Rangers were working together. So what other explanation could there be? I supposed it was possible that the demons just happened to be in that isolated part of the forest, but that seemed like a huge stretch.

I also wondered about that one demon who'd stayed in the back. His coloring suggested he was a relatively new demon, and yet his demeanor seemed to indicate that he was in a position of power. Instead of taking part of the fight, he'd seemed to be supervising it. Was it possible that he was too important to be involved? Why was he here, then?

But that wasn't what was really bothering me. It was that there was something familiar about him.

I couldn't put a finger on what it was. While we waited, I asked Mitch, but he hadn't gotten a good look at the demon. And neither Torr nor Noel recognized him either.

It was possible that I remembered him from my previous time in Hell. I did actually recognize Abaddon, or at least I'd had a feeling of recognizing him.

But this felt different, although I couldn't quite figure out why. I didn't know what to make of it. But the fact that someone was familiar was novel. And that alone made me wonder what was going on.

Up ahead, the gates for the Seraph Academy stood open. Today there were four Rangers at the front gate instead of the usual two. Like everywhere else, Graham had increased the security here as well.

During the day, the gates were kept open, but they could be closed quickly in the event of an attack. At night, they were always closed. As the Rangers on duty caught sight of us, surprise flashed across their faces.

"Mitch?" I asked, not taking my gaze from the Rangers.

"I know two of them," he replied. "They're okay. The other two I don't know."

"Which two don't you know?" I asked.

"The two on the left."

Narrowing my gaze, I noted they were older than the usual recruits. They looked to be in their mid-thirties, which wasn't unusual for a Ranger. Rangers oftentimes joined later in life and stayed up until the time that they could no longer fight.

I got no sense of alarm or concern from the two Rangers that Mitch knew, although I did get the sense that they were curious about us. That seemed reasonable, though. After all, Torr was walking with us, as was Grunt. And neither of them was shielded from view.

A hurried whisper from one of the other Rangers had the two nodding and then lowering their staves. Mitch strode forward. "We need to speak with Graham."

One of the newer ones nodded and ran ahead. We made our way slowly through the gates.

"Is everything all right, Mitch?" one of the Rangers asked.

"I'm not sure yet," Mitch said. "How are things here?"

"Quiet. No demon activity."

Noel grunted. "Yeah, well, aren't you lucky."

Mitch quickly explained about the situation in the woods and that there would be Rangers coming up that would need to be brought down to the cells.

As Mitch made arrangements, I ushered the others forward. We were halfway across the space between the gate and the academy entrance when the door opened, and Graham strode out.

He hurried down the path toward us. Concern flashed across his face as he took in our disheveled state and the wound in Grunt's side.

Glancing across us, I realized what a motley group we must look like. Torr, Noel, and I looked the worst. All of us had blood splashed on us. We'd tied the bandage to Grunt's side, but it had turned red on the walk here. Noel's shirt was ripped, and Torr was shirtless.

Micah was the only one who was relatively clean. But apparently, he'd taken a spill along the path somewhere because his pants and arms were covered in dirt.

"What happened?" Graham asked, his alarmed gaze roving over all of us again, as if to make sure he hadn't missed an injury the first time around.

"A lot. We need to talk," I said, nodding toward the doors. The sooner we were inside, the sooner Grunt's wound could be seen to.

Graham led us to the third floor where the Rangers had apartments. We took the lift, which was operated by hand. No one wanted poor Grunt to have to climb the stairs. And I could tell that even though she might deny it, Noel was on the edge of collapsing as well. That attack had taken more out of her than she realized.

And the fright had taken a lot more out of me. Already, I could feel the tremors starting to work their way up my arms as I thought about the danger the kids had been in.

As the doors to the lift opened, I flicked a glance down the hall. The third and fourth floor contained the Ranger apartments. They were all along the wall, and a banister lined the courtyard below.

No one was in sight today, for which I was very grateful. Stepping into Tess's apartment, Graham pushed me and Noel toward Tess's bedroom, promising to look after Torr and Noel.

With a nod, I headed in and grabbed a shower first, then pulled on some of Tess's clothes. I left a set of clothes on the bed for Noel as I moved out into the main room. Torr looked up from where he sat next to Grunt. Dr. Jade was carefully stitching up his side.

Getting up, Torr walked over to me and nodded at the door. "Graham called Dr. Jade for Grunt. Now he's making arrangements for the Rangers being brought in."

"I hope he makes it very uncomfortable for them," I said with a growl.

"From the look in his eyes, I'm pretty sure that was the plan," Torr replied.

The two of us sat back down on the couch as Dr. Jade finished up with Grunt. She told us we should try to keep Grunt from moving too much so he didn't rip the stitches. We promised to do our best before she took her leave.

As Noel stepped out of the bedroom, I ran my gaze over her, noticing the redness in her eyes. She had cried. That was good. Noel tried to bottle up all her emotions, but I was glad she had let some out, even if she had done it in private. Today had been a lot.

By the time Graham stepped back into the room ten minutes later, we were all sitting in Tess's living room eating. Torr had raided the fridge and grabbed some sandwiches and snacks. Beth apparently had stocked this fridge as well.

Grunt lay by the fire, looking happily content, the result of a mixture of the meds Dr. Jade had given him and the four roast beef sandwiches he'd polished off.

Graham hadn't returned alone. Vera was with him. As she stepped into the room, her eyes grew wide. "What kind of mess did you guys get yourselves into?"

We quickly explained about the Rangers coming to get the kids and leading them into the woods, followed by the demons showing up.

Vera pursed her lips. "Someone wanted to use you guys as bait."

"Yeah, we were thinking the same thing," I said.

Graham paced along the windows of the room. "I knew that there were traitors amongst our Rangers, people that sided with D'Angelo. But I never thought they'd take it this far, to be aligned with the demons."

"We need to talk to D'Angelo," I said.

Shaking his head, Graham said, "Yeah, I don't think that's going to happen."

"What do you mean?" I didn't like the tone of his voice.

"The Council has declared that we are not allowed to go near him until after his trial."

I stared at him, hoping he was joking. It would be in poor taste, but it was better than his words being the truth. He didn't even crack a smile. "And when will that be?" I asked.

"They've set the time for two months from now."

"Two months?" That was insane. We needed answers from D'Angelo now. We couldn't wait two months. The demon invasion would have begun by then.

"Apparently they want to make sure he has time for a good defense," Graham growled.

"Or they're hoping we'll all be dead by then," Vera muttered.

Micah's head shot up. "What?"

Vera winced. "Sorry, kid. Just saying things that I don't really know to be true. Don't listen to me."

"Well, we need to find out what's going on. And we need to find out soon," I said.

After grabbing a chip from Torr's plate, Vera sat back on the couch. "You need your father."

"Why?" Graham asked.

Vera smiled. "No one's better at getting people to talk than Lucifer."

CHAPTER 20

D'ANGELO

Word should have arrived from the Rangers by now. D'Angelo's heart pounded as he paced along the confines of his bedroom.

He ran a hand over his mouth and then through his hair. His whole body felt out of sorts. It was a big risk they were taking, grabbing Noel and Micah. If it went sideways...

D'Angelo didn't even want to think about that. If they were caught, they could tie everything back to him. And then he wasn't sure even the Council would be able to get him out of it.

"You always were a worrier."

His hand going to his throat, D'Angelo whirled around as Brock appeared on the balcony. "Get in here before someone sees you," D'Angelo hissed.

Brock walked in slowly.

Hurrying over, D'Angelo quickly slammed the doors shut. He pushed back the curtains and glanced outside, craning his neck to see if anyone was looking. But no one seemed to have noticed his old friend's arrival.

Taking a breath, D'Angelo turned to Brock. "What are you doing here?"

"Your little plan didn't work. Addie wasn't distracted. She arrived to help her wards."

"It wasn't my plan," D'Angelo screeched before he got a hold of himself. He took another breath.

"It wasn't my plan," he repeated in a calmer manner. "You were the one who came up with it. I merely suggested the location."

Waving away his words, Brock plopped into the chair by the fireplace. "Nonetheless, it didn't work. Addie arrived and dispatched two of my people."

D'Angelo groaned. "What about the Rangers?"

Brock shrugged. "They were alive."

Gritting his teeth, D'Angelo searched for his inner calm. "Yes, but were they captured?"

"I believe so. I didn't stay around to watch."

"Oh my god." D'Angelo whirled away from Brock, his hand on his forehead. This was horrible. If they were interrogated . . . No, he couldn't let that happen. He hurried to the door.

"Where are you doing?" Brock demanded.

For the first time since Brock had reappeared, he did not intimidate him. No, Brock was not his current worry, that was reserved for thoughts of the vengeance a certain winged woman would bring down on him if those Rangers talked. "To make sure that none of this comes back to bite me."

CHAPTER 21

ADDIE

Graham dispatched Rangers to Blue Forks to find Lucifer. While they waited, Graham had Noel and Micah go over everything that the Rangers had said to them.

When they'd run through their story twice, he stood up. I nodded toward the kitchen. "Why don't you guys see if there are any cookies?"

"I'm not hungry," Noel said.

"No, but Micah is, and I'm sure Grunt could go for some more food." I gave a meaningful nod to Micah.

Noel read my look and stood. "Right. Micah, come on, let's see what we can find."

While they were distracted, Graham and I moved over to the side of the room. "Well?" I asked.

With a look toward the kitchen, Graham dropped his voice. "I don't know the Rangers that are involved in this. They were brought in when I was under Michael's control. Two of them are from the Chicago area."

"And the other four?"

"I have a group out searching for the one who got away, but I don't even know who the other three are. I have no background on them."

"Is it possible that they're not Rangers at all?"

"I don't even want to think about that. Can you imagine if we have people in our ranks who aren't even supposed to be here?" Graham let out a breath. "I'm going to have to go through and check every single Ranger. I need to find a way to test allegiances, and that's going to upset even the ones who are loyal. But we can't have Rangers that are working on the side of the demons."

He shook his head. "I can't believe I even have to say that."

I didn't know what to say to that and was saved from having to find something because Lu showed up in the doorway.

Tess was with him, and she looked around the room in surprise. "Well, I see no one's worse for wear, and you've all found my food."

"Sorry about that," I said as we moved back toward the couch.

"I'm not. Glad someone's eating it. Beth always loads the fridge up like she's expecting a siege. Are you guys okay?" she asked as she crouched next to Grunt and rubbed his belly. He gave a tired wag of his tail.

"Physically, yes, but I'm pissed," I told her.

"You're not the only one," Tess said, her eyes flashing as she stood. "Mitch brought me up to speed. I don't like what I'm thinking."

"Neither do I," Graham said.

Lu hurried over to Torr. "You weren't injured?"

"We're fine. Noel, Micah, and I weren't hurt. But Grunt was." He nodded to where Grunt lay.

Crossing the room, Lucifer knelt down and rubbed a hand over Grunt's head. "Thank you for protecting them."

Grunt preened under Lucifer's attention.

Then Lucifer returned to Noel and Micah. "I hear you to comported yourself incredibly well."

"I just ran away," Micah said, staring at the ground.

"No, you brought in the reinforcements they needed," Lu said. "If you hadn't, Addie wouldn't have known where to find you. So don't sell yourself short."

A small smile crossed Micah his face, even though he kept his face turned down.

Lu turned to Noel. "And I hear you held your own against Rangers. That is impressive."

I knew that Noel was still a little wary of Lucifer, and I couldn't really blame her. She took a long time to warm up to people. But Lucifer was definitely making strides. And complimenting her ability to take care of herself and others was a smart move on his part.

I could tell she was pleased, although she was trying hard to hide it. She gave a shrug. "It was nothing."

"Not having an ego is a good thing, but you should also feel proud when you've done something worthwhile. And you protected my son, your brother, and yourself. You should be proud of that," Lucifer said, placing a hand gently on her shoulder.

She looked up at him and gave him a nod.

Then Lucifer crossed the room toward me. His face hardened as he joined us. "I don't like this."

"Neither do we. We need to interrogate the individuals involved, and Vera suggested that you might be the man for the job," Graham said.

Vera cackled. "Oh, he's the man all right."

His eyes hard, Lucifer nodded. "Show me where they are."

CHAPTER 22

It was agreed that Noel and Micah couldn't be left on their own, which neither of them was happy to hear. I knew that they worried that they were being treated like children, but it wasn't that. If the threat was against Tess, I would have had people surrounding her as well.

As it was, Tess and Vera agreed to keep an eye on them while Graham, Lucifer, and I went down to talk to the Rangers. Two of them were in the infirmary while two were down in the cells.

The cells were on the lower level of the academy, vestiges of a time long past. They weren't used very often anymore, but recently they'd had one long term resident: Michael.

In the past week, I'd thought about making the trip down here to visit him. I knew I would need to talk to him at some point. He no doubt had useful information locked in that devious mind of his.

But honestly, I just wasn't up for seeing the man. And I wasn't sure how much information he could or would provide.

Although perhaps now that Lu was back, maybe *he* could have a chat with his brother and see what he could glean.

As a group, we made our way down the cold dark steps. A shiver ran through me at the change in temperature. It had to be at least twenty degrees cooler down here.

The stairs ended in a small room. A Ranger stood on duty, and he nodded at us. Straight ahead the walls and floor were both carved from stone. Torches lit the way. Squinting up ahead, I saw that some of the walls seemed to have been dug from the ground itself rather than stone.

Noting my attention, Graham explained, "The prison level was dug right out of the earth. Most of it sits on a rock bed, but some of it is actually just hard-packed dirt. As a result, this place stays cold and a little damp. It's not somewhere anyone wants to spend a lot of time."

"Do you use this place very often?" I asked.

Graham shook his head. "There hasn't been a need. The last time this place was used was about five years ago. Michael's the first real resident since then. Before that, the most time someone spent down here was a few hours, sleeping off a drink."

"Where is he?" Lucifer asked.

"He's down that hall, the second-to-last cell on the right. He's got a guard twenty-four seven." Graham nodded to a hallway that jutted off to the right.

"How's he doing?" I asked, making no move to head in that direction.

"He's quiet. He hasn't made so much as a murmur. I've personally chosen the guards that have sat with him and have one of the Seven checking in on him each day just to make sure."

"His wounds?" Lucifer asked.

"He's healing, but slowly." Graham paused. "I think he may be fully human now."

"He is," Lucifer said softly, his gaze straying to the hall where his brother was held. "We angels can sense one another, and I can't sense him any longer. He has no more grace left."

Even with everything that he had tried to do, I still felt some sympathy for the man for his change in stature. That would be awfully difficult to accept.

"As for the Rangers, I had them put them in the cells up here to the left." Graham nodded in that direction.

We turned down a different hall and immediately saw two bodies lying stretched out across the hallway.

Graham was sprinting down the hall before I fully registered what the bodies meant. Then I ran down the hall after him with Lu right behind me.

Graham reached the first one and felt for a pulse. "He's alive."

Hurrying past him, I crouched down to the second one and touched his throat. "So is this one."

Lucifer had made his way to the cell. He looked inside and shook his head. "But these ones aren't."

I jumped to my feet and hurried over to his side. I pulled on the door, and it swung open easily. It hadn't been locked.

Stepping inside, I shook my head at the senselessness of the violence. The soldiers from earlier, the ones who'd tried to take Noel and Micah, lay on the ground in different positions, their throats slit.

"Somebody is making sure we can't question them," I said.

"And I think we all know who that someone is," Lucifer said quietly.

"D'Angelo," Graham seethed.

CHAPTER 23

The Rangers in the sublevel weren't the only ones who could provide answers. And none of us believed that they would have been overlooked. We turned and rushed back down the hall. As we sprinted back up the stairs, Graham issued orders to two Rangers coming down.

Unfortunately, as fast as we ran, it wasn't fast enough. An inspection of the medical wing showed the same issue. All of the Rangers who had been involved in the attempted kidnapping had been killed. This time instead of knocking out the medical staff, they had called away the doctor and the nurse, claiming that there was a medical emergency out on the training yard. When they returned, Dr. Jade had found the Rangers dead.

The guard who'd been on duty had been called away as well, told that there was a demon incursion in the left wing of the academy. He was shaking his head at his gullibility at leaving his post.

The guards at the gate said that two Rangers had come in just after the individuals from the attack had been brought in, two scruffy-looking Rangers, but they'd had the password. They'd been allowed in and had left only a few minutes later.

They had to be the individuals who had killed the others.

And while they'd gotten a description of them, Graham and I didn't have a lot of hope that we were going to be able to track them down.

If they were smart, they would have gotten out of town. If they weren't smart, they went back to D'Angelo and now were as dead as the others.

Frustration twisted up inside of me. If we'd talked to the Rangers sooner, we could have tied D'Angelo to all this and closed down at least one threat. But instead, he'd beat us to the punch, snipping the string that could have tied him to the attack.

One look at Lu's face told me he felt the same way. He knew what the kids meant to me, but he also knew that I was the main target in all of this. He flicked a glance back toward the entrance to the dungeon. "I think I need to go have a chat with my brother."

He didn't wait for a response, just stalked toward the stairs. I wondered for a moment if the Rangers would try and stop him but knew they wouldn't. Lu was an archangel. They would get out of his way.

Graham tugged on my shirtsleeve and nodded his chin down the hall. I turned and followed him. He led us back to his office. Closing the door, he leaned against it, looking at me. "Are you okay?"

Shaking my head, I ran a hand through my hair. "No. They came after Noel and Micah. And then they killed all of the ones that tried to hurt them. It feels like things are speeding up. And this was a coordinated attack. The demons in Blue Forks tried to occupy us so I wouldn't be around when Noel and Micah were grabbed. If they had grabbed them . . ."

My knees buckled at the idea of Noel and Micah being in the clutches of the demons or worse.

Graham was across the room in a moment with his arms wrapped around me. "Don't think about that. It didn't happen. You got to them in time."

I leaned against his chest, closing my eyes, using his strength to hold me up. "But time's the problem, isn't it? It seems to be slipping away. And we're no closer to figuring out how we're going to stop this than we were a week ago."

He leaned his chin on my head. "We'll figure it out, Addie."

But I wasn't so sure. Killings and disappearances had been increasing everywhere for the last week. It was like the demons realized they needed to ratchet things up. And now that we knew that the angels were helping them, the idea of that was even more terrifying.

We needed to figure out a way to at least strike a small blow to slow their momentum. I slipped my hand into my pocket and pulled out the bracelet I'd taken off the demon. "I took this off of one of the demons before he could disappear."

He smiled down at me. "See? We're making progress."

I gave a little laugh as I stepped out of his arms. "Yeah, we got one bracelet." But then I paused as I stared at it, an idea forming. "But what if we could get more?"

Graham frowned. "What do you mean?"

"When we were last in Hell, I saw Uriel hand over a bag of stones. All of them are going to be used to make bracelets."

"Yes."

"What if we could stop them from making them? I mean, I don't think the demons are going to be the ones making them. Have you seen their hands? They're like big meaty paws. No doubt it's humans making the bracelets. So maybe we could kill two birds with one stone: get in, figure out where they're making the bracelets, destroy their capability to do that, and then rescue a bunch of humans while we're at it."

"Well, I like the idea in theory. But we need more information. Do we have any idea where they're making the bracelets?"

I frowned. Cornelius had explained that he'd been in a camp that made bracelets when he first arrived. But that camp had long been destroyed. "Maybe my father knows where they are."

"Wouldn't he have already told us?"

My shoulders slumped, realizing that was true. That was not information that he would keep from us. "Yeah, you're probably right. If he knew where they were making them, he would have told us. And being he and his people have been rescuing people from camps, if he hasn't mentioned it yet, he doesn't know."

"And Cornelius doesn't know?"

"We can ask him again, but I don't think so."

"If only there was someone who actually knew everything that was happening in Hell. Maybe we could see if Abaddon would like to share information."

I chuckled. "Oh yeah, he's a big sharer. I'm sure he's got a map with every important camp labeled on it that he'll hand right over if we ask nicely." My mouth fell open as a face flashed across my mind.

"What is it?"

A smile slowly spread across my face. "I don't think Abaddon's going to help us, but there just might be someone else who will."

CHAPTER 24

Speaking with Lucifer after he met with Michael, he confirmed that he didn't know where any of the bracelets were being made. And also that Michael wasn't saying much. He was so wrapped up in self-pity for the loss of his grace that he was barely saying anything at all. Lucifer would keep trying, but right now, it wasn't going to happen.

But that was okay, because we had another possibility.

We called a meeting of the Seven. An hour later, all of us sat in the Seven conference room along with Vera, Torr, Grunt, Noel, and Micah.

There was no way the kids were going to be left alone, and we needed everyone that could possibly have information on the next steps to be part of this conversation.

The last to arrive was Cornelius. Glancing around, he gave a nervous smile before taking a seat next to Tess.

Vera looked around the group and grinned. "So, we're finally taking the fight to the demons."

"Maybe," I said before I quickly explained my idea. "If we can stop their production of the bracelets, that would at least stem some of the tide."

"If we could grab the stones, that would be even better," Tess said.

Donovan leaned forward. "I agree. If we could take some of that off the table, that would be helpful. But I'm not getting how we're going to find this camp. I mean, if Lucifer doesn't know, who would?"

I flicked a glance at Cornelius, who nodded back at me. "When I was down in Hell, Cornelius took me to a market. It's pretty bare bones, but there was a woman there named Agnes. She seems to know all the ins and outs of Hell. Information is how she trades. I'm betting she would know the location of the camp."

"But she won't just give it to you. You'll have to trade her something for it," Cornelius reminded her.

"I know." I pictured the young girl that I had seen in Agnes's tent. "And I know exactly what I'm going to offer her in trade."

CHAPTER 25

The portal rippled in front of us. It was the one not too far from the academy. Anticipation and nervousness rolled through me as I stared at the swirling mass.

Graham stood next to me, scowling at it. "I don't like this."

"You don't have to. But it needs to be done."

He looked like he wanted to argue. But we'd already done that. We were at the point of only dangerous choices. Not doing anything could be even more dangerous for all of us down the road, so he simply nodded.

It was decided that Cornelius, me, Lucifer, and Tess were going to go back into Hell. Lucifer was going to go and check on his camp, and we would meet up with him back at the portal. I was thinking we'd take all of his people out of Hell. That would mean that Lucifer would be free to focus on the battle ahead instead of splitting his time between us and Hell.

I was surprised when Lucifer agreed, but I suppose I shouldn't have. He would be happy to see his people out of Hell. He was still amazed that I had brought Cornelius over.

Part of me worried that it had been a one-time fluke, but

even if it was, with the bracelets, we would be able to get people over.

For now, Lucifer was just going to check on the camp and tell everyone to get ready. And then he would meet up with us, and we would figure out exactly how we were going to do this.

But first we needed to get the location of the bracelet production camp.

Vera was going to stay with the kids, along with Grunt and Torr, until we got back. I felt better knowing that she would be keeping an eye on them.

Lucifer told us not to worry about him and that he would find us when we were over there. He'd already gone through a different portal earlier this morning. He didn't want to set off any warning bells by coming through the one close to Sterling Peak. It was the one that we were going to have to go through because it was the closest to where we needed to be. We didn't have time to travel to one of the other portal sites. I could get there quickly with my wings, but it would take too long to get Cornelius and Tess there.

"How exactly are we going to find your father again?" Tess asked.

"He said he'd find us," I said.

She raised an eyebrow. "And how exactly is he going to do that?"

I shrugged. "He's Lucifer."

Tess nodded. "Right, well, let's get this show on the road," she said, tightening the straps on her pack. She rubbed the bracelet on her wrist and stared at the portal. "I hope this works."

"Be careful," Graham said, meeting my gaze.

"I will."

I looked at Cornelius, who stood on my other side with a bracelet around his wrist. He hadn't hesitated to volunteer to join us, even though I knew going back to Hell was the last thing he wanted to do. And none of us were sure if he would be able to get out again.

But he gave me a nod.

Taking a deep breath, I stared at the portal. "Remember, as soon as we go through, there will be guards. Be on the lookout."

Both of them gave me a nod. Taking a deep breath, we stepped through.

CHAPTER 26

As soon as we stepped through the portal, a surprised yell rang out from my right. My sword already pulled, I plunged it into the gut of the demon standing there. I yanked it out before he could do so much as move.

His eyes widened, his mouth opening in an O before he pitched forward.

At the other side of the portal, Cornelius and Tess intercepted the other guard. Cornelius went low, cutting the demon at the back of the legs before Tess impaled him through the heart with her sword. He was dead before he hit the ground.

Despite the fight, the area around the portal remained quiet. I looked around, surprised that there weren't more guards.

"Why aren't there more here?" Tess said, asking my question aloud.

I shook my head, not sure what to make of it. "Maybe they weren't expecting us to come through. After all, what would we be doing here? They're expecting us to wait on the other side for them to bring the fight to us."

The bodies of the demons still lay where they fell. I tilted my head as I glanced at them. Death was a closed-loop system down here. They could be killed, but then they ended up right back here. They should have started to disappear. I glanced down at the bodies before I looked at Cornelius. "What happens to these bodies?"

He frowned as he stared at them. "They must not have been dead when they were brought to Hell, otherwise they would have disappeared already. These ones were just killed. Their souls are now in limbo. It could go either way. They're probably in Purgatory."

I raised my eyebrows at that. "I didn't think Purgatory was real."

"Me either. It really exists?" Tess asked.

Cornelius nodded. "Yes. It's rare, but some people actually end up in Hell after Purgatory. They tend to be the ones that the demons embrace. I've heard a few stories of them."

I had a vague idea of Purgatory. It was where someone, God, I suppose, determined if you were going up or down. The legend was that some people spent a long time there while that determination was made. For others, it was a short trip. Their actions while alive made it clear where they belonged.

I grunted. I hadn't really thought of how that all worked out. In my head, I pictured long rows of people lining up at tables to have their worth measured. "Well, we're going to need to hide these bodies, then. We can't just leave them here."

Tess nodded to the outcropping of rocks. "I'm afraid that's the best we can do. The ground is too packed to dig, not that we have anything to dig with."

Nodding my agreement, I grabbed the arms of one and started to drag him. Cornelius and Tess grabbed the arms of the other and followed me. We positioned them behind the rocks, and then Cornelius and I covered bodies with some smaller rocks while Tess went back to hide the drag marks.

Stepping back, I frowned at the little their mounds that we had created. The demons were, for the most part, hidden, but anyone who came near would notice that it wasn't a natural formation. But there wasn't anything else we could do about it. That was as good as it was going to get.

Cornelius nodded to the left. "We need to head that way to get to the market."

Stepping back around the rocks, I glanced over toward Jabal City. Once again, it looked dark and foreboding. But there were no cries of alarm coming from inside of it. It looked like we hadn't been discovered yet.

"Let's go quick before anybody comes to replace these guards. If we're lucky, they'll think the Damned got them," Tess said.

Both Cornelius and I were in complete agreement. We hurried across the open space. My skin tingled, waiting to hear a yell from someone as they caught sight of us. But no sound came from the city. In fact, there was no sound anywhere around us.

Without any issues, we managed to slip into a cusp of trees. Moving quickly, none of us spoke as Cornelius took the lead. All around us, it was eerily quiet. I found myself stepping more lightly, not wanting to add any noise.

For over an hour, we traveled like that. I'd gotten so use to the quiet that when a noise finally reached my ears, I immediately froze. I put out a hand to the other two before pointing to my ear.

Tess's eyes widened when she heard the noise as well. She nodded to a row of boulders. Hurrying over to them, we crouched down low.

It took only a minute or two before the cause of the noise became clear. Two Damned came into view. Their bare feet dragged along the ground as they walked. Their mouths gaped open as they stared straight ahead. The skin around their eyes was darkened, their frames skeletal. But these two must have been relatively new, as their skin hadn't deteriorated as badly as the other ones we'd seen. In fact, this was the first time I'd had a chance to see them up close.

These two were a man and a woman. Both had dark hair, the woman's long and nearly down to her waist and matted. The man's was shorter, although his hair still came to his shoulders and was similarly disheveled. Their clothes hung on their frames in strips and were soiled.

A wave of compassion rolled over me as I watched them. This was no way to live. And who knew why they were in Hell? Maybe they had been pulled in as well.

But there was nothing I could do for them, so I simply had to sit and watch as they shuffled past. We stayed there quietly for a few minutes until we could no longer hear them, and then we stood.

Tess cast a glance after them. "That's not an existence I would ever want."

"Me either," I said softly.

His gaze still staring in the direction the Damned had disappeared, a look appeared on Cornelius's face I couldn't decipher. Catching me looking at him, he seemed to give himself a shake before nodding in the direction we had been heading in before the Damned had interrupted us.

"We should get going," he said and hurried ahead before I could say anything.

Tess and I exchanged a glance and then followed him.

Cornelius was quiet by nature, but he'd seemed even more subdued since we'd stepped through the portal. It must be tough to come back here. He'd finally escaped, and now he found himself back in Hell. Besides bringing up all sorts of horrible memories, it had to be messing with his sense of reality.

I wasn't sure if I should say anything. I mean, what could I say that would actually make it better? I could assure him that we were going to get him back home with us, but he knew that already.

The thoughts and fears rolling through his mind were his, and I didn't have the right to intrude on them. So, I'd have to leave him with his thoughts and hope that he could sort them out himself.

We walked for a good two hours before Cornelius put up a hand, a finger to his lips. We slipped off the path as sounds reached us. This time, when we hid, it was behind thick trees.

A woman hurried past, but she was no Damned. She flicked a glance over her shoulder and hurried forward, her shoulders hunched, as if trying to make herself as small as possible.

I wanted to reach out to her and tell her to wait, that we could help her, but we couldn't reveal ourselves just yet.

Once again, I wondered about the existence of Hell. I didn't doubt that some people belonged here. D'Angelo came to mind as a prime candidate for residency. He was someone who deserved a nice long, extended stay. But I also didn't believe that most people deserved to spend their eternity here. Who knew what kind of person D'Angelo might have been if he had been raised with kindness and decency rather than entitlement and arrogance?

This whole system had to change.

Originally, at least according to my father, it had been set up in a fairer way. People would come here, but when they had changed, when they had finally seen the error of their ways, they moved on. Hell was never meant to be an eternity. It was meant to be a learning ground.

Somehow, though, Abaddon had changed all of that.

And I couldn't help but wonder if the angels had something to do with that too, if Michael had something to do with that. Had he somehow stopped the flow of souls from heading to

Heaven? It didn't seem out of the realm of possibility, given what the man thought of humanity.

But it also was a shocking thought, nonetheless. Could he really sentence humans to an eternity in Hell when they didn't deserve it? Even when they had finally redeemed themselves? Of course, being he was in cahoots with the demons to destroy humanity, that didn't seem like too much of a stretch.

Cornelius tapped me on the shoulder. He nodded to the path. "The market is just another hundred yards ahead. There will probably be guards."

I looked over at Tess, who nodded, her face determined. "Well, there's no time like the present."

CHAPTER 27

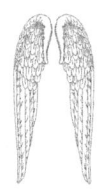

Once we were sure the coast was clear, we stepped onto the path and made our way cautiously toward the market. Usually, markets were something you could hear from a good distance away. People would be chatting. Traders would be calling out, hawking their wares.

But the markets in Hell were nothing like that. They were silent places. The transactions occurred in whispers.

Before we stepped out of the trees, we peered ahead and could see the market in the distance. Once again, it was located in the gully with rock faces on either side. A canyon that was inescapable except through the main pathway and the secret tunnel underneath Agnes's tent.

We lucked out, and there didn't seem to be any demons on guard duty today. Once again, I wondered why Abaddon wasn't shoring up some of these locations. Maybe he figured he didn't have to.

Unlike the last time, I was prepared. We'd taken cloaks from Blue Forks that were ratty and a little stained. The three of us slipped them over our shoulders and pulled up the hoods to cover our faces as best we could before we stepped onto the path again and walked toward the market.

"Hunch your shoulders more. You look too confident," Cornelius said.

Both Tess and I obeyed, making our steps more halting while turning our head this way and that, as if casting around nervously.

"We need to fix this, Addie," Tess said, her gaze hard as she got her first look at the market.

I nodded my agreement. We were too close for me to say anything else.

The market looked much the same as it had the last time. There were stalls lining each side, but they were nothing like the stalls back home. These were made out of scraps of wood, and sometimes there wasn't even that. It was just a scrap of cloth placed on the ground. The food tent was the most popular, but even there it was just an old blanket propped up on four slim sticks of wood that looked like it would blow over with a good breeze.

And the food, if you could call it that, was decidedly limited. It looked like some sort of beef jerky and a few tiny rolls that I had no doubt would be stale.

All of the people we saw were similarly clothed as we were. Almost all of them also had their hoods up. None of them were demons because demons were muscular and tall. Everyone here was shorter and gaunt. The few faces that I did catch a glimpse of were drawn and cast about nervous glances.

We shifted our way through the crowd, careful not to touch anyone. It was another behavior in Hell. People tried to avoid any sort of contact.

Up ahead, I saw our destination. Agnes still had the only fully standing tent. It was red, although faded by time and sun.

We reached its entrance. The same two guards from last time

were on duty. A man and a woman, both were more muscular in appearance than a lot of the other humans, but still they looked emaciated.

Cornelius stepped up and spoke quietly to the woman. "I need to speak with Agnes. Tell her it's Cornelius."

The woman looked up into his face with a frown before her eyes widened. With one last curious glance at Cornelius's face, she stepped through the opening in the tent.

I wondered about her look for a moment and then realized Cornelius's appearance had changed. A week of good food and decent sleep had made him look completely different than he used to. Gone were the gaunt cheeks and the dark circles under his eyes. He looked healthy, if on the thin side.

The guard returned a moment later. She held open the tent and waved us in.

The last time we'd seen Agnes, demons had stormed into the market looking for us. We'd escaped through Agnes's tunnel, but I had to think that the demons had been unhappy to say the least.

I worried about what kind of reception we might receive from her, being we had to have brought some difficulty down upon her. But it was too late to second-guess ourselves now. I stepped into the tent, feeling Tess tense beside me.

The tent looked the same. Lyra, the small girl I had mistaken for a boy, now stood behind Agnes's chair, peering out at us.

Agnes sat in her chair with the regal bearing of a queen. Her hard gaze flicked over the three of us, her eyebrows rising as they caught my gaze and then shifted to Cornelius with a frown. "Cornelius?"

He stepped forward. "Hello, Agnes."

Her mouth fell open as her eyes traveled from his boots to the top of his head. "What happened to you?"

Cornelius nodded back at me. "She did."

CHAPTER 28

Agnes's curiosity about Cornelius was a palpable thing. But my own curiosity was just as great. I noted the new tears in the side of the tent.

"Did you have any trouble after we left last time?" I asked.

Agnes pulled her gaze from Cornelius. "A little. They were very adamant in their search for you. But alas, they couldn't seem to find you anywhere. They couldn't seem to quite figure out how you had disappeared."

"Thank you for your help."

"My help doesn't come free." She shifted her gaze to Cornelius. "You've changed. You're clean."

Cornelius nodded. "I am," he said, falling silent.

We hadn't discussed how we were going to explain Cornelius's new healthier appearance. It was possible Agnes thought he'd linked up with Lucifer. She knew about his camp. Originally, we had planned on telling her that's where he had been.

But as I stared at the woman, I realized that approach would be a mistake. Agnes was too shrewd for any flimsy excuses. She could smell a lie from a mile away.

I took a step forward. "It appears I have a new gift that I didn't realize. I can take people through the portal."

Flicking a gaze at Cornelius before returning her attention to me, Agnes frowned. "What do you mean?"

I nodded to Cornelius. "I took him back with me. He left Hell. He lived in our world and only returned here in order to help us."

Agnes sat back, her mouth falling open. She looked completely stunned, and I had to think that she was someone who wasn't shocked very often. "That's not possible."

"I assure you, it's very possible. And it happened. Cornelius returned with us." I nodded to Lyra, who looked out curiously from behind the chair. "And I can take her back with me."

Lyra led out a little gasp and turned to Agnes.

Agnes stared at the young girl for a long moment before turning back to me. "You will take both of us."

I had known she was going to say that. "That will cost you extra."

A small smile appeared on Agnes's lips. "I expected no less. I assumed you weren't here just to repay your debt. What is it you want?"

"I need to know where they are creating the bracelets that the demons wear."

Agnes frowned. "What bracelets?"

I could hear the challenge in her voice. She wasn't going to give away any information for free.

I slipped one out of my pocket and showed it to her.

Agnes sucked in a breath. "Where did you get that?"

"I took it off a demon I killed."

Agnes's eyes glittered as she stared at it. "There are rumors about what these bracelets do. That they give strength to the wearer or that they could even make them invisible."

I shook my head, slipping it back into my pocket. "It does neither of those things. But it does allow the demons to cross into our world."

Shock once again slipped over Agnes's face before she could conceal it. "Well, you certainly have learned a lot since the last time we saw one another."

I shrugged. "We have a lot of people gathering that information. And now we need a little bit more. We need to know where these bracelets are being made."

Agnes drummed her fingers on the side of her chair. "And what will you do with this information?"

"I think you know," I said, staring into Agnes's eyes.

She gave a laugh. "I have no doubt."

Turning to Lyra, she stared at the young girl for a long moment before straightening her shoulders and looking back at me. "If we go with you, the demons will notice our absence. Abaddon keeps a close eye on the market. My stall being closed, it will draw attention."

I'd been thinking the same thing. I had an idea for how to avoid that, but I wasn't sure Agnes would like it. She surprised me by coming up with the idea herself. "I will have to stay. But Lyra will go with you."

"No," Lyra said. She came around the side of Agnes's chair and latched onto her arm. "I won't go without you."

Agnes gripped her arm tightly. "Yes, you will. You will go, and you will get yourself safe."

Her voice was harsh. But the gentle hand she then ran over the young girl's face softened the rebuke. "This is the safest way. There are others in those camps. And if the demons get through the portal, then you are in danger. This is how I keep you safe."

Lyra lowered her head, leaning into Agnes's chair. "I won't go without you," she said, her chin trembling.

"You will do as I say. And I will come through and find you after I help them with the camp." Agnes gave me a hard glare.

I nodded my agreement. "Yes, we'll take you then."

"As well as my two guards. They have been faithful and loyal. And they deserve a chance."

I didn't hesitate. "Agreed."

Agnes released Lyra's hands. The young girl slipped back behind her chair again, tears tracking through the dirt on her face.

"Then our deal is struck," Agnes said with a nod. "Lyra, get me paper and a pencil. We must show them where the camps are and get you on your way."

CHAPTER 29

We stayed in Agnes's tent for a good hour as she drew out the map and explained its layout. I questioned her repeatedly, as did Tess, looking for all possible details that could help us in our assault. Finally satisfied, I sat back, feeling a crick in my neck from having stayed hunched over for so long.

"How do you know all of this?" Tess asked.

Agnes shrugged as she sat back. "I trade in information."

"But this is not easy information to come by. And the camps can't allow people in and out of them easily. So how do you know this?" Tess pressed.

I looked between the two of them, wondering what Tess was getting at. "What's going on?"

Tess didn't look away from Agnes as she spoke. "She trades information with the demons."

My mouth fell open, and then I turned to Agnes, who met my gaze unflinchingly. She nodded. "Yes, I do."

I stood up quickly. "How do we know that you won't trade information on us?"

"You don't. But it's not in my interest to betray you." She nodded to Lyra. "After all, I'm giving you a prized possession to take care of."

"How could you trade with the demons? After all they've done?" Tess asked.

Agnes stared her down. "I live in Hell. It's not a rhetorical statement. It's a fact. I will do whatever is necessary to survive and keep those I care about alive."

She huffed. "You come in here as if you know what this world is like, but you have no idea what I have been through, what those of us who have been around for centuries have been through. Cornelius knows. He could tell you stories that would terrify you... and they should.

"I do not apologize for keeping myself and mine safe," Agnes said, lifting her chin. "You would be no different in my position. Death is not even an escape here. The only thing different is that Hell becomes more painful. So don't look down at me."

Tess met her gaze for another long moment before giving her a nod. The tension in the tent ratcheted down.

One of the guards slipped into the tent and paused, seeming to sense the hostility in the air. She raised an eyebrow at Agnes, who waved her in. "What is it?"

"Night is falling. We need to get somewhere safe."

Agnes sighed, for once looking weary. "Very well. We'll stay in the tunnels tonight. But first we're going to escort these four to its exit."

If the guard was surprised by the statement, she didn't let it show. She merely nodded. "Of course, Agnes."

A few minutes later, we were slipping into the tunnel underneath Agnes's tent. I knew it would be pitch black, but luckily one of the guards led the way with a torch.

Cornelius followed behind him, and then it was Agnes

holding onto Lyra's hand, followed by myself and Tess, and finally the second guard.

No one spoke as we walked. Every once in a while, I would catch Lyra glancing up at Agnes as if looking for something from her, but Agnes kept her focus straight ahead.

It would have seemed cold if I hadn't noticed that every now and then, Agnes took a deep breath, like she was steadying herself for the goodbye to come.

An hour after we started, the guard put up a hand, and everyone stopped. She handed the torch to the guard in the back. "It's another ten feet until the opening. I'll go check and make sure it's clear," she said.

Tess stepped forward next to me. "I'll go with her," she whispered.

The two of them disappeared into the darkness. The rest of us stood waiting.

Lyra leaned into Agnes. Wrapping an arm around her, Agnes ran her other hand over the young girl's head. Lyra tucked her head into her side, bowing her head low.

Agnes was tough and no nonsense, but she obviously cared a great deal for the girl and vice versa. This separation was going to be difficult for both of them. Who knew how long the girl had been down here? And Agnes had been her protector. I wondered how the two of them met.

The girl had to be traumatized from her time here, and stepping into a whole new world would be difficult for her. I had to find a way to keep her safe, to give her a sense of normality.

Sheila automatically popped into my head. Marjorie was home during the day while Sheila was at work. Perhaps Sheila would agree to take the girl in. She would be a good caretaker for Lyra. Strong, confident, she was a lot like Agnes in some ways.

Part of me thought that I should take responsibility of the girl myself, but I didn't see how that would be possible. I needed to keep Noel and Micah under guard. And if I put the girl with them, she would just be in more danger. No, I needed to find other accommodations for her.

Agnes spoke low, her voice caring in the dark tunnel. "I'm giving you my most precious gift. You will keep her safe."

"I promise I will. I'll do everything in my power."

Even in the dim light, I could feel Agnes's penetrating gaze on me. "Your power is more considerable than you know. You need to use every ounce of it."

I frowned, wondering at Agnes's words, but before I could ask, the guard and Tess returned. "The way's clear. You should go now," the guard said.

Cornelius stepped forward, heading toward the exit. Tess joined him, and I turned to Agnes. She knelt down to meet the girl's gaze. "I will see you in a few days. You are going on to a good life, Lyra. You will be safe, and you will be happy. You will see sunlight again. So embrace it." She wrapped the girl in a hug.

Lyra's shoulders shook as she cried, holding on to Agnes tightly. Agnes closed her eyes, her face dissolving for one brief moment, the only moment she would allow herself. And then she composed herself. She pulled back, nodding at the girl. "Now go. It's time."

As she stood, she nodded at me. I put my hands on the girl's shoulders. She jumped in response.

"Go on," Agnes said.

I gently started to pull her down the tunnel. Lyra reached back, her hand holding on to Agnes until the very last moment. Then Agnes let her go. The other guard came to stand next to her.

Lyra kept her gaze focused on Agnes the entire time we walked, even long after Agnes was lost to the shadows.

"It will be all right, Lyra."

The little girl finally faced forward. "You don't know that," she said, sounding much older than her appearance would indicate.

CHAPTER 30

The tunnel spit us out about a mile away from the portal. We were coming at it from a different angle than we had before. Once again, it was quiet, with no Damned or demons in sight. The air above had darkened during our long walk.

As I walked, I kept a hand on Lyra, in part to comfort her and in part to make sure she didn't run back to Agnes. She made no move to do so, but tears rolled down her cheeks.

A few dozen feet from the tunnel exit, Cornelius stepped to her other side. Reaching down, he took her other hand without a word. The girl gripped his hand and took a smaller step closer to him. I smiled, knowing that if anyone could help her through this, it would be Cornelius.

In silence, we made our way to the portal with Cornelius directing us. He used hand signals whenever we needed to shift our approach. My mind flitted back over the directions that Agnes had given us.

Apparently the bracelets were made in one central camp. There were three areas, one where the metal was melted down, one where the bracelets were formed, and one where the stones were inserted. But they all happened within the same massive camp. Any sort of assault would need to be equally massive.

I worried a little bit about what that would mean. Going against the demons was not going to be easy. We would need all of the resources we could come up with, plus any extras we could manage.

Two of those resources were Vera and my father. I was hoping that they would be able to help with the battle as well. Having two angels on our side would definitely be an advantage.

Even with them, though, it was going to be difficult. But we had to make this work. Cutting down the number of demons that could come through to our side would be a game-changer, a world-saver.

Once we overtook the camp, the really big part of the plan needed to begin: me bringing the prisoners in the camp back to Earth. That was going to be another whole huge undertaking.

Part of me hoped I would be able to use the bracelets that we found in the camp on the prisoners. Worst-case scenario, I could have somebody on the other side immediately removing the bracelet and coming back with them so that we could get a steady flow of people through. But that was still going to be time-consuming.

All of the different permutations and all of the problems rolled through my mind in a never-ending stream. Tess bumped my shoulder, pulling me from my thoughts.

I looked up at her, and she nodded. I glanced up. We had reached the edge of the warren of rocks we'd been walking through.

About three hundred yards away stood the swirling portal. There were two guards standing at it. They didn't seem alarmed. Maybe they believed the other guards had been chased off by the Damned.

We were still hidden by the rocks, so they hadn't seen us yet. I rolled my shoulders, knowing that I needed to cover the space fast. They needed to be taken down quickly so that they couldn't raise the alarm.

"I'll take them." I handed Cornelius the bracelet. He slipped it onto Lyra's wrist. "As soon as the portal is clear, you three go through. If I'm not with you, don't wait for me."

"Addie," Tess said, a warning in her tone.

"I'll be right behind you. I said *if*. This shouldn't be—"

A shout rang out across the space. My head jolted up, looking for its source.

"There." Tess pointed farther to our right.

Squinting, I tried to make out what was coming.

My mouth dropped as Lucifer, his wings extended, flew over the land. Four demons rushed after him. The two at the portal gave a yell and ran to intercept him.

And that's when I noticed the body in Lucifer's arms.

CHAPTER 31

The body was small, maybe about the same size as Micah's. Although Lu was still a good distance away, I could see the red staining the shirt and skin of the boy he held.

"Oh my god." I looked at Cornelius and Lyra. "Cornelius, get her through the portal."

"But—" he started to protest.

"No, Cornelius. She's the priority. Get her to safety," I said before I took off to intercept the demons.

Tess had already stepped forward, pulling out her bow and lining up her shot. She let one fly, and it caught one of the demons from the portal in the back of the thigh.

Taking to the air, I surged forward, my wings engulfed in flame as I soared toward my father. One of the demons took a running leap. I put on a burst of speed and tackled him just before he grabbed my father's leg, dragging him into the ground. I quickly rolled off as one of the other demons swiped his large hand down toward me.

Rolling onto my back, I slammed a kick into his groin,

followed by a round kick to his knee. He wobbled.

Jumping up into the air, I grabbed the back of his head and slammed my knee into it.

A second demon rushed toward me from behind. With the barest of thoughts, the flames on my wings burned hotter. He screamed as the flames caught on his pants and set them aflame.

The other demons continued after my father. The one that I kneed in the face had stumbled back but now righted himself. I slammed another side kick followed by a back-kick into his chest, and he went flying back. I tore off after my father.

Pulling my sword from the scabbard as I flew, I slashed at both of the demons following my father at the back of the knee. With screams, they crashed to the ground.

Both of the demons from the portal lay face down. Six of Tess's arrows punctured each of their bodies. They didn't move. Tess sprinted for the portal. My father had just touched down ten feet away from it.

With a burst of speed, I caught up with them, looking at the face of the child my father held. I sucked in a breath, recognizing him. It was the boy from the camp, the one we had met that first night we had been there. "Samuel."

Lucifer thrust him into my arms. "Take him through."

"What happened?" I asked as I gripped the boy.

The look my father gave me spoke volumes. My heart dropped. Before I could ask more, Tess let out a yell.

"Incoming!" She let loose two arrows in quick succession, but the demons coming at us swiped them out of the air with their swords.

"Tess, go!" I yelled. Without hesitating, she dove through the portal.

"Dad, no. Let's go," I yelled as my father turned to face them.

He looked at me and smiled. "You called me Dad."

I rolled my eyes. "Get through the portal or I won't do it again."

The two of us turned and sprinted for it, both of us feeling the demons hard on our heels.

Careful to keep the boy curled into my chest, I jumped through, trying hard not to jostle him and cause him more pain. It looked like he had already been through enough.

CHAPTER 32

My landing wasn't as gentle as I would have liked. I hit the ground hard, but I managed to stay upright, taking a stuttering run forward. The boy was heavy in my arms and made me top-heavy, but I managed to keep the two of us from falling.

Tess had apparently hit the ground. Now she got to her knees, wiping dirt from her chest and pants as she stumbled to her feet. My father came through, graceful as ever, touching down lightly with a running walk.

Cornelius and Lyra stood behind Donovan, who stood in front of the portal, ready to defend them against whoever came through.

Donovan raised an eyebrow. "What happened?"

"Get him some help." I quickly handed the boy to Tess.

Tess gave me a look as she took the boy, flicking her gaze toward the portal. I knew she wanted to stay and fight, but now wasn't the time. She grabbed the boy and hurried over to Cornelius and Lyra.

"Heads up," Donovan called.

I whirled around as the first demon stepped through.

"Dad," I yelled, tossing my sword to him. He grabbed it midair and slashed it across the demon's chest. The creature fell face first, half his body in this world and half still in Hell.

The other demon started through, and with one swipe of the blade, my father took off his head.

Donovan walked up, his eyes wide. "So I guess the trip didn't go smoothly?"

The demon's head rolled to a stop only a few feet in front of me. "No. It was definitely not smooth."

CHAPTER 33

Neither my father, Donovan, nor I were willing to leave the portal unguarded, so we waited for another thirty minutes to make sure no one came through.

By that time, Tess had made it back to the academy and sent two more guards to replace Donovan. Once they arrived, we quickly turned and headed to the academy.

"So what happened?" Donovan asked.

"I know where the camp is. I got the information. We're going to need to be there in two days' time."

"We should be able to do that," Donovan said.

I wasn't so sure. The size of the camp still made me nervous. But that wasn't the top priority right now. I turned to look at my father. His face was ashen.

"What happened?" I asked softly.

He shook his head as if he wasn't going to answer, but then I realized he was just trying to shake the thoughts out of his mind. "The camp... it's gone."

My heart stuttered. "What do you mean *gone*?"

"I went through early at a portal closer to the camp. There

were two guards at the portal entrance, and I dispatched them. Then I headed on to the camp. I made it through the Field of Sorrows without any problems.

"But Akira and Sibon didn't come to meet me. That was strange. They always come to meet me. They always sense where I am. So I knew something was wrong. I hurried, but it wouldn't have mattered. I saw the first body in the fields. There were dead everywhere."

Picturing all the people from my father's village, I sucked in a breath. From *my* village. "I'm sorry."

I'm not sure he even heard me, his eyes still looked so lost. "I made my way through the village looking for someone, anyone who might still be alive. I found Samuel. I thought it was a miracle that anybody had survived. But then I realized I'd only seen about a dozen dead. The rest were simply gone. I hope that maybe Ian managed to get them out."

"Was Ian among the—" I couldn't even bring myself to say the word.

Lucifer shook his head. "No, I didn't see him. I think he's alive."

"What about the dead?" I asked

His face grew even more drawn at my question. "Half of them had been pulled through by demons. Now they're dead for real."

My heart ached. Hopefully they ended up in Purgatory and eventually went on, although that thought brought me up short. Something was wrong with Purgatory, and those souls were being sent down to Hell. So there was no hope for those people. They would return to Hell, and this time my father wouldn't be there to greet them.

"You found Samuel, though," I said softly.

"They wanted me to find him. They left him alive to draw me in. They were waiting."

I sucked in a breath, fear lancing through me despite the fact that my father stood next to me. "How did you get away?"

The briefest of smiles flitted across his face. "I'm not so easy to take down. I fought them off, grabbed Sam, and ran. But they were looking for me. I knew that I couldn't go through the portal with Sam. I needed you to get him through. If that didn't work, I was going to kill one of the demons and take their bracelets, but none of the demons that I fought had a bracelet on them.

"I'd all but lost hope when I remembered that you would be coming through the Jabal City portal. I hastened there but drew the attention of a scout. They fell on me, and I barely managed to get away. And then we ran into you."

I couldn't help but picture the people from the village again. They'd been good people, kind people, peaceful people. And then I pictured all of the new refugees who had already been terrorized by the demons who dragged them into Hell.

None of them deserved that. And those refugees had been the lucky ones. My father and Ian had managed to grab them from the demons. Not all refugees were so lucky. And a good portion of those were going to be in the camp that Agnes had indicated.

But they weren't the only people who were trapped down there. There were humans in Jabal City. And there were people like Torr who were fighting the process, not wanting to become the full demons that Abaddon wanted them to be.

Fear, uncertainty, and doubt warred within me. But I shoved the feelings aside as I pictured Abaddon's face.

He'd crossed a line going after the people of my father's village. And whatever it took, I was going to take him down.

CHAPTER 34

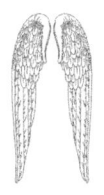

By the time we got to the academy, Sam was being examined in the medical unit. Tess had sent Cornelius with Lyra up to her apartment to get a shower and something to eat.

Stopping in at the medical wing first, I found Dr. Jade, who told me that Sam was resting and that she'd given him some meds to keep him asleep while she set his arm, which was broken, and wrapped his ribs. She'd also stitched up a gash on his thigh and another on his shoulder.

My heart broke for him. "He has family over in Blue Forks. Could you send one of the Rangers to find them?"

Corey, the Ranger I'd first met when Tess and I were sneaking back into the academy through the library, had been standing nearby. He stepped forward, looking down at the boy. "I'll do it."

I told him everything I could remember that Samuel had said about his family. Corey took his leave to see if he could find them.

When I stepped out of the medical wing, I turned to head up the stairs toward Tess's apartment.

"Addie."

Graham's voice stopped me. He hurried down the hall and hugged me tight.

Exhaling, I let myself sink into the hug, wrapping my arms around him and leaning against his chest. He seemed to know that I needed a moment, so he held me without asking any questions. Finally, I leaned back.

"Are you all right?" he asked.

"Physically, yeah, I'm fine. You know about the boy?"

"Yes. Mitch just gave me the rundown and told me you also brought back a young girl?"

I nodded, heading toward the stairs. "Cornelius took her upstairs. I'm heading there now."

Graham took my hand as we started up the steps. I gave him a brief report on the situation in Hell, both what my father had been through and what we had learned. Then I handed him the map that Agnes had drawn. "I'm afraid staging an armed assault against a camp is not something I have any experience with. I'm hoping maybe you might come up with some ideas?"

He took the paper and unrolled it. Glancing at it, his eyebrows rose before he rolled it back up with a nod. "I'll come up with something. How long do we have?"

"Two days."

The fact that Abaddon had set a trap for my father made me worry about what plans he'd already concocted. And the fact that the demons and some of the Rangers were working together concerned me even more. Agnes had said two days. I thought that it was too short a time for everything that needed to be done.

But now I worried that it was too long.

CHAPTER 35

The water was running in the bathroom in Tess's apartment when I stepped inside. Graham had headed downstairs to start going over the camp's schematic in detail and try to figure out some options for an assault. He was going to call in Donovan and Mitch to aid him, along with some of the more senior Rangers who were in town.

Part of me thought I should be helping him, but like I'd told him, that wasn't really my strong suit. And right now, I really needed to see that Lyra and Cornelius were all right.

I'd sent a note to Sheila explaining the situation and asking if she would be willing to help out. I was hoping the answer was yes.

Cornelius looked up from where he sat on the couch. He started to get to his feet, but I waved him back down. "How is she?"

Cornelius opened his mouth to answer and then closed it, shaking his head. "I don't know. She hasn't said a word."

I didn't know what to make of that, but it didn't sound good.

The water had turned off in the bathroom as I walked into

Tess's room. I headed for the closet and rifled through it, grabbing some pants and a T-shirt. I knew that they'd be too big for the girl, but they'd be better than the clothes she'd been wearing. I grabbed some socks and underwear as well.

Walking over to the bathroom, I knocked softly on the door. "Lyra? It's Addie. I have some clothes here for you."

There was silence for a moment before she spoke. "Come in."

Opening the door, I spied Lyra. She sat in the tub with bubbles up to her chin. Her hair was wet, and her skin had started to prune. Placing the clothes on the sink top, I smiled at the sight of all the bubbles. Cornelius had taken care of the little girl the best way he knew how.

Grabbing one of the towels from the closet, I put it on the sink next to the clothes. "There's a towel here for you whenever you're ready to get out."

The girl nodded, staring straight ahead.

Not sure if I should say something or try and help her, I decided to just step out and give her a little privacy. Closing the door behind me, I slid down against the door to wait.

It was ten minutes later when I finally heard the splashing of the bath water and knew that she

She'd stepped out. I gave her another fifteen minutes before I stood up and knocked softly on the door. "Lyra? Are you all right?"

"I'm okay," came the soft reply.

Hesitating for a moment at the closed door, I said, "Is it okay if I come in?"

She didn't reply for a long moment. "Okay."

As I opened the door, it took me a moment to spot her. She was sitting in the corner of the bathroom behind the vanity, her knees tucked up to her chest, her arms wrapped around her legs. She looked up at me with big eyes.

Careful not to touch her in case she didn't want that, I sat down next to her. "This must all be pretty overwhelming for you."

She nodded. "I don't remember a lot before Hell."

"Do you know how long you were down there?"

The girl shook her head. "No. I remember my parents' house, but I can't picture them anymore. We didn't have anything like this," she said, indicating the bathroom.

I had a feeling that wasn't because they couldn't afford it but because perhaps modern plumbing wasn't a part of her world.

She looked up at me and swallowed. "They died, didn't they?"

I nodded. "I don't know for sure, but yes, I would think they're dead by now."

Lyra leaned her head on her knees. "Do you think they're in Hell somewhere too?"

The thought brought me up short and I wasn't sure what to say. "I don't know."

"I hope not. Nobody should have to live there. Nobody," Lyra said, her eyes seeing something that I couldn't.

A tear rolled down her cheek. I held out a hand, and she grasped it. I leaned back against the wall, prepared to sit and stay with the girl as long as she needed.

CHAPTER 36

I stayed with Lyra for a good hour before Cornelius knocked on the door to let me know Sheila had arrived. It took some doing to convince Lyra to trust me enough to go with her, but eventually I managed it.

Cornelius promised to go down and see her as soon as he finished up at the academy. Then we headed to the conference room where Graham was meeting with the others to go over the map and create a plan.

Now as I stared down at the map, the sheer size of the operation was hitting me yet again.

But I was going to take every refugee that we came across back home with us. Agnes had explained that the camp was made up entirely of refugees, people who'd been stolen from our world, not people who'd died. As a result, all of them should be able to come back through the portal.

According to Agnes, there were at least a hundred souls within its boundaries and at least a dozen or more demons keeping watch.

Each week, the bracelets were collected and given to Abaddon. If we didn't get there within the next two days, then the delivery would be made and the bracelets would be gone.

We would still be able to retrieve the stones, but we needed those bracelets.

It was a rush but a necessary one. As I looked around the room at the Seven, I couldn't help but note that everyone was concerned about how little we actually knew of the conditions in the camp.

"So these points here where the guards are supposed to be, are they stationary or do they roam?" Donovan pointed to the X's that Agnes had placed on the map to indicate the guards positions.

"Most stay where they are. There are four entrances to the camp, with two guards stationed at each entrance. But then there are another four that roam throughout," Tess said.

"And what about portals? Are there any nearby?" Graham asked.

Lucifer leaned forward. "There's one about a quarter of a mile away from the site. That must be the one that they come through when they bring refugees in."

Tess frowned. "I still don't understand how those portals work. The one outside of Jabal City, that one's permanent, like the one in the woods, right?"

"Yes," Lu said. "Other portals are a little bit more flexible in where they'll take you. You merely have to have a destination in mind. And when you want to return, you simply think about where you want to go back to."

"That's how all the demons disappear," Laura said.

Lucifer nodded. "Yes. They come through one of the other portals, and then when they want to return, they don't need a portal to return. They simply think their way back."

Donovan ran a hand through his hair. "We know there's at

least a hundred refugees in the camp. How many bracelets have we gathered so far?"

"I have all of the cities rushing them over to us. From last count, it looks like it's close to fifty," Graham said.

"And remember, as long as someone is touching hands with someone wearing a bracelet, they should be able to get through the portal," I said.

"Should?" Mitch asked, raising an eyebrow.

I shrugged. "Yes. Should. The demons don't put bracelets on the people that they take through from our world. So we figure it has to work the same way in reverse."

"That's a pretty big assumption," Mitch said.

Graham blew out a breath. "True. But this whole thing is a risk. And we're at the point where we need to take risks. We have to cut off the demons' ability to come through that portal. We have to do something to reduce their numbers."

"But if they can simply hold hands as they come through, doesn't that mean that this won't change anything? Won't they all still be able to come through that same way?" Donovan asked.

"So far, we've cut down their number by at least fifty by taking down the demons here and removing their bracelets," I explained. "If we can stop the manufacturing of this latest batch of bracelets and remove the heavenstones, we're definitely going to slow their ability to come through the portals."

Donovan chuckled. Everyone turned to look at him. He shrugged. "What? I'm just picturing all the demons having to come through holding hands."

I admit that the image did bring a smile to my face as well.

"And you've never seen this camp before?" Tess asked.

Lucifer shook his head. "No. We were never able to find it."

"So how did Agnes?" Tess asked, turning to Cornelius.

Cornelius shrugged. "Agnes has this way of getting information.

She's very good at ferreting it out. I don't know the extent of her network, but it's pretty big, and it includes people and possibly demons in Jabal City as well. If Agnes says that this is where the camp is and that this is the layout, then we would be wise to believe it."

I didn't doubt that Agnes's network was extensive. I did, however, wonder whether or not we could completely trust her. I suppose the fact that we had Lyra gave us a little extra comfort that the women wouldn't intentionally try to lead us into a trap.

But Abaddon had to, at the very least, be aware that we would be coming for the bracelets. Or maybe he wouldn't. Abaddon seemed awfully sure of himself.

"I just wish we had more intel," Laura said.

There were murmured grunts of agreement around the room. And my grunt was one of them. It felt like a reckless move.

But Graham was right. Reckless was necessary at this point. We needed to slow the tide of demons coming through the portal. And while this was a risk, if it paid off, it could at the very least give us more time to prepare. And at worst...

I shook my head, not wanting to think of the worst.

"There is one more source that could possibly provide us with more intel on this camp," Tess said slowly.

"He's not talking," Lucifer said. "I've visited him three times each day so far. He's so angry and bitter that nothing seems to be getting through to him."

"Then maybe we need to try a different approach. Or maybe just an approach by someone different," I said.

CHAPTER 37

The cells in the bottom of the academy were still empty as I made my way down to them. I couldn't help but think that D'Angelo deserved to be rotting in a cell. From what I had heard, he was having food delivered to his home regularly. He was even entertaining guests. Apparently even the members of the Council had been by to visit with him.

I rolled my hands into fists in frustration. That man had caused so many problems and yet he was still sitting in the lap of luxury. Such considerations would not be extended to a Demon Cursed if they'd been charged with the same type of crime as D'Angelo. But this was hardly the first example of an Angel Blessed receiving special treatment.

In D'Angelo's case, however, it went beyond his Angel Blessed status. Members of the Council were actively looking out for him.

Even now, when they were well aware of the impending war with the demons, they were still looking to make life more difficult for the Demon Cursed. I'd gotten word about them wanting to round up the Demon Cursed to make sure they didn't help the demons when they invaded.

As if the demons held any allegiance to the Demon Cursed. They thought no more of them than they did the Angel Blessed. In fact, I wasn't sure the demons were even aware of the distinction between the two groups. And if they did, they certainly wouldn't care about it.

The Council also argued that only Rangers who were Demon Cursed should be put on guard duty at the portals to raise the alarm when the demons appeared. I knew in my gut that they thought they would be the first to fall and that would be less of a loss.

My steps were muffled by the heavy stone walls. Up ahead, I saw a Ranger standing guard ten feet down from Michael's cell. He gave me a nod as I approached.

"How is he?" I asked.

"Quiet. Marcus was down earlier speaking with him, but he hasn't made a sound since then."

Marcus was Michael's other regular visitor. He'd been trying to get any information at all he could about Michael's involvement with the demons. But I had no doubt he was also trying to ferret out everything he could about the angels and Heaven. Not from the standpoint of trying to fight them, of course, but out of pure academic curiosity.

Having Michael sitting in a cell was absolute catnip for the professor. He'd already been hounding both Vera and my father to get them to answer some questions for him. It had gotten to the point that I'd seen both of them disappear into rooms, and in one memorable case with Vera, out a window as soon as they caught sight of Marcus.

I was going to have to speak with him to get him to quit pestering the archangels, Vera especially. Because unlike my father, I wasn't entirely sure that Vera wouldn't just tell Marcus where to go and how to get there if he bugged her once too often.

When I reached Michael's cell, I peered inside. The cell was eight feet by eight feet. The back of it was a rock wall, and three sides were lined with thick metal bars. If he'd had his strength, he would have been able to get out of here with no problem.

But now that he'd lost his grace, he was no stronger than a human and therefore no more capable of breaking out than a human was, perhaps even less so. At least with a human, there might have been a chance that they knew how to pick a lock. But Michael had no need of such skills when he could rely on his strength.

The former archangel now lay on his cot, on his back, his eyes closed. His skin was ashen, probably because of the air. It was dank down here. And his cheeks looked a little gaunt, as if he hadn't been eating. He was a far cry from the Michael I'd seen arrive at Graham's estate that day in a ball of light.

"Michael."

His eyes flicked open. He glanced over at me before sitting up slowly. "Daughter of Lucifer. What is it you want?"

"I want to know about you and Uriel's deal with Abaddon."

A slow chuckle emerged from the former angel's chest. "And why would I help you?"

"Because the demons are coming. And they're not going to spare you simply because you once were in cahoots with them. Without your powers, you're of no use to them. And if they roll through Sterling Peak, they'll kill you just like everyone else or worse. They'll just leave you in this cell to die, no food, no water. You'll just waste away."

Despite his haggard appearance, Michael's eyes blazed as they stared at me. "I'm not going to help you. You're an abomination. You never should have existed."

"You know that's not true. And you know your anger for my

father is misplaced. He was sent down to Hell. He was meant to keep the demons in line."

Michael scoffed. "And what a fabulous job he did."

Anger burst inside of me, bright and hot. I took a deep breath, willing it back. My father had taken on the duty in Hell even though he knew the hardship it would create for himself. But he'd taken it on like a good soldier.

"My father was and is a good and dutiful soldier. He did what he was told to do. He followed orders. What orders are you following, Michael?"

Michael stood up quickly and swayed for a moment. He gritted his teeth as he walked closer to the bars. "There's no way your father was sent down as part of a mission. He betrayed all of us."

I shook my head. "You know that's not true. You want it to be true, but you know it isn't."

"All I know is that no one stopped me when I first reached out to Abaddon. Which means that my actions were ordained as well."

Stunned, I stared at him. "You can't honestly believe that. You can't believe that wiping out humanity is somehow following God's rule."

A bitter laugh escaped Michael. "Does it really matter? Humanity is a stain on this planet. Humanity is the favorite. Why? All your fighting. All your cruelty. Even with all of that, somehow you have attained the honored position. You never earned it. You don't *deserve* it."

"You're jealous," I said softly.

Michael snorted. "Jealous of what? Your short life spans?"

I shook my head. "No, of our freedom, of our lives. They're filled with happiness and, yes, sadness at times, and even pain. But there's such joy in the lives that we lead that that the memories can carry us through the moments of pain and sadness. You don't have anything like that."

"I don't *need* anything like that."

For a moment, as I looked at him, he was no longer the archangel Michael. He was a small little boy who felt alone. "It's all right, Michael. You're human now. You'll experience all of that one day yourself."

He sneered at me. "I have no interest in any of your human experiences. And I certainly have no interest in any compassion from you. You're not even worthy of the breath it takes to speak to you." He turned his back on me and stomped back to his cot.

My mind whirled at his choice of words: not worthy. "You don't think any of us are worthy, do you?" I asked softly, my mind spinning. My mouth fell open as it hit me. "You're the one who stopped the souls from going to Heaven, aren't you?"

"They are not worthy of His grace."

"How did you do it? How did you stop them?"

Michael smiled. "I don't know what you're talking about."

"Lying? The great archangel Michael has now stooped to lying?"

He glowered at me. "Humans don't deserve to be allowed into Heaven. They haven't earned it. They never will. It is a privilege well above them."

"So, you locked them away from it. You kept them in Hell. You doomed all of them. All of us."

"It is where you all belong."

I stepped closer to the bars. "But you seem to have forgotten something, Michael."

He looked up at me. "And what is that?"

"You're human now too. Which means when you die, Hell is where you'll end up as well."

CHAPTER 38

To say the conversation with Michael didn't go well was an understatement. I'm not sure why I thought he would help. At least now I knew he was the one behind the souls being barred from Heaven. But what I could do about it was yet another question I couldn't seem to answer.

And what about Michael claiming his action was ordained because he wasn't stopped? Where exactly was God in all of this? Shouldn't he be part of this?

"Addie?"

I looked up as Marcus hustled down the stairs. "Hey, Marcus."

"Were you visiting Michael?"

"Unfortunately." I explained how our conversation had gone.

Marcus leaned against the wall. "I've been wondering about Purgatory and the souls. There has to be something in Hell that's drawing the souls down there. Perhaps I'll be able to tease it out of Michael's recollection."

"How are your conversations with him going?"

"Actually, not bad. He wants to talk. And I suppose with me, he holds no anger. I think in part it's because he's bored staring at four walls. It's not an existence that he's ever experienced before."

I grunted, realizing that was probably true. "If you find out anything, please let me know as soon as possible."

"I will. And good luck on the mission, Addie. I know you'll succeed," he said before heading back downstairs.

As I watched him go, I couldn't help but wonder if I should try again with Michael. But in my gut, I knew I wouldn't be the one who got through to him. But maybe my words would make him talk to Marcus. Because what I said was true: If the demons won, they'd kill everyone they came across.

Which meant Michael was bound for Hell just like the rest of us.

CHAPTER 39

The next two days were a rush of activity getting everything ready for the assault on the camp. The last of the bracelets from the other cities arrived the night before.

There were forty-eight of them. I hoped they were enough, but I just didn't know. We weren't even sure if the bracelets would work the same for humans as they did for demons. Theoretically, they should, but there was no way to try it out.

I also wasn't sure if something had changed in the humans who'd been pulled down there. But the bracelets had worked for Tess and the others, so I had to hope that they would be just as effective for those that had been pulled in by demons.

The other issue was whether or not they could indeed extend that ability to travel through portals to someone whom they were holding onto. That worked for the demons, but again, we were just guessing that it also worked for humans.

We were also only guessing at the number of people in the camp and the number of guards, as well as the camp's location.

In fact, there was so much we were relying on Agnes and her map for that it was keeping me up at night.

But there was no helping it. We needed to at least take some of the demons' ability to cross the portals off the board. And this was the only way we were going to do it.

Plus, part of me wanted to strike back at Abaddon and let him know that we weren't going to simply sit back and wait for him to invade.

For the last two days, I'd barely seen Graham. He'd been arranging for the raid, hand-picking each person who'd be going in with us to make sure that every single one was loyal to the mission and not to D'Angelo.

I could see the stress on his face that D'Angelo's maneuvers had caused. And once again I wished that that particular Angel Blessed had been taken out during the training yard incident.

D'Angelo, though, was too slimy for that. He'd made sure he wasn't there. As a result, everything tying him to Michael was simply hearsay, a point certain Council members continually stressed. And from the way the Council was talking, or at least half their members, they were going to make sure D'Angelo suffered little for his actions.

That whole situation was a headache we didn't need right now. Graham needed to be in charge of the Seraph Force. He needed to be the one leading when the demons invaded because if it were D'Angelo, he would probably just open the doors for all of them.

It still stuck in my craw that a human would turn against their own kind. The demons' plan was quite literally to wipe out most of humanity, which would send most of them to Hell. And then they would rule over what was left.

How could a human possibly go along with that? Was D'Angelo stupid enough to think that the demons would somehow give him a position of power? He'd be their lap dog at best.

Nonetheless, that was the route that we suspected D'Angelo had taken. I wasn't sure if he was motivated by arrogance or fear. But either way, he'd ended up in the same place: united with the demons against humanity.

But now it was time to take that first step to make sure D'Angelo's plans failed.

We'd traveled this morning to the portal that was an hour from Sterling Peak. My father knew of it and had led us here. It was set in the middle of a clearing. I could see it, as could Vera and my father, but the rest wouldn't be able to see it until they were wearing the bracelets.

We handed the bracelets out to our forces. Twenty Rangers were joining us along with my father, most of the Seven, and Vera. Torr was also here. Grunt was back at the academy with Noel and Micah.

Donovan was there as well, much to his chagrin. He was still healing, and we needed everyone to be in top form when they went into the camp, so he would keep an eye on them along with Lyra until we returned. He wasn't happy about it.

Graham walked over to me and looked into my eyes before casting his gaze across the assembled group. "It looks like we're ready."

Everyone knew what the plan was. The portal would take us to a spot only a quarter of a mile from the camp. Lucifer had arranged it so that we would arrive in a secluded location. Then we would make our way to the camp and hopefully catch them unaware.

But there was no guarantee of that.

The individuals arrayed around me looked confident and ready for the fight to come. My gut churned as I turned toward the portal and hoped that they were.

CHAPTER 40

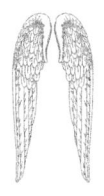

My father, Vera, and I stepped through the portal first. We looked around, listening for any sound that might alert us that someone was aware we were nearby.

We didn't take to the air to search because we'd be too easily seen, but each of us spread out, walking the distance to the camp and keeping an eye out. The camp was up ahead beyond a series of rocks that Agnes had drawn on the map.

As I reached the rocks, I had a birds eye view of the camp. It was surrounded by an eight foot rock wall with three separate entrances. And as Agnes had described, there were three massive tents.

The tents weren't enclosed making it easy to see inside them. The two on the right had a mass of bodies lined up at tables where the bracelets were put together.

Flames could be seen from the first tent where the metal was melted down. The heat inside must be excruciating.

Even as I watched, one man dropped, although whether it

was from exhaustion or the heat, I didn't know. He was pulled to the side, another man quickly taking his place in the line.

There had to be easily three hundred refugees, triple the number we suspected, and all of them looked exhausted. I was surprised to see that some were like Torr: partway through their transformation.

Everything seemed calm. The guards seemed relaxed as they stood at the camp's entrances.

Footsteps to my right sounded, but I wasn't alarmed. I was expecting them. Agnes and her two guards stepped out of the path.

"You made it," I said.

"Of course. How's Lyra?" Agnes asked.

I pictured the young girl. She didn't talk much. She seemed to be withdrawn, but she was eating and seemed to be comforted by the presence of Noel and Micah. I guess she was just looking for people closer to her own age. "She's good. She'll be happy to see you. Any changes?" I asked, nodding to the camp.

"No. They don't seem to be aware of anything, but I can't guarantee that," Agnes said, her gaze direct.

"Understood."

Agnes looked around. "Where are the rest of your people?"

"We came out first to see what the situation was before the rest of them arrive."

"You didn't trust me?" Agnes asked with a smile.

I returned the smile. "There's trust, and then there's trust."

Agnes chuckled. "I understand." She nodded to her two guards. "They would like to join in the rescue attempt."

I looked at them and nodded. "Good. We'd be grateful for the help. And you?" I asked Agnes.

She shook her head. "Fighting is not my forte. My strengths lie elsewhere."

That was most definitely true. Vera appeared on the path to our right and hurried toward us. "We're all clear," she said.

My father appeared from the path on the left. "Here as well. I saw a herd of Damned in the distance, but they shouldn't be a problem."

That was a relief. I was worried that the Damned would kick up a ruckus if they were nearby alerting the guards.

Agnes's eyes widened as she looked between Lucifer and Vera.

"Agnes, this is my father, Lucifer. And this is our friend Vera."

Agnes turned to Vera, her eyes widening even more. "You're an archangel."

Vera raised her eyebrows. "How do you know that?"

Agnes's expression immediately shifted to neutral. "Just a guess," she said, looking away.

I frowned, studying her. "That was a pretty good guess."

Agnes shrugged, not meeting my gaze. "So what's the plan now?"

"I'm going to go back and get the others and let them know they can come through. Why don't you come with me?"

With a nod, Agnes turned to her two guards. I was surprised when she walked forward and gave each of them a hug, whispering good luck.

I was even more surprised to see the emotion on her face. I'd thought Agnes's affections only ran to Lyra, but apparently she'd grown close to her guards as well. There was a bright sheen in her eyes as she turned toward me and nodded. "I'm ready."

"I'll be right back," I said to my father and Vera before heading back the way we had come.

We walked through the path in the trees. Agnes looked around constantly, her eyes wide. "Are you all right?" I asked.

Agnes took a shuddering breath and then gave a little laugh.

"Believe it or not, I'm nervous. For so long, I've wanted to get out of here, and yet now that it's happening, I'm just nervous."

"It's understandable. You don't know what's on the other side. How long have you been here?"

Agnes shook her head. "I don't really know. I died so long ago that I'm just not sure. Time, it's tricky here. Sometimes it seems to speed by in the blink of an eye. And other times it seems to crawl by and practically stop."

"Well, Lyra is waiting for you. And I know she'll be happy to see you."

"And I will be more than happy to see her."

The portal appeared up ahead as we rounded a bend.

I reached out my hand toward Agnes. "You'll have to take my hand. It's the only way you'll be able to go through."

With a nod, Agnes clasped my hand without hesitation. A little gasp escaped her as her eyes locked on the portal. "I've never seen one before. I mean, I knew where they were, but they just seemed so unreal at the same time because in all my time here I've never been able to see them." Her chin trembled.

"Are you ready?" I asked.

Straightening her back, she nodded.

"Here we go." Keeping a firm grip on Agnes's hand, I stepped through.

As we touched down on the portal on the other side, Agnes stumbled. I wrapped my arm around her waist to keep her from falling. She didn't even look at me, her gaze focused on the people surrounding us and the trees above. A tremor ran through her. "It's so colorful."

Then Cornelius pushed through the crowd. He stopped in front of her. "Hi, Agnes."

Agnes let out a laugh and wrapped her arms around Cornelius with a sob. Her reaction touched everyone around her.

More than a few looked away, but I caught the sheen of tears in a few people's eyes.

I nodded at Cornelius, who walked Agnes to the back of the group. A group of ten younger recruits were stationed there. Their job was simply to take care of the refugees as they came through, herd them together, and get them back to the academy.

Graham stepped next to me. "No problems?"

"No. Everything's as it should be. We're ready," I said.

"Then let's do this."

CHAPTER 41

Silently, I led the group from Sterling Peak toward where I had left my father, Vera, and Agnes's two guards. I kept casting a glance around, looking for anything that might alert the camp that we were nearby. Luck seemed to be on our side, and this part of Hell was quiet.

As I scanned the area looking for threats, I caught more than a few of the shocked expression on our team's faces.

I knew exactly how they felt. I felt the same way when I'd first stepped through the portal as well. And these people had all grown up with stories of Hell being the worst place imaginable. The fact that they'd been willing to come here said a great deal about their strength and bravery.

Up ahead, my father stepped onto the path and waved us forward. "Any problems?" he asked.

"No. You?" I asked.

"All quiet. The camp is just going through its normal routine. I detected no heightened sense of awareness. I don't think they know we're coming."

Releasing a short breath, I nodded. I'd worried that Abaddon might somehow learn what we were up to. He always seemed to know what was going on. But maybe, just maybe, we'd managed to keep this one under the radar.

Quietly, Graham broke us up into the three separate groups. All of the members of the assault force had bracelets. Each group had one person who had a few extra bracelets to give to the refugees.

But we were planning on using the bracelets from the camp itself to get the refugees through. Even with that, the plan was for everyone to go through the portal in twos.

It wasn't going to be a fast process, but there was no other way. Once someone stepped through, their bracelets would be collected. And each time, they reached ten someone would dash back through with the bracelets to hand out to more people.

Lucifer, Vera, and I were split amongst those three groups as well. We figured that it was best to have one person who could fly within each group.

We were going to be the strongest fighters, and we wanted to make sure that everybody had an equal chance of getting out. There was no conversation as we split up. Lucifer and Vera each headed off in opposite directions. They would come at the camp from different sides. I stood waiting with Tess, only giving Graham a quick kiss before he disappeared with Vera's group.

My heart was in my throat as I watched him go, but I had to have faith that he would come out of this all right. That all of us would. But it was difficult to stand there and wait. I wanted to rush down into the camp and get this started.

Instead, we slowly made our way along the cliff toward the edge of the camp. Then we stopped, staying hidden, and waited.

The call of a bird sounded across the camp. "That's the signal," Tess said.

I nodded as I stood, my wings unfolding from my back. "Let's go."

CHAPTER 42

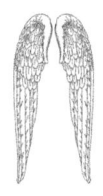

Taking off into the air, I flew straight for the entrance of the camp. One of the guards had his back to me. The other was leaning down to scratch his leg. I slammed into the one leaning down with two feet. He went flying.

Without saying a word, I pulled my sword from its scabbard and ran it through the one who'd been scratching his leg. As he stood up, surprise flashed across his face before he keeled over.

The second guard stumbled back to his feet. Before he could get fully upright, I slashed my sword toward his face, but he jolted back. Soaring forward, I sliced my sword up from his groin to his shoulder. Then with one last swipe, I took off his head. The body dropped.

A cry went up through the camp. Behind me, Tess led the rest of the charge.

Another demon guard, this one a towering beast more muscular than any I'd seen before, rushed forward with a yell from behind the tent.

Before he could reach me, two arrows crashed into his chest. He stopped moving forward as a third arrow lodged in his neck.

Turning, I caught sight of Cornelius with a bow. He gave me a nod and then hopped up on the wall, his bow and arrow at the ready. Two other members of our forces leaped up next to him, keeping watch across the camp, looking for any movement.

I hustled toward the tent in the middle. This was the one that manufactured the frames. As I burst into the tent, people cowered away.

There had to be over fifty people in here.

Tess was right next to me with the bag of bracelets. She quickly started to move through the crowd. "We're here to get you out. We need you all to come with me."

Nobody moved. All of them seemed to be frozen in place. Cornelius hurried into the tent and stopped next to me.

"What's going on? Why aren't they moving?" I asked him.

"They're scared. They think this is some sort of demon trick."

Motioning for Cornelius to back away, I stepped forward and set my wings aflame. "We're not working with the demons. We're here to help. You don't belong here, and we're getting you out."

A woman with long gray hair stepped forward, her eyes locked on my wings. "Are you an angel?"

I didn't think now was the time to go into a long treaties on my unusual genetic heritage, so I simply nodded. "Yes, come with me. Let me help you."

Nodding, the woman took a step forward. Her actions seem to spur everyone else into motion.

People started rushing. I held up my hand, calling out. "No, we have to do this organized. Everyone who has a bracelet needs to link up with someone who doesn't."

Three more Rangers hustled into the tent. We grouped the people together and started them toward the exit. I stepped out of the tent and saw Vera soar up into the air and then over to me.

"Demons coming, a lot of them," she said before she rushed back to her tent.

I closed my eyes. Damn it.

CHAPTER 43

I took off into the air to get a visual of the demons heading in. Sure enough, there was a large group coming from the direction of Jabal City. I was less concerned about them, though, because they seemed far enough away that it shouldn't be a problem.

The six heading to the portal however were going to be a problem.

"Tess!" I called down. "There's a group heading to the portal."

"Go! I'll be right behind you," she said, already grabbing two of the Rangers and running for the exit of the camp.

Flying over the group from the camp, I did a quick calculation, happy to see that dozens of people were already being led to the portal.

Putting on a burst of speed over them, my wings left trails of fire through the sky. I heard the gasp of the people below.

With my sword leading the way, I headed toward the group of demons on an interception course with the portal. Focused on the demons, I narrowed my eyes. Thirty feet away. I'd reach them well before the first group from the camp. It would be okay.

Something slammed into me on the side and then wrapped around me. I plunged to the ground with a cry.

CHAPTER 44

The air rushed from my lungs as I hit the ground hard. Rolling onto my side, I lay gasping like a fish on land. It took me precious seconds to get my breath back. When I did, I realized that there was a net wrapped around me. Someone had launched a net at me.

My wings were flattened against my back.

Closing my eyes, I sent a burst of energy out through my wings. They flamed hot and high, ripping through the net.

I'd just managed to scramble to my feet when a demon swung a mace at my head. My sword had fallen from my grasp when I hit the ground, and I didn't have a chance to grab it before I had to move.

Barely managing to duck the demon's attack, I felt the wind of the mace's movement push back against my hair. Shifting to the side, I shot out a kick into the side of the demon's knee.

The demon stumbled.

Not letting him recover, I climbed up his back, pulling the knife from the holder in my thigh and plunged it into the demon's neck.

Blood sprayed across the dry ground. Dropping to his knees, the demon gurgled as he grabbed for his neck. Pulling my knife free, I jumped off him as a second demon let out a bellow and went low to grab me around the waist.

Gripping the back of his head I pulled him forward while simultaneously twisting him to the side. With a cry, he fell onto his back and rolled a few feet away.

A third demon pulled his sword, slashing at my face. Once again, the blade was too close for comfort. I ducked to the side and backtracked, moving quickly before taking off into the air.

Tess slid in behind the demon, slicing him along the back of his knees before she slashed straight between his legs. He let out a cry before Tess stood up and plunged her sword into his back and twisted it.

Spying my sword on the ground, I dove back for it. Snatching it up, I finished off one of the other demons while Cornelius and Laura took care of the third.

But we weren't done yet. I turned for the other three demons. One of the Rangers had intercepted one and dispatched it. But the action had cost him. He was bleeding from a wound in his ribs. Another rushed toward him. Racing forward, I slammed my feet into a demon's shoulder, sending him flying.

"Help the refugees," I told the Ranger, who grimaced as he grabbed his side. He nodded and hurried to the refugees who were just cresting the path.

With a quick slice of my sword, I ended the demon that I'd shoved and turned to help with the other two to find that Tess, Cornelius, and the two other Rangers had already taken care of the problem.

Another Ranger darted forward and pulled all the bracelets off of the demons before they disappeared. But these weren't slipping away. This was their first death. Somewhere deep inside of me, I felt bad about that, the taking of a life, even though I knew we had no choice. I shoved that feeling down deeper. The demons deserved no sympathy from me.

The first of the refugees appeared at the portal. Cornelius urged them through. They hesitated. Cornelius quickly dove through the portal and then reappeared, showing them it was safe. The first two then stepped through. Once the initial few went through, the rest moved quickly.

I hurried over to Tess. "I'm going back to the camp to make sure everything's all right. You got this?"

Tess nodded. "We'll stay and guard the portal, make sure nobody else shows up."

Nodding, I was already launching myself into the air and heading back toward the camp.

A long line of refugees snaked all the way back to the camp. They were different ages, different genders, different races, but they all seemed to have the same look on their faces: a mixture of fear and hope.

Following the trail back to the camp, I scanned the area but didn't see any Damned or demons nearby. I dropped down outside the middle tent and looked around. Across the way, Vera was herding what looked like the last of the group from her tent to the exit.

"You good?" I called out.

She gave me a thumbs-up as she headed for the exit. At the other tent, my father had a small child who couldn't be more than four in his arms as he ushered his own group of about six toward the exit.

Moving to the middle tent, I hurried into it. There were long tables, probably about three dozen of them. Boxes were underneath to hold the frames of the bracelets.

After one last check here, I'd go catch up with everyone at the portal. Hurrying down each row, I made sure that no one had been left behind.

A sniffle sounded from somewhere farther in the tent. Stopping still, I tried to pinpoint its location. Crouching low, I spied a small face two rows over.

I leapt over the two rows, landing just in front of the table. A cry rang out from underneath it. Dropping low, I met the eyes of a young girl. She had dark skin and long hair braided behind her.

And behind her were another six children.

Feeling time slipping away, I had to force myself to keep my tone calm. "Hi there. We're getting everybody out. I'm going to need you to come with me."

"But the demon said we have to stay here," the little girl said.

My heart broke at the fear on her face. "I know. But we've taken care of those demons. And I need you to come with me so that I can get you somewhere safe."

The girl shook her head. "There is no place safe."

My heart broke again at her words. I extended my hand. "I promise you there is. I just need you to be brave for a few minutes, and then I can show you."

The girl looked deep into my eyes, and I could tell she wasn't sure. A little girl who looked too much like her not to be her sister crawled up to her side. "Alice, I want to go with her."

Alice looked down at her little sister, and then back at me. I could tell she was weighing the best approach. It was too big a decision for such small shoulders. "Let me help you," I said softly.

Finally, Alice nodded.

"Okay, come on, guys. We need to get out of here." I hustled all of them out of the tent. We were closer to the back of the tent, so I hurried them out that way. As we came around the side, I saw the last of the refugees disappearing through the camp exit. "Almost there," I said.

Picking up Alice's little sister, who couldn't be more than four, I held her in my arms as we hurried forward. Alice herding the others. A little boy latched onto my other hand. I gave it a squeeze as I led them toward the entrance. I cast a glance over my shoulder looking for any threats.

A cry burst from Alice. "Fire."

I whirled around. A wall of fire raced along the wall of the camp, blocking off the entrance. I pulled the kids to a stop and then turned to use one of the other entrances. But the fire was moving too quickly. In seconds, the fire had encircled the entire camp, blocking off all the exits.

We were trapped.

CHAPTER 45

A deep voice chuckled behind me.

I put the girl down and gently pushed the boy behind me as I turned. Three demons stood, their legs braced as they stared me down. "You're not getting out of here," the one in the lead said.

"Neither are you," I said, narrowing my eyes.

He laughed. "Doesn't matter what happens to us. Don't you get it? We're already in Hell. You kill us, we just show up back here again. Our job is to keep you here until Abaddon arrives."

My heart pounded in my chest. It was a never-ending cycle. We killed them, they ended up back here. They came to our world, we killed them, they end up back here. The futility of it all rolled through me.

One of the kids whimpered behind me. My anger grew hot at the idea of them being terrorized yet again.

"Stay here," I told the kids as I bolted forward.

There was no time to fight each of these guys individually. They needed to all go down together.

Energy welled up inside of me. I held up my hand as a ball of fire appeared in my palm. I tossed it at the demon in the front.

He ducked, but that only left his partner exposed. The flames engulfed him. He let out a scream and started to run.

The other demon stared after him, his mouth falling open.

I used the distraction to throw a fireball at him. Catching the movement from the side of his eyes, he ducked out of the way, but I'd already moved and brought my sword across his chest.

The leader of the group grabbed a hold of me and pulled me up by the neck. "Stupid little abomination."

"Look who's talking," I gasped out before kicking him in the groin.

His eyes bulged. He held my neck with one hand, and my sword arm with the other.

I kicked him in the groin again, and then ran my feet his chest and slammed my foot into his neck. He gasped as the pain shot through him and loosened his grip just enough for me to yank free.

Falling backward, I used my wings to keep me from hitting the ground. He lunged at me with a scream. I brought my sword up and impaled him right through the heart.

Shifting to the side, I pushed him to the ground and shoved my sword in deeper, twisting it. The light dimmed in his eyes, and he went still.

Pulling the sword from his chest, I wiped it on his pants and then slid it back into my scabbard. Turning, I was faced with the children who looked between me and the demons with expressions of shock on their faces.

Hurrying back over to them, I looked at the wall of fire. It roared up ten feet in spots. An accelerant must have been used on the wall itself. I'd have to fly each of them over it. I could probably take them two at a time, but that would still take three trips.

A bellow went up across the camp. I looked over as demons put out the fire near one of the entrances.

My heart jumped into my throat. I didn't have time to take them out two at a time. I wouldn't even make it back after the first jump before the demons would be on the other four.

At least a dozen demons streamed into the camp. They caught sight of us and started to charge.

No, no. I wasn't going to be able to get them all out in time. And I couldn't fight off that many, not while keeping the kids safe.

I needed a portal. I needed a portal right now. Right here.

The air started to waver to my left. One of the kids let out a little cry. I stared in disbelief as a portal formed. I had no idea where it would take us, but anywhere was better than here. "Everybody grab hands," I instructed.

The kids all linked up. I picked up Alice's little sister. "And everybody stay with me. And don't let go."

Taking a deep breath and praying that this portal didn't shoot us right into the middle of Jabal City, I stepped through.

CHAPTER 46

I stumbled as I touched down on the other side of the portal. My head whipped up as I looked around and recognized Sheila's backyard.

Confusion rolled through me. How on earth were we in Sheila's backyard?

"Where are we?" Alice asked, pulling me from my shock.

Ignoring her question for a moment, I did a head count and realized that everybody was here. Letting out a breath, I slowly lowered Alice's sister to the ground. "We're at a friend's house," I said softly.

The back door flew open. Sheila darted out, her eyes wide as she looked at the group of us. "Addie? What's going on? How are you here?"

I shook my head. "Honestly, I have no idea."

Grunt burst out of the door, hurrying toward us.

The kids let out a cry, some of them starting to run. I quickly moved to block their exit. "No, no. It's okay, he's friendly."

The kids stopped but looked at Grunt with wide eyes.

"Grunt, sit," I ordered. He immediately lowered his butt to the ground.

Alice's little sister giggled.

"Grunt, down." Grunt immediately flattened on the ground.

"Grunt, sleep," I ordered. He rolled onto his back all four paws up in the air. "See? He's friendly. He just looks scary. Grunt, come," I ordered.

Jumping to his feet, Grunt walked slowly toward me, his whole body vibrating with excitement. I reached out a hand and rubbed him on the head. "Hi boy."

The kids moved forward slowly, each one touching him, smiles quickly spreading across their faces.

Noel appeared at the door and hurried down the steps. "Addie? I thought you wouldn't be back for at least another hour."

The strangeness of what had just happened hit me. That portal had appeared out of nowhere. "We shouldn't be. I'm not quite sure how we're here."

Concern lacing her face, Noel frowned. "Did everything go okay?"

"Honestly, I'm not sure," I said before I turned to Alice. "Alice, this is Noel. And that's Sheila over there. They're going to look after you. I need to go make sure everybody else got back okay. All right?"

Alice looked from me to Noel and then Sheila and Grunt before she nodded. "Okay."

I ran a hand over her head and then burst up into the air.

Soaring across Sterling Peak, I headed as fast as I could to the portal that we'd gone through earlier. As I flew, my mind raced. That portal had just appeared. And it had taken us exactly where we needed to be.

I'd thought about where the kids would be safe, and I'd pictured Sheila's house.

Was it possible that *I* had somehow summoned the portal? I mean, that seemed the only possible explanation. But at the same time, how was that possible?

My father never mentioned anything about being able to create portals. So how on earth was I able to create one? Yet another question in a long line of questions, but I shoved it aside. I needed to get to the others. They would have no idea what had happened to me.

And I wasn't sure what they would do when they realized I wasn't there.

CHAPTER 47

By foot, traveling to the portal had taken an hour. But at the speed I was traveling, I managed to get there in mere minutes. Even from some distance away, I could tell there was a disturbance over by the portal's entrance.

As it came into view, I saw Lucifer step back through, shaking his head. "I can't find her," he said, his face bleak.

With a determined stride, Graham moved toward the portal. Tess stepped in front of him, holding him back. "Where do you think you are going?"

"Exactly where you think I'm going."

"Graham, we can't just go in there."

"Get out of my way, Tess. I won't leave her there." He started around her.

I touched down just a few feet away from them. "And you don't have to."

All of their eyes turned toward me.

Graham strode across the space, grabbed my face in his hands, and kissed me until my knees went weak. Then he released me and pulled me tight. "Don't ever do that to me again," he said, his voice shaking.

I hugged him back just as fiercely.

Vaguely, I was aware that the rest of the refugees were being escorted over to the path and toward Sterling Peak.

But I stayed with Graham, feeling his heart pounding in his chest, knowing he needed this moment to be assured that I was all right.

And honestly, I needed this moment with him too. The last few days had been so chaotic that we'd barely seen one another. And right now, I think it was hitting home for both of us that life was short. These next few days were going to be extremely dangerous. It was possible that one of us, if not both of us, wasn't going to make it through.

Tess cleared her throat. "Not to break up this little moment, but, uh, where the hell did you come from? No pun intended."

Graham finally pulled back. He moved a stray piece of hair from my forehead to behind my ear before stepping aside and standing next to me. Vera, my father, and Tess all stood looking at me expectantly.

"I found a group of six kids hiding in the middle of the tent. I grabbed them and headed for the exit, but a wall of fire blocked it off. Three demons were there. Another group was heading quickly toward us.

"I dispatched the demons, but I wasn't going to be able to get the kids out in time. I wished that there was a portal, and then there just sort of *was* one there. I stepped through with the kids, and we ended up in Sheila's backyard."

"A portal just appeared?" Vera asked with a frown.

Looking at my father, I nodded. "Have you ever heard of that?"

He shook his head. "No. I didn't think that was even possible."

"Who first created the portals?" Tess asked.

Lucifer opened his mouth and then closed it. "I don't know. They've always just kind of . . . been there."

Vera's gaze stayed locked on me as she spoke. "Addie created the portal."

I nodded my head slowly. "Yeah, I get that, but I just don't understand how."

"Maybe it's because you're a child of both worlds," Vera said. "You're a child of Hell but also a child of a human mother. So you can cross realms."

I looked at her, mulling it over, and then shrugged. It seemed as good an explanation as any. After all, I could even take the dead through the portal.

Which reminded me . . . "Was there any problem getting anybody through?"

Tess shook her head. "No. From what I could gather, everyone that was at the camp was someone who had been pulled and not someone who had died."

"So everyone was a kidnapped soul. I wonder why that is," I said.

Vera held up a bag. "Because you can only have the unblemished touch heavenstones."

"What?" Tess asked.

"The stones that they use for the bracelets, they're called heavenstones. The Damned can't touch them. I think that's why they put them in the bracelet. It protects them. It would burn them otherwise."

"So the bracelets allow them to go through the portals and also keep them from getting harmed from the heavenstone itself," Tess said.

Vera nodded. "Yes. And we got two hundred bracelets, along with this bag of untouched heavenstones. We made quite a dent in Abaddon's plans."

I grinned. "That's good."

Graham slipped his hand into mind. "That's great."

"It's so great, I think we should all celebrate," Tess said.

"There's still a war coming," I said.

Tess nodded back at me. "Yes, there is. Which is even more of a reason to enjoy the moment."

CHAPTER 48

Although initially surprised by the suggestion, everyone warmed to the idea of a celebration. No one was downplaying what the refugees had been through, what all of us had been through, but the idea of one night where we just had some fun was something everyone could get behind.

Getting the refugees settled first was priority number one though. The Rangers had already set up beds in the community center to get everyone processed. The people of Blue Forks and Sterling Peak had also donated clothes, food, and medical supplies to the effort.

By the time we arrived, it was controlled chaos. A group of refugees was being tended to by medical volunteers being overseen by Dr. Jade. Another group was doling out food to the refugees as they made their way through the food line. One group of refugees seemed to be just staring, and more than a few were crying.

Other Rangers walked through carefully, placing blankets around refugees' shoulders, especially the ones who looked like they were going into shock. I stared at all of the people, wishing I could have done more.

"Addie," Sheila called as she walked through the crowd.

I smiled as I walked over to her. "Hey. How are the kids?"

"Good. I brought them over here. Noel, Micah, and Lyra are here too. They wanted to help."

I nodded, understanding the impulse.

Scanning the swarm of humanity, I did a double take, recognizing two of the individuals. Agnes sat on a chair with Lyra curled up in her lap. Her arms were wrapped around her, her head resting on Lyra's.

Agnes met my gaze and gave me a nod with a smile before closing her eyes and just holding Lyra. Her two guards walked over with plates of food and sat near them, leaning against the wall, small smiles on their faces as well.

My chest felt lighter as I looked around the room. It was true, a war was coming. But at least for this moment, it felt like a victory.

CHAPTER 49

That night, we decided that we would have a feast down at the community center. A band was even brought in from Blue Forks. A small dance floor had been created in the middle of the room, and the refugees, who at first were hesitant, soon crowded the floor.

Table after table of food lined the sides, and refugees and Rangers alike took advantage of it. A party atmosphere filled the space, and I looked around, wanting to remember this moment. It was a good one.

In one corner of the room, Grunt was entertaining Alice and her friends, who all seemed to be enamored with him. Noel and Micah were nearby, keeping an eye on the kids. And Torr was there, although he still kept himself invisible.

It didn't seem necessary, though. There were more than a few individuals who looked like Torr. While some of them seemed to fit right in with the others, more than a few kept to themselves away from the celebration.

I hoped that once the shock of everything wore off that we'd be able to find a way to assimilate them all into society a little easier, Torr especially. I didn't want him to spend his life separated from the world. He deserved to be a part of it.

Farther to my right, my father sat speaking with Ian. He'd been amongst the refugees, along with most of the members of the village. Ian still looked a little haunted. It would be a long road for him to come back. It would be a long road for all of them. But they all seemed to be making an effort to at least enjoy the moment.

More than anyone, the refugees seemed to realize that life was short. You needed to take your happiness where you could find it.

An arm slipped around my waist, and I leaned back into Graham.

"Dance with me," he whispered into my ear.

Nodding, I took his hand. He pulled me out onto the dance floor and into his arms. He wrapped his arms around me, and we swayed to the music as it slowed down. I looked up at him, arching an eyebrow. "Did you plan this?"

"I may have made a request of the band," he said.

Leaning my head against his chest, I took Tess's advice and dropped thoughts of everything else. It could wait.

Graham and I danced for five songs straight. The first song was the only slow one. The rest were fast-paced, upbeat tunes. I was breathless by the time we were done.

Graham led me over to a spot where Tess and Donovan stood along the back wall. "Anybody want a drink?" Graham asked.

"I could definitely use one," I said, my throat feeling dry.

Graham kissed my cheek. "Your wish is my command."

He hurried toward the food line, and my heart expanded even more as he got in line rather than cutting ahead of the refugees patiently waiting.

"Well, I could have used one too," Tess said, glaring at Graham's back.

Donovan pushed himself off the wall. "Allow me, fair lady," he said, heading over to join Graham.

I leaned back against the wall and looked around at the group. A few people still looked bewildered. I was sure part of it was just the absolute difference between what their lives had been like this morning and what they were experiencing right now.

Most seemed to be enjoying themselves. I hadn't seen any tears except happy ones. But I knew in the days to come that they would no doubt go through a range of emotions.

Right now, though, this was good. "This was a great idea Tess."

Shifting to lean back against the wall next to me, Tess grinned. "Occasionally I do have them. We all need to take a break sometimes." She grunted with a nod toward the main entrance. "Some more than others,"

Turning, I caught sight of Marcus, who'd just stepped into the room. He looked around anxiously. Catching sight of me, his eyes widened and he started to work through the crowd in my direction.

Tess pushed herself off the wall. "You know, I'm having a really nice time tonight, and I think I'm going to keep doing that. So you are on your own."

"Chicken," I murmured as Tess headed away.

"Bok-bok," she called over her shoulder.

I laughed at the sound and was still smiling when Marcus reached me. "Hey, Marcus. You finally came to join the festivities?"

He frowned, and then finally seemed to take note of the party happening around him. "Oh, no. That's not why I'm here."

It was a struggle not to roll my eyes. "I figured. What's going on?"

He nodded toward a door a few feet to our left. It led to a

hallway. "Do you think we could go talk out there where it's quieter?"

A knot formed in my chest, and I realized I should have gone with Tess. Marcus definitely had a look about him that said he was going to steal some of my happiness. But I resigned myself to it and nodded. "Sure."

Catching Graham's gaze over at the food line, I pointed to the door, and he nodded.

Then Marcus and I headed out into the hallway. Once we'd closed the door behind us, the volume dropped precipitously. Now the party was just a dull murmur.

Marcus moved a little down the hallway and then stopped. "I was speaking with Michael."

Leaning against the wall, settling in for what I was sure was going to be a long conversation, I nodded. "Okay."

But Marcus surprised me by being brief. "He let it slip that Abaddon's amulet is what's keeping the souls from going to Purgatory and then on to Heaven. If you destroy that amulet, the souls will be freed."

CHAPTER 50

The party had been a welcome respite for the Rangers and a good way to introduce the refugees to their new lives. Everyone was looking a little more content, a little more secure, and a little less fearful as the night drew to a close.

It wasn't going to be a late night. The refugees weren't up for that, and the Rangers had to get back on duty.

Rangers had shifted in and out throughout the night, depending on what duties they were on, and it seemed like all of them had cycled through at one point or another. Now Graham and I were helping make sure that the refugees all had beds for the night.

An hour after the band had played their last song, the food had been packed up, and the refugees had all found a spot to lay their heads. Graham and I walked outside, arm and arm.

Donovan stood by the main entrance and grinned at us.

"Heading back to the academy?" I asked.

He shook his head. "No. Six of us are going to keep an eye on things down here just to make sure everybody feels safe. I'll stay until morning when someone comes to relieve me."

I reached up and kissed him on the cheek. "You're a good man, Donovan Gabriel. No matter what Graham says."

Donovan faked outrage. "And just what has he been saying?"

"Only the truth," Graham said, slapping a hand on his back.

"Well, that's all right, then. You two have a good night." He grinned as he headed back inside.

Graham pulled me close. "*Are* we going to have a good night?"

"In maybe an hour?" I asked. "I promised Tess that I would do a quick patrol through Blue Forks. There are some people there who are getting nervous, and she said seeing me may help calm some nerves. She even suggested I fly over and make sure that my wings are fully inflamed."

Graham chuckled. "Well, I'd offer to join you, but I actually promised that I would go give a report to the Council." His face darkened.

"Do you have to do that tonight?"

"They wanted one earlier in the evening, but I thought it was important that the refugees see me at the gathering."

"A few of the Council members were there," I said, picturing Javier and Elaine.

"Yeah, but they're not the ones we have to worry about," he said.

I knew that was true. Javier and Elaine were probably the only ones not trying to make Graham's life difficult.

I leaned my head on his shoulder and pictured sometime in the future when these walks could be commonplace.

"What are you thinking about?" he asked.

"I'm thinking that I like this. You and me walking together. No screaming, no yelling, no demons in sight."

Graham grimaced. "Are you trying to jinx us?"

I laughed. "No. It's more that I find myself thinking about the future and feeling hopeful."

Graham pulled me to a stop. He tipped my chin up and smiled down at me. "And you have every right to be hopeful. We are going to have a future together, Addison Baker. That I am sure of."

He leaned down, his lips softly touching mine.

Wrapping my arms around his neck, I pulled him closer. But I couldn't seem to get him close enough. I wanted more. More than stolen kisses when we had time. I wanted his undivided attention and to give him mine.

Actually, right now, I wanted nothing more than to find a bed. But as always, duty called. I pulled back, breathing hard. "Later. I just need to go to Blue Forks, and then later..."

"I'm going to hold you to that," Graham said, his eyes dark.

Tingles ran over my skin at the promise in his eyes. "I hope so," I said, backing away but keeping my gaze on him.

Finally, I turned and took off into the night. My wings burst into flame, and I smiled, picturing the evening to come.

CHAPTER 51

Blue Forks was quiet as I walked through the streets, but more than a few residents pushed their curtains aside to glance out at me. I made sure to wave or acknowledge each of them.

A few even came out to talk and ask about the fight to come. I assured them that if the demons reappeared, protecting the people of Blue Forks was a priority for the Seraph Force.

By the time I was done, I felt like I had calmed some nerves, and I found myself moving quickly across the celestial bridge. Reaching the halfway point, I looked up at the dual statues of Michael and Gabriel.

The artist had gotten Gabriel completely wrong, making her a man. And Michael they had gotten wrong as well, at least in terms of his appearance. But the cold look on his face they'd gotten right.

Hurrying across the bridge, I waved at the guards on the Sterling Peak side as I scooted around the barricade. Tess was just coming off Highbridge street, which ran along the river and called out to me. "Hey, Addie."

I stopped so that she could catch up, even though I was anxious to get to Graham. I hoped his meeting with the Council was over and that he was home waiting for me. I'd check in on Noel, Micah, and Torr, and then it was time for Graham and I to have our own quiet time. We'd waited long enough.

"How's Blue Forks?" Tess asked.

"Quiet, if a little nervous."

"Same here. A few of the Angel Blessed stopped to tell me that they were concerned about the number of refugees being brought in. They want to know when they would be moved over to Blue Forks." Tess rolled her eyes.

I shook my head. Angels Blessed really weren't known for opening their doors to the less fortunate. Apparently even being sucked into Hell didn't win you any compassion from them.

"Where are you heading?" Tess asked.

"I was hoping to see Graham after his meeting."

Tess shook her head. "I just stopped by there. They're still going at it. I think it might be a while."

"Great," I sighed.

"I was going to go check in on Donovan and see that all the refugees are settled in."

Up on the hill, I could see Graham's house was all lit up. "I was going to go check on the kids."

"I think only Micah and Grunt are up at the mansion. Torr and Noel came back to the refugee center with some toys for the kids to help them sleep."

"Well then, I guess I'm heading to the refugee center, as well. I'll make sure those two head back home."

Tess and I turned down the street toward the center. It was a nice night. A light wind blew, but it was still warm.

"Today was good," Tess said softly. "We need more days like this."

"And hopefully we'll have them. More wins against Abaddon are what I'm looking for."

"Me too."

A feeling of contentment wafted through me. It was small, but there nonetheless. Tess grabbed my arm pulling me up short. I frowned. "What's wrong?"

"I don't know. I thought I heard –"

A scream shattered the night air.

CHAPTER 52

"That came from the refugee center," Tess yelled as she took off at a run.

I burst into the air as more screams broke through the silence of the night. I prayed that whatever was causing it was not a demon attack.

With my speed, I reached the community center before Tess and kicked in the doors, bursting into the space. I took it all in in a glance.

Donovan and two other Rangers were fighting off three demons. Two refugees were pulling away a third refugee as blood poured from a wound in their thigh.

Four other bodies lay sprawled on the ground behind all of it.

Noel and Torr stood in front a group of children, fighting off a seven-foot-tall demon. Noel slipped to the side as the demon focused on Torr. She brought a sword to the back of his thighs, slicing it along both of them.

He cried out and turned to swipe a meaty paw at her. Ducking, she rolled to the side as Torr took his knife and plunged it into the creature's gut, twisting it as he did so.

The demon slammed a fist into Torr's face, sending him flying back.

With a yell, Noel thrust her sword into the creature's back. Torr scrambled back to his feet. Yanking his knife out of the creature's gut, he drove it into his neck. The demon crashed to his knees and then toppled forward.

For a split second, Noel met my gaze across the space. She gave me a nod and moved to stand once again in front of the children. Torr took up position next to her.

My heart swelled with pride at the two of them.

A demon let out a roar and swiped its nails across one of the Ranger's shoulders. He screamed as he fell backward. The demon moved in for the kill.

"No!" I burst across the space toward him, my wings shooting fire and brightening the entire area.

Energy wound up in my chest, and I threw a fireball at the demon. He was engulfed in flames in seconds. I kicked him to the back of the room, where he wouldn't be near any other refugees. Most were now in a panicked race for the exits.

To my right, one of the other demons pulled back a massive claw, going for a kill shot as Donavan stumbled with a wince of pain. Pulling my sword, I managed to get there in time to block the hit.

Donovan let out a grunt, and I watched from the corner of my eye as he got pushed back. Tess burst across the room, working her way through the refugees, swarming in the opposite direction.

One of the demons met my gaze and smiled. Then he darted toward a group of refugees. I sprinted after him and plunged my sword into his back before he could reach them.

The group scattered with cries as the demon fell face forward. A short distance away, Donovan and Tess held off the one demon that remained.

I turned over the demon that I'd stabbed. He glared up at me even as his blood seeped into the tiles below him. "You can't stop us," he growled.

"How'd you get here?"

The creature smiled, his teeth stained red with blood. "You brought us here."

"What?"

Seeing my surprise, the demon grinned wider. "Abaddon sent us. He knew you'd come for the refugees."

From one heartbeat to the next, the truth hit me. I recognized the clothes that the demon wore. Disbelief sent me back on my heels. The demons hadn't entered through a portal. *We'd* brought them here. These were the refugees who'd only gone through the partial shift. I'd assumed they were like Torr, but they weren't. They *wanted* to transform.

"What does Abaddon want? What did he promise you?"

"He promised us access to his ranks. We just had to wait until you came for one of the camps. He wants all of them"—he scanned the refuges cowering away—"to know there's nowhere they can hide from him. He wants *you* to know that he'll always be one step ahead."

I shook my head. "You could have had a life. You could have lived here. Why would you do this?"

"I don't want the life that you can offer me. I want the life Abaddon can. We will live here, and we will rule you all."

"Not you. You're dead."

The demon smiled. "Yes, but Abaddon has made it so that doesn't matter either. After all, where do you think I'm going when I leave here?" he said as the light faded from his eyes.

I stared at him and then backed away, a chill rolling over me.

He was right. He would go right back to Hell, and then Abaddon would let him fall into his ranks. And one day he would return when Abaddon made his move.

Tess walked over, blood splattered across her tunic. "Addie, you okay?"

Suddenly feeling the hopelessness of it all, I shook my head. "No, not even close."

～

THE REFUGEES WERE TERRIFIED, and I couldn't blame them. And I couldn't work up the words to reassure them. Extra Rangers had been called to round up the refugees and get them re-settled. But from the looks on their faces, none of them would be getting any sleep for the rest of the night.

Graham came striding through the doors. His measured gaze took in everything quickly before he walked up to Donovan. "Report."

Donovan winced as he stood up. The bandage on his side was leaking blood again. He must have pulled his stitches in the fight. "The four half demons that we brought back from Hell, they killed some refugees, and then they transformed into full demons. I was across the room and wasn't able to get to them in time. By the time I reached them, they'd already taken four lives. They morphed right in front of us. It was the creepiest thing I've ever seen."

"That's all they needed, four lives," I said softly.

Graham turned to me. "What do you mean?"

"To become a demon, it's a process. They put Torr through it, but he never completed it, no matter what they did. The last step is for someone to take the life of an innocent." Unbidden, my gaze went to the spot where I'd seen the four bodies sprawled earlier.

I stood up. "Abaddon sent these four here. He knew that we were going to hit the camp. Although he didn't know which one, he wanted to send a message. He wanted us to know that he is always one step ahead."

"He planned all of this," Graham said, his hard gaze roving about the room.

Nodding, I stared out at the room that hours ago had been full of celebration and people excited about starting their new lives. But now all of those people looked absolutely terrified. We'd promised that we would protect them. We'd promised that we would keep them safe.

And we had failed.

CHAPTER 53

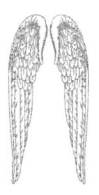

Despite the trauma of the evening, these events made it clear that we couldn't waste any time. We needed to speak with the refugees and get an idea of what had gone on in the camp and gather any intel that we could from them.

Staking out a small office at the back of the first floor, I spoke with six different refugees. Unfortunately, none of them could tell me much beyond their experience in the camp. All had been new arrivals. The demons had snatched them and brought them to the camp, leaving them bewildered, lost and terrified.

As for the six who'd turned, they'd either already been in the camp or brought to the camp in their partially turned phase. They'd only arrived a few days earlier. Which meant, just as the demon said, Abaddon had planted them there hoping that we would come across them.

Conferring with the other Rangers doing the interviews, they all got the same information. After another dozen, I knew I needed to call it a night. After the attack, I'd stayed at the refugee center. I knew that I wouldn't be able to sleep, so I figured I might as well let the refugees try to get some sleep.

Of course, that didn't happen either.

Most of them stayed awake. The lights were dimmed, and every once in a while, I would hear the soft cry of someone. It was a tough night for everyone.

When morning dawned, no one felt refreshed, least of all me. Torr and Noel had stayed. They had curled up with the kids, trying to make them feel safe. But I couldn't help but notice that more than a few were frightened by Torr's appearance among them.

And my heart broke just a little bit more. All my hopes for Torr being able to slip back into society seemed to dissipate right in front of my eyes. It seemed he would always be looked at with distrust, especially after last night.

I rolled my hands into fists.

Abaddon was always one step ahead of us. Everything we did, every step I thought we were taking forward, he was already two steps ahead of us.

How was it possible that he knew we were going into the camps? That seemed like such a stretch. It was a huge risk and not something we would take. He couldn't have just known, could he?

A new set of Rangers had relieved us, but I wasn't quite ready to leave, so I moved back to the small office I'd used for interviews last night.

It was a nice office with ivory colored walls. The fabric on the furniture was a soft blue and was comfortable with its thick wooden frames. There were landscapes and forest images framed on the walls. One of the windows even overlooked the river. Most importantly, it had a large picture window that overlooked the room where the refugees were staying.

But that wasn't the window I was focused on. Right now, I

watched the water roll by, letting my thoughts drift with it. I pictured Abaddon as I'd last seen him. Then I pictured Torr and my father speaking, finally getting the chance to know one another.

I remembered Noel and Micah as I'd first seen them, comparing them to how they looked now. Then I thought of Michael wasting away down in the cells.

And then finally, my thoughts returned to Graham, how he'd been overtaken by Michael and now was back to himself. Through it all, the images flipped by, fast and furious, some of them bold and clear and others more feelings than anything else.

For some reason, the scene with D'Angelo slipped into my mind. It was before all of this had started. There'd been a guest at the Uriels, a friend of Hunter Uriel, that D'Angelo had been trying to impress.

To do so, he'd acted as if he was one with the Demon Cursed. He'd been trying to win over Michael family from Chicago. He wanted to secure a marriage with that branch. If he'd succeeded it would have elevated him above Donovan in the rankings and made him second of the Seraph Force.

He was always so duplicitous. He always seemed to have an angle. The face he put forward was never truly an honest one.

Turning away from the view of the river, I moved to the other window to watch the refugees below The fact that I'd failed to give them a safe harbor burned through me. Instead of leaving, I found myself pulling over a chair to watch over them from above.

And that's where Lucifer found me. I'd watched as he made his way through the crowd, trying to ease people's worries.

When he appeared in the doorway of the office, he didn't say anything. He simply pulled up a chair next to me. "Are you all right?"

Weariness had overtaken my bones. I couldn't even work up

the energy to sigh. "No. This was supposed to be a victory for us. But this doesn't feel like one."

"We underestimated Abaddon."

His words caused me to narrow my eyes as I stared out over the room. He was right, but only partly. "No. This is more than just us underestimating him. Someone's been telling him what we're up to."

As soon as the words left my mouth my head jolted up, and my eyes narrowed as a face swam across my mind. It couldn't be. But he'd worked with Michael. And if he'd worked with Michael, what would stop him from working with someone else? Someone even worse? I stood up.

"Where are you going?"

"To talk to a traitor."

I strode to the door. It opened, and Tess looked surprised as she caught sight of me. "Hey. I wanted to check if you wanted another refugee. I was thinking maybe you need a little break."

Shaking my head, I strode past her. "I don't need a break. But what I do need is to speak with D'Angelo."

Falling in step next to me, Tess grinned as she took in my face. "Well, this should be fun."

CHAPTER 54

The streets of Sterling Peak were quiet as Tess and I strode toward D'Angelo's home. Lucifer promised to keep an eye on the refugees.

The wind had picked up since yesterday and blew hard against us as we headed up the hill. There was a bite of something in the air, but I wasn't sure what.

Fear most likely. The few people that we'd seen were hurrying to their destination their gazes quick as they hurried on.

There were more Seraph Force on patrol than I'd ever seen before. They all gave Tess and me a nod as we passed.

"Graham's really got the preparations going. Another hundred soldiers arrived this morning," Tess said. "And speak of the devil..."

Both Graham and Donovan were heading toward D'Angelo's estate. Catching sight of us, Graham's eyes widened in surprise as he stopped at the edge of D'Angelo's family's estate to wait for us.

As we caught up to them, I nodded toward the estate. "Going to chat with D'Angelo?"

Graham nodded, a grim set to his mouth. "Yes. I think he knows more than he's telling."

"I came to the same conclusion," I said.

"Look at that, the two of you identifying the same conspiracies. How adorable," Donovan said teasingly.

I rolled my eyes at him but couldn't help but love how in tune Graham and I were.

"Shall we?" Graham asked, waving a hand toward the drive and raising an eyebrow.

Despite the easygoing tone in his voice, I could tell that he was angry. Actually, he was beyond angry.

And that was good, because so was I.

CHAPTER 55

The Rafael home sat slightly down the hill from Graham's. I'd never been inside it, but it was hard not to notice it. It stood out even amongst all the other ostentatious homes on the hill. Beyond just its enormous, monstrous size, there was the equally enormous and monstrous statue of cherubs frolicking in a pool in the front drive.

Marble stairs led to two massive doors that had knocker shaped in the form of more cherubs. The door opened before we'd even reached it. I recognized the Ranger who was on duty. It was Corey. He stepped back to let all of us in.

"Where is he?" Graham asked without preamble.

Corey nodded toward the stairs. "He's in his room. He's always in his room. His mother was just here and brought him a meal."

Graham gritted his teeth but said nothing. He led the way up the stairs.

As we walked, I couldn't help but notice how extreme everything in the house was. The doorways were just a little bit larger, the paintings and furnishings just a little bit grander. Everything was just a little bit extra.

It was nauseating.

I'd known a few members of D'Angelo's family's staff, just in passing. They'd all seemed exhausted. From what Nigel told me, the Rafaels were an incredibly demanding family. They let people from their staff go for the slightest infractions. Being late, even during a storm, wasn't an option. Showing up looking bedraggled, even if there was a rainstorm, was reason for people to be dismissed as well.

It was insanity. But the Angel Blessed didn't care about the hardships they inflicted on those below them. They believed that they had earned their exalted position in society, and no one believed that more than D'Angelo's family.

My blood still boiled when I thought of all of the policies that they'd put in place to make the lives of the Demon Cursed more difficult. They believed that the Demon Cursed were descended from demon and human interactions.

Personally, I'd never heard of such a birth, although I suppose it wasn't out of the realm of possibility. But there was no chance that half of society was the result of such unions.

The same way there was no chance that the other half of society was the result of unions between humans and angels. Yet the Angel Blessed clung onto the belief in their own heritage to justify their exalted position within society. And they lorded that position over the Demon Cursed with brutality.

What did it say that the people who were the cruelest within society took on the moniker of angels?

We reached the landing and walked down the hall, our footsteps muffled by the thick carpet. Donovan grunted when we were about halfway down the hall.

Tess eyed him. "You feeling okay?"

Donovan had been hurt pretty bad before the debacle in the

community center. It looked like he was getting a little bit better. The sling was no longer on his arm. That didn't necessarily mean that it was healed; it just meant that Donovan was sick of wearing the thing. Plus, he'd definitely agitated his stitches in the fight at the refugee center.

"I'm fine. I just hate this place," he said.

I knew there was no love lost between Donovan and D'Angelo. D'Angelo had been good friends with Graham's older brother and Donovan's younger one. The three of them had been a destructive force in the world before Brock's death.

And although it was uncharitable of me, I was kind of glad that Brock was gone. From the stories that I'd heard, he was on par with D'Angelo in his view of the Demon Cursed, and a few steps above in his violent cruelty. If his reign had gone on much longer, I had no doubt that he and D'Angelo would have truly destroyed the lives of the Demon Cursed. They'd probably all be enslaved at this point.

And I guess so would I.

At the thought of it, I shook my head. What a waste. If I'd been enslaved, would I have even known about my abilities? And if I had, would I have bothered to help the Angel Blessed? If anything, I could see me starting a civil war between the Demon Cursed and the Angel Blessed. And then when the demons had invaded, we would have been in even more trouble than we were now.

Yeah, it was a good thing that Brock was no longer around.

But I jolted at the next thought. If souls weren't going to Heaven, that meant that Brock was somewhere in Hell.

I flipped a glance at Graham, noting his determined expression. I wondered if that thought had crossed his mind yet. We hadn't talked about his brother, but I knew how cruel Brock had been to him in particular. Brock seemed to want to get his brother out of the way and had sent him on increasingly dangerous missions to accomplish that.

Graham had gone to work for Marcus because he'd known that if he stayed here any longer, he would probably be dead.

I wasn't going to be the one who mentioned that Brock was probably somewhere down in Hell and that with a little work, we might be able to find him. I doubted Graham would want that particular reunion. And with my abilities, I would be able to return Brock to life.

But given what I'd learned about the man, he was exactly the type of individual Abaddon was looking for. No. I definitely was not going to bring his brother up.

Two Seraph Force soldiers stood about a quarter of the way from the end of the hall. Graham nodded at them as we strode past. The hall was long, and D'Angelo's room was apparently at the end of it.

Again, I was struck by the complete and total waste. This home could house dozens of families from Blue Forks. Yet Blue Forks people scrimped by in little more than shacks. Whole families were living in rooms that were no more than ten by ten feet.

Yet here was D'Angelo in this monster of a home, just for himself.

The demons were the priority right now, but once that situation was handled, if it was handled, I was going to make sure that there was a little more equity in this society. People like D'Angelo were given everything by virtue of their birth, and they'd done absolutely nothing to deserve it. Meanwhile, the people in Blue Forks, also by virtue of their birth, were sentenced to a lifetime of struggle. It couldn't continue.

And I would make sure that it didn't.

Graham didn't even slow as he reached the double doors at the end of the hall. He flung them open.

D'Angelo had been standing in the middle of the room, his

back to the door. He whirled around, his mouth falling open, his eyes widening in shock. But none of us paid more than a second of attention to D'Angelo.

No, all of us immediately focused on the demon standing at the far end of the room.

CHAPTER 56

No one spoke for the barest of seconds. In that time, I realized I'd seen the demon before. He was the one who'd been out in the woods. The one who'd been waiting for Noel and Micah to be delivered to him.

Even with the proof staring back at me with a smug expression, I couldn't believe that D'Angelo was actually consorting with the demons.

While part of me thought that maybe he was a traitor, another part thought maybe it was just my intense dislike of the man that had me wandering down that particular line of thought. But as I stared at the demon across the room, I knew that I'd underestimated his duplicitousness. D'Angelo truly was a traitor to his own species.

I pulled my sword from its scabbard. Flames engulfed it immediately.

D'Angelo let out a cry and darted to the side of the room. Tess bolted forward and tackled him to the ground, yanking his arms behind his back, and holding him there.

I lunged toward the demon.

"Not quite yet," he said with a smile before he slowly started to fade away. My sword cut through the air where he'd been standing a split second too late.

He was gone.

My chest heaved as I stared at the spot. Then I turned to look at where Donovan and Graham stood. Neither of them had moved a muscle nor made a sound. They still didn't. They acted as if they were glued to the floor.

I looked over at Tess, who stared at them with a concerned look on her face. Her brow furrowed as she caught my gaze and shook her head.

Sheathing my sword, I walked back toward the two men. "Graham? Donovan? You two okay?"

Donavan didn't look at me or Graham when he spoke. His eyes stayed locked on the spot where the demon had disappeared. "Tell me that's not who I thought it was," he murmured.

Graham simply shook his head.

I flicked a glance back over my shoulder as if it would help me remember what the demon had looked like. I remembered that sense of familiarity when I'd first seen him in the woods.

And now as I pictured him and looked back at Graham, my heart dropped. "No. It can't be."

Graham's stricken gaze met mine. He didn't say a word. I shifted my gaze to Donovan. "Tell me what I'm thinking is wrong."

Donovan shook his head. "I can't."

I walked up to Graham and gently placed a hand on his arm. "Graham?"

Slowly, he turned his head and looked down at me. His eyes locked with mine, pain, heartache, and fear all rolled together in his gaze. "That was my brother."

CHAPTER 57

No wonder he'd looked familiar to me. I'd seen photos of Graham's brother in his home. I'd only stopped to look at them once. And now, in his demon form, he looked so different and yet somehow still the same. He'd been just over seven feet tall and extremely muscular, as they all were. But his face had somehow remained unchanged and easily identifiable.

"Get off me," D'Angelo yelled.

D'Angelo's yell seemed to pull Graham from whatever hellscape his mind had been thrown in. He narrowed his eyes as he stared at D'Angelo, who squirmed underneath Tess.

Tess slammed a fist into his side.

D'Angelo grunted before he spit out, "Do you know who I am?"

"A traitor," Tess growled.

"Get him up," Graham ordered.

Donovan stormed across the room and helped Tess yank D'Angelo to his feet. D'Angelo turned his eyes to Graham before they shifted to me and returned again to Graham. "I can explain."

Graham crossed toward him in two steps and slammed his fist into D'Angelo's stomach. D'Angelo's eyes bulged as he bent at the waist, gasping for air.

"Explain? You're working with them," Graham seethed. "You told them we were going to the camp."

Donovan and Tess grabbed D'Angelo by the shoulders, yanking him upright. With a wince, D'Angelo shook his head. "No, no, I didn't."

"How long? How long have you been talking to my brother?" Graham demanded.

D'Angelo let out a strangled cry. "I-I had no choice. He's a demon now. He came to me and threatened me. I had to do what he said. You don't understand."

Graham leaned forward until he was a mere inch from D'Angelo's face. "I don't understand. I *know* who my brother was. You know who he is, what kind of man he is. You could have come to me. We could have come up with a way to handle this. We could have set a trap for him. And then we could have used *him* for information."

D'Angelo shook his head. "He never would have fallen for that. He's too smart." A cruel look flicked across D'Angelo's face as he glared at Graham. "He's always been smarter than you."

Graham's face tightened, but he didn't strike D'Angelo again, even though I could tell he itched to. Instead, he took a step back and nodded to Donovan and Tess. "Find out what he knows," he ordered before turning and striding from the room.

I watched him go and had every intention of going after him, but there was one thing I had to do first.

Quietly, I walked toward D'Angelo. His eyes widened as I approached, but Tess and Donovan held him in place. I stood in front of him, waiting until he met my gaze. He swallowed nervously.

I spoke quietly so he had to really listen to hear me. "If you've done anything that will harm the humans in the fight to come, Brock will be the least of your worries. I promise you that. And if you have done anything that will harm Graham in particular, I assure you that my face will be the last one you ever see."

CHAPTER 58

Leaving D'Angelo with Tess and Donovan, I strode out of the room looking for Graham. There was no sign of him outside the room. I reached the end of the hall and looked at the two guards. "Where's Graham?"

Instead of indicating the hall that led to the stairs, they pointed in the opposite direction.

Following their directions, I headed down a new hallway just as ostentatious as all the others. This one seemed to be animal themed with stuffed animals mounted on plaques on the wall and standing along the wall. There was even a polar upright halfway down.

As I made my way along, I peered through the open doorways catching signs of more animal prints and art but no sign of Graham.

Finally, at the end of the hall, I reached a solarium. Two baby giraffes stood on either side of the entrance. My heart broke at the thought of their lives cut short to be stuffed and made into art.

As I opened the door, a wave of warm air wafted over me.

Heat enveloped me as I stepped inside. Despite the ugliness of what I had just witnessed, I could appreciate the beauty of the spot. It was a massive room, with large fruit trees growing on the second story of a home. I didn't know that was possible. Flowers dotted the space, and there was even a lush vegetable garden that took up a space about the size of my entire apartment.

I found Graham sitting underneath an avocado tree. I walked up to him, not sure how to approach him. Brock had been his tormentor growing up. He'd tried to kill him when he was the commander of the Seraph Force. Now he was working against humanity.

And D'Angelo, that little weasel, had helped him.

I stopped when I was only a few feet away. Graham seemed to be staring off into space. I wasn't sure if he even knew I was there. But then he held out his hand.

As I reached out and took it, he pulled me close. I sat next to him, holding his hand. "You all right?"

He huffed out a laugh. "No. I can honestly say I am most definitely not all right." He went quiet for a moment. "I should have known."

Now it was my turn to laugh. "You should have known that your brother would turn his back on humanity?"

Graham didn't join in my laughter. Instead, he nodded seriously. "Brock, he's always looked for the angle. He's always looked for the way to gain a little bit more power. I'm not surprised that he's become one of them. I should have foreseen it. He wouldn't be one of the nameless masses in Hell. No, he'd want to be part of those in power. He'd want to be the *one* in power. I have no doubt that he's already plotting how he's going to take over."

"Take over the demons?" I asked.

"Take over everything. Brock never suffered from a smallness when it came to his plans." He ran a hand through his hair. "It was just such a shock seeing him there."

I curled my legs underneath me. "Do you think D'Angelo has been feeding him information all along?"

"Of course he has. It was one of the reasons I wanted to keep him locked away in the dungeon. I wanted to keep access to him tightly controlled. But here, that's impossible. Of course, then I was only worried about him selling us out to other humans."

Graham shook his head. "D'Angelo's always had an extensive network of informants. I'm sure they've been telling him everything we've been doing. That's how Abaddon knew to put someone into the camps. They knew we were coming."

"It doesn't mean that we can't still win this."

Graham raised an eyebrow at me. "You think we're going to win this?"

"I do."

"And tell me, what makes you so sure?" he asked.

I didn't let him look away as I spoke. "Because we have to."

CHAPTER 59

Graham and I stayed in the solarium talking about Brock and D'Angelo and what they'd put Graham through when he was younger. I hated all that he'd experienced at their hands, but I also understood that what he'd experienced had caused him to become the man that he was today.

And sitting there, listening to the deep timbre of his voice, I also realized that I loved that man. He was good and he was strong. And he put others before himself.

He was also awfully easy on the eyes.

But right now, he needed to talk. He was the commander of the Seraph Force, the one who everyone turned to for answers. The one who everyone looked to. He set the tone.

At this moment, though, he wasn't the commander of the Seraph Force. Right now, he was a man struggling with the reappearance of the person who'd made his life a living hell. And he simply needed someone to listen.

I'm not sure how long we sat there. But my blood boiled more than once at the stories that Graham shared. Brock truly had been a monster long before his exterior matched his interior. I couldn't imagine what he had in store for humanity now.

The fact that he'd been the one who'd wanted to grab Noel and Micah both terrified and incensed me. And while the anger burned through me, it wasn't the only emotion. A cold ball of fear erupted in my chest at the idea of someone like that getting his hands on them.

Brock was going to have to be taken down. If Graham was right about Brock's ambitions—and I had no doubt he was—he was too dangerous to be allowed him to live, in any realm.

But those were not thoughts I could share with Graham. As much as he despised his brother, I didn't think it would be so easy for him to kill him.

So I would make sure he wouldn't have to. That would be a burden that I would make sure I took on. If only to save him from one more horrible situation that Brock had placed him in.

Eventually, Graham fell quiet. I leaned my head on his shoulder, my arm wrapped around his. "It's amazing you turned out the way you did."

"And how's that?"

I smiled. "Is somebody fishing for compliments?"

He shrugged. And for the first time, I saw the little boy who'd watched his family dote on his brother and leave him behind. As much as he loved Mary and Franklin, it didn't erase the hurt caused by his biological family.

"You are strong, you are kind, you are fair, and you are brave. You are a good man, Graham Michael. And I am so glad that I met you."

He leaned forward. "Right back at you," he said before his lips touched mine.

As they did, the world fell away. The upcoming war, D'Angelo's betrayal, the attack on the refugee center, all of my worries and fears for what was to come just disappeared at the touch of

Graham's lips on mine. For this moment, there was only him. He was warm and he was safe, and he was mine.

He pressed his body into mine, and I wrapped my arms around him, deepening the kiss. He started to lower me to the ground when the doors of the solarium burst open. With a muttered curse, his forehead touched mine before he pulled away. "We are going to make time for us."

I groaned. "Can't we just shoot whoever is about to disturb us?"

Graham chuckled. "Only if it's D'Angelo." Sitting up, he reached down and helped me stand as he did the same. Wiping the dirt off our clothes, we'd just stepped back onto the brick path as Tess came hurrying down the aisle.

One looked at her face, and I knew that something horrible it happened. Pulling my hand from Graham, I stepped forward.

"What happened?" Graham demanded.

Tess swallowed. "The demon war. It's starting in two days."

CHAPTER 60

Two days. We had two days before all the demons in Hell invaded.

The air seemed to rush out of my lungs, and the world seemed to spin for a moment. We weren't ready. We had hundreds of Seraph Force officers across the country, but we weren't ready.

Graham automatically slipped into commander mode. "Where?"

"They're going to make their breach here, in Sterling Peak," Tess said.

"How many?" he asked.

Tess swallowed. "All of them. They're going to wipe Sterling Peak off the map. As the head of the Seraph Force, they figure that once it falls, the rest will be easier to take over."

Immediately my thoughts jumped to Noel and Micah and then slipped to all the other children that that lived in Sterling Peak and Blue Forks. "The children," I whispered.

Tess gave me a nod, her mouth a tight line.

"We can't know for sure that they're all going to be heading here. It could easily be a simultaneous attack. They could be feeding D'Angelo false information," Graham said.

Tess nodded. "I know. But what if they're not?"

Graham looked over at me. He gave me a quick kiss on the cheek. "I have to go."

"I know. Go."

With a quick look, he hurried out of the solarium. I watched him go, my heart plunging. Two days. Two days until literally all hell broke loose.

CHAPTER 61

The next twenty-four hours were a rush of preparations. Certain areas of Sterling Peak were fortified in order to hopefully funnel the demons into kill boxes, where it would be easier to attack them.

Many of the Angel Blessed immediately departed, heading for other towns, hoping that that would keep them safe.

But I knew it wouldn't. If Sterling Peak fell, it would only be a matter of time before the rest of the world did. It was a smart move to target here first and no doubt Brock's.

Once the demons took out the command of the Seraph Force even if the other soldiers in other parts of the country survived, they'd be demoralized by the loss. The battle would feel hopeless. And with good reason: it would be.

The strongest fighters were in Sterling Peak. If they were overcome, it was only a matter of time before the rest of the world followed.

The children of Blue Forks and Sterling Peak were being evacuated from the area. They were being sent to a town two hundred miles away.

Most of the refugees were going with them. Physically, they were in no shape to fight. They would simply be lambs to the slaughter. The same went for the residents of Blue Forks and Sterling Peak who wouldn't be able to fight.

In this battle, everyone was going to be on the front lines whether they wanted to be or not. And if someone wasn't in shape emotionally, physically, or mentally to fight, we needed to get them out of the way.

For the last day, I'd spent most of the time showing the ones who'd stayed behind the best way to fight demons in teams, even though I knew that if it came down to the civilian forces, there was only a slim chance that they would survive. But I needed to give them some chance to hope.

George from the Uriel's home was right next to me, helping to get the civilians up to par. He was a strong, steady presence, his usual humor absent as he focused on the task at hand. And I could see the Ranger he'd once been.

The only time I saw him falter was when his nephew joined the civilian ranks. Nathan had just turned fifteen, making him old enough to be trained. The look of anguish in George's eyes as he spotted him cut right through me. But then he rolled back his shoulders, strode over to him, and explained exactly what he needed to do.

I wish I could say it was as easy to shove my emotions aside, but it wasn't. I tried to get Noel, Torr, and Micah to leave town, but they wouldn't.

I tried to pull on Noel's guilt, saying that if she didn't leave, then Micah would stay. But even that didn't work. The two of them were training as hard as they could, but all I could picture was what would happen if they slipped up or if they were caught unaware.

Now I stood at the back of Graham's estate watching as

Micah hit sent arrow after arrow into a target in the distance. Not all were bull's-eyes, but they were pretty close. Torr stepped next to me and nodded. "He's getting good."

"He is. But I don't know if it's going to be good enough."

Torr nodded to Grunt, who'd latched himself onto Micah. "Grunt will stay with Micah."

It was a small consolation. But I would take any that I could get. Taking a deep breath, I turned to Torr. "Torr, I need you to promise me something."

He glared at me. "Don't tell me to leave this fight."

"I'm not. I'm telling you to get them out of it. If things go bad, I need you to promise me you will grab Micah, Noel, and Grunt and run. Run as far as you can."

My brother looked deep into my eyes. "And where would we go, Addie? Is there a safe place that we could all escape to?"

I looked back at him, my heart breaking before I shook my head.

"Whatever's going to happen is going to happen. And if we fall, I'd rather we fall together. Otherwise, we're just postponing the inevitable," he said.

My chest tightened, even though I knew he was right. What was going to happen was going to happen. If Sterling Peak fell, the rest of the world would fall as well. And Torr was right. He and Noel and Micah would just be running to postpone their fate, not avoid it.

I could picture their terror-filled days as they tried desperately to stay out of the reach of the demons. And then, one by one, they would fall too. I closed my eyes as if I could will the images away. "I hate this. I hate all of this."

"I know."

Reaching over, I pulled him into a hug. "I'm glad that I found you. I wish we had more time."

"I'm glad you found me too, Addie. When you came into that cave and rescued me, I didn't know what to think. When Mom died, I thought I was lost. But you showed me that I wasn't. And I will always be grateful for that. And then you gave me Noel and Micah. I've had a family these last few years because of you. And that's more than I ever expected."

Tears pressed against the back of my eyes as I looked at him. Ever since Tess had broken the news, tears always seemed to be threatening to fall whenever I was with my family. During the other times, I could lock it all away.

But it was at times like this that the real cost of the battle ahead weighed heavily on me. People were going to lose their lives. People who loved one another as much as I loved my family.

And there was nothing I could do to stop it.

There might not be anything I could do to stop the violence coming for my family either. A feeling of helplessness threatened to consume me.

Torr pulled his arms away, clearing his throat. "I'm going to go work with Micah now. His, uh, sword fighting still needs a little help."

Taking a deep breath, I nodded, trying to will the tears back yet again. "Okay." I nodded toward where Tess was working with Noel. "Tess could give you guys some pointers too."

"Good. Maybe I'll—"

"Addie."

I turned as Vera walked out of the house. "I need to speak with you for a moment," she said.

Nodding at her, I turned back to Torr. "I'll join you guys in a minute."

He flicked a glance a at Vera before slipping away.

Vera stood with her hands in her pockets, looking over at

where my little group had gathered on the grass. Tess was running them through different movements with their swords. Neither Vera nor I spoke for a moment as we watched them go through the drills.

It was good that they were learning some things, but I also knew that nothing they did this late in the game would help. Micah was too small to take on a demon. Although maybe with the help of the other two and Grunt, they could take one down.

I looked over at Grunt, who lay on his back, swatting his paw at a butterfly that floated above him. I couldn't help but smile at how peaceful he looked. But I'd seen him in battle. He could be ferocious when he needed to be.

And when it came to protecting Micah, Noel, and Torr, I needed him to be his most ferocious.

Next to me, Vera grunted and nodded toward Grunt. "Your father went back to Hell."

My head jolted toward her. "What?"

"He's just going to retrieve the rest of Grunt's herd. He thinks he knows where they are, so he'll grab them and bring them back with him. They'll be another line of defense."

My heart, which had raced at Vera's announcement, slowed. I felt dizzy. "Oh, okay."

But I realized that that was more than okay. Grunt's species was incredibly fierce. Grunt was a tiny ganta, just a baby, really. But the others were the size of elephants. I smiled. That would be good. I'd seen them wipe out dozens of demons. That could definitely help.

"When will he be back?" I asked

"It might take him a while to get to them. He probably won't be back until tomorrow."

"Tomorrow." The day the invasion was supposed to start, if Abaddon stuck to the schedule. Brock no doubt had informed him that we'd seen him at D'Angelo's. He could easily move the timetable up.

Unbidden, my gaze strayed to the tall structure that had been constructed at the edge of the forest. I could see the two Rangers on duty. Although from this distance, I couldn't make out who they were.

There was another similar structure farther into the woods, keeping an eye on the portal. As soon as a demon emerged from the portal, they would set off the alarm, and everyone would get into position.

Even before that, there were at least two dozen Rangers stationed just at the edge of the forest as the first line of defense. They were being rotated on four-hour shifts until the war began. Graham wanted to make sure that everyone was as fresh as possible. Four hours was as long as he was willing to let them be on duty before they were replaced.

Graham had been busy contacting Seraph academies across the nation. Rangers were racing to Sterling Peak. But not all of them. They still had to leave some behind in each of the cities in case the intel they'd received was false and the demons were going to do simultaneous attacks on all of the cities.

In my gut, I didn't think that was going to be the case. Simultaneous attacks like that would be a long fight. Abaddon was going to want this over in one quick move. One decisive victory and then small little attempts from that point on.

I hadn't seen Graham except in passing since our time in D'Angelo's solarium. He was too busy arranging troop movements and planning strategies.

The rest of the Seven had been just as busy. This was the first time I'd seen Tess since the solarium as well. And although she was smiling with the kids as she taught them the moves, I could see the stress on her face and the stiffness in her posture. She kept glancing around as if she expected a demon to pop out from behind a tree.

"There's something else I need to tell you," Vera said.

Her words pulled my attention back to her. For the first time, I noticed the seriousness on her face. "What is it?"

"I need to leave."

CHAPTER 62

I need to leave. Vera's words rang through my head. My mouth fell open, but no sound came out. I must have misheard her. She couldn't have said that. Yet I didn't seem capable of speech, so getting her to clarify was going to take a moment. Finally, I managed to stutter out a question. "What? Why?"

Vera shifted her gaze to the sky. "I need to speak with my brothers and sisters and see if I can get them to intercede."

I pictured the angels that I'd seen at the training yard. They'd watched as Michael tied Vera to the hellstone, weakening her. They'd stood back and done nothing. They believed that she deserved to die for turning her back on the angels.

"Vera, you can't. They'll kill you."

She gave me one of her smiles. "No, they're beyond that now. With Michael and Uriel's betrayal, they're probably just confused. Thinking for themselves is not really high on an angel's list."

"You and Dad seem to do that just fine."

She cackled. "We do indeed. But we're cut from a slightly

different cloth. My job is to interact with humanity. I needed to be able to think for myself. And your father, with the mission he was given, he needed to be able to think for himself too.

"For the others, though, it's more a matter of being given orders and just carrying them out. So learning that Uriel and Michael had betrayed them and had been working with the demons, that's going to take some time for them to come to grips with."

"How much time?"

She shrugged, but the worry in her eyes wasn't nearly so nonchalant. "I don't know. I'm hoping I'll be able to speak with them and convince them that they need to intercede on the behalf of humans like we did before."

In theory, that sounded good. But I also knew that when the angels had been part of the Angel Wars earlier, collateral damage wasn't a big consideration. Defeating the demons was all that mattered.

"Are you sure that's such a good idea? Last time, they weren't exactly worried about protecting human life."

"I know. But I'm hoping that things may have changed. I know that my living on Earth caused quite a few of them to take a closer look at what humans are like. I'm hoping that closer look has changed how they view all of them. And I will be sure to make them understand that humans need to be protected at all costs."

It was a risk. But the reality was that without angelic intervention, I just didn't see how we were going to survive. So finally, I nodded. "Okay. Good luck."

Vera hugged me tight. "I am privileged to have known you, Addie. You've shown me what an incredible woman you are. If I hadn't already been convinced that Nephilim could be good after my son, you definitely would have shown me. And you may be the one who convinces the angels that there's a need to help humanity."

I wasn't sure what to say to that. It felt too lofty for me. Instead, I nodded toward the kids. "You see those three? They are the reason that the angels should help. They've all been through hell, Torr quite literally. And yet there they stand, ready to defend each other and the rest of humanity to the best of their abilities. They're good people. They deserve a chance to have a life. They're who you need to show your brothers and sisters, not me."

"I think perhaps I'll show them the whole family," Vera said as her wings extended beyond her.

In a flash, the Vera that I knew with the gray hair, the braid, the old jeans, and T-shirt disappeared, and standing in her place was the young, vibrant warrior. I raised an eyebrow at the change.

She shrugged. "Appearances matter, even for angels. I'll be back as soon as I can."

Without another word, she disappeared into the sky. I watched her go with dread in my chest. "Hurry, Vera. Hurry."

CHAPTER 63

ABADDON

The preparations were underway. Abaddon stared out over his troops. He'd come down to the training yard to see the progress. Gorge, one of his lieutenants, hustled up to him.

"Report," Abaddon demanded, not taking his eyes from the masses going through attack maneuvers in front of him. These were the newer demons. The ones learning different fighting techniques. Some grasped them quickly while others looked as if they never would. They were too cocky with their size, thinking that when going against humans, that alone would be enough. And for some it would be. Some humans could be killed with just one blow.

Not all would be so easily felled. He pictured Addie.

"We're short two hundred bracelets," Gorge said.

Abaddon growled. The raid at the camp had been too successful. He'd known that they were going to hit one of the camps, but he'd counted on his people being able to stop them before any real damage was done.

He hadn't, however, counted on Lucifer and Vera being there as well. They'd made it difficult to succeed.

And then with Addie being there, success had proven impossible. They'd gotten away with all of the heavenstones and some of the completed bracelets. There was no way to make that up, and Uriel, that bastard, hadn't returned with a new supply.

"What do you want me to do?" Gorge asked.

Abaddon stared out over the trainees. His gaze locked on the four who'd been amongst the refugees of the camp, the ones who'd turned when they were in Sterling Peak. He smiled at the thought of it, wishing he'd been there to see the humans' faces when they realized that he'd outsmarted them.

His patrols had picked up the four just the day before. They were brutes without much finesse, but finesse wasn't necessary for certain endeavors.

"We'll do what they did. Have them go through two at a time to make sure that everyone gets through."

Gorge paused for just a moment. "But they won't be able to get back if there's a problem."

Abaddon narrowed his eyes. "Are you expecting a problem?"

"Of course not, sir. I'll make sure your orders are relayed."

Abaddon nodded, leaning against the railing and staring out over his troops.

Soon.

CHAPTER 64

GRAHAM

The Council had called an emergency meeting.

Anger thrummed through Graham as he made his way up the hill toward the Seraph Academy. He did not have time or energy to waste on useless politicking.

Donovan strode next to him, his face grim. "You need to tell them where to go. We don't have time for civilian oversight in the middle of this."

Graham completely agreed.

The Council was waiting for him in one of the conference rooms. They'd balked at first, saying that they were not going to hold one of their meetings up at the Seraph Academy. Even though they were on the brink of war, the Angel Blessed still wanted the comforts of their homes around them.

That, as far as Graham was concerned, was not even worthy of consideration. He told them that they were meeting at the conference room or nowhere. They'd been shocked and angered but had finally agreed.

"I think you might need to calm down there a little bit, my friend," Donovan said.

Graham just grunted in response. Donovan was right, but he didn't think that was an option. There was simply too much that still needed to be done to not be angered at being pulled like a dog on a leash.

In less than twenty-four hours, the demon invasion would begin. Rangers were rushing in from all parts of the country. And even as he prayed that they arrived in time, he worried that they were being played the fools and that the demons were going to attack on mass across the globe at the same time. If that were the case the battle was lost before it began.

But a decision had to be made. And he'd decided that they would make their stand at Sterling Peak. Because if the academy fell, the country would fall soon after.

It wasn't that he thought that Sterling Peak was more important than any other city. It was just that the Seraph Academy symbolized the fight against the demons. It was the beacon in the dark. And when it fell, the reverberations of that throughout the land would be swift and severe.

Plus, with Brock involved, he knew in his gut that this was where it would all start. His brother would want his pound of flesh. He would want to prove to Graham once and for all that he was the more powerful.

So the stand had to happen here.

He still couldn't get that image of Brock out of his head. Seeing him standing there had rooted him in place. Donovan had been the same next to him. Only Addie and Tess had been unaffected.

Addie had burst toward Brock while Tess had taken down D'Angelo.

But Graham wasn't sure he would have been able to move if a whole horde of demons had arrived at that moment. Brock was working with the demons. Brock *was* a demon. It was as if a circuit had tripped in his brain, and he could not think of anything beyond that. Moving, fighting, breathing, they'd all seemed beyond him at that moment.

He'd always secretly thought that his brother was evil incarnate, but to see that thought made flesh...

D'Angelo had been working with him. He'd been feeding him intel all along. D'Angelo now rested in a cell in the academy dungeons, one block over from where Michael was being held.

And D'Angelo's network of information had dried up. There'd been about a dozen or so Rangers who'd gone missing once news spread about the impending attack. Graham had no doubt that they were the ones loyal to D'Angelo.

The families that were loyal to D'Angelo had disappeared as well. To be honest, he was shocked that the Council members were still here. He thought they would have been on the first ship out of town.

But they seemed to think they had pressing business to discuss with him, and he had no idea what that might be because he doubted they were here to offer their suggestions about military strategy.

Up ahead, two Rangers stood on duty outside the conference room doors.

Graham gave them a nod as he strode past them and flung the doors open.

The members of the Council turned quickly at his entrance. Elaine Remiel sat at the end of the table glaring at Sasha Gabriel who stood over by the window with Angela Rafael, D'Angelo's mother.

Donovan's father frowned as Graham and Donovan stepped up to the table. With an annoyed wave, he indicated the empty side table. "There is no food. There are no snacks or drinks. This is not how we conduct a meeting."

Donovan's mouth fell open as he stared at his father. "We're on the verge of war. We don't have time for catering."

Angela narrowed her eyes. "You're not a member of the Council. You have no right to speak here."

"Enough," Graham said, his voice cutting through the room like a knife. "I do not have time for this. What do you want?"

Sasha's back straightened at Graham's tone. He narrowed his eyes. "You forget yourself. We are the Council. We are—"

"Getting in the way. Whatever you need, spit it out now," Graham ordered.

Sasha opened his mouth, his face turning red, but D'Angelo's mother spoke before he could. "My son is being held in the dungeon. He needs to be released due to the oncoming threat."

Graham gaped at her. "Are you kidding?"

Angela looked taken aback. "Of course not. And we need to discuss your overreach in placing him in the dungeons. You will need to provide an accounting of why you think such an egregious action was taken, and then we will discuss your punishment."

Graham stared at her for a long moment and then started to laugh.

"Stop laughing," she said.

But Graham couldn't help himself. In fact, her words only made him laugh harder. He grabbed onto his stomach as tears rolled down his cheeks.

"Stop laughing!" Sasha yelled, his face an alarming shade of red.

Graham finally got ahold of himself, wiping the tears from his cheeks. "You people are ridiculous. We are on the verge of being completely wiped out. Instead of concern for that, you come here demanding I release the spoiled little brat who betrayed us to the demons?"

He stared at Sasha and Angela, shaking his head. "I will not hear any more of this. We are all about to be killed. Every last one of us. And that mewling spoiled little brat is a big reason why. He's been feeding information to the demons for the last few weeks at least. He told them we were going into Hell. He warned them."

"Going into Hell?" Elaine asked with a frown.

"That is another problem," Donovan's father said. "We never gave permission for such an excursion. And now we have refugees that we have to deal with. They are taking up valuable resources that—"

"That was a military decision, and it is not up for discussion," Graham said.

Sasha narrowed his eyes. "Perhaps it should be. From what I've heard, the demon that D'Angelo was threatened into speaking with is your brother."

Graham crossed his arms over his chest. "So?"

Sasha smiled, the sight chilling. "How do we know that your loyalty is not compromised? Perhaps you've been working with your brother all along and merely created this charade to make D'Angelo look guilty."

Donovan scoffed but said nothing, although the look he gave his father spoke legions.

"If D'Angelo is guilty of betraying us, I don't see why we should believe you haven't as well. After all, we only have the word of you two, Tess, and the half-breed," Angela said with a derisive sniff.

"What did you call her?" Graham asked softly.

Sasha sneered. "She called her a half-breed. Why we should take her word on anything is beyond me. She was a *maid*. And now she's all of a sudden got these powers, and she's supposed to be someone that we listen to? I think not. When it comes to the four of you versus D'Angelo, I'll take D'Angelo's word. And he says that he was framed."

Graham stared at the faces looking back at him. Only two looked at him with faith. The others looked at him with derision.

These were the people he was fighting to save.

He wanted to just throw up his hands and leave them all to whatever happened and take off with Addie and the people he cared about.

But the reality was that these were not the most important people. In fact, these were the least important people of the ones who were in danger. And he was done with all of this. He leaned his hands on the table and glared across the space. "The Council is dissolved."

Sasha sputtered. "What? You can't do that."

"Actually, he can," Donovan said cheerfully. "Marcus had some time to go through the charter for the Council. In times of war, the Council can be dissolved so that the governing of the country rests solely with the commander of the Seraph Force. And just this morning, Graham officially announced that we are at war."

"No, we won't allow this," Sasha said, looking to the other members of the Council.

"You have no choice. Now, unless you're planning on helping with the war effort, I suggest you get out of my academy," Graham said.

"But my son—" Angela said.

Graham turned to look back at her. "Is exactly where he deserves to be. And unless any of you want to join him . . ." He scanned the room. "I suggest you get out of my sight."

CHAPTER 65

ABADDON

The brandy swirled in Abaddon's glass as he held it up in front of the fireplace. He liked to watch the changes in the color caused by the flame.

Taking a sip, he enjoyed the warmth sliding down his throat. Shifting in his seat, he let out a sigh. This was why they were leaving Hell. Not the brandy in particular, but all of the treats that the real world had to offer. In Hell, there was no fine liquor. Everything seemed to be covered in a layer of ash. Everything tasted like ash.

Abaddon wanted more. He wanted the life that he had seen. The life that caused him to rip off his wings and fall. He wanted to return to that world. And in just a short while, he would. Finally, after all this time, his visions for his future, for himself and his brothers and sisters, was coming to fruition.

He smiled as he pictured the heavenstones that made it all possible. All these years, getting to Earth had been the stumbling block. Demons could exist on Earth but only if they could get through the portals. And getting through the portals required special stones.

They'd gathered a few over the years that some unlucky souls had brought down to Hell with them.

But once Uriel had started delivering the stones, that was when things had really changed. Slowly, Abaddon had sent his forces out to test the humans to see what kind of resistance they offered.

And the truth was they offered very little. They were terrified at the sight of his soldiers, and well they should be. After being stuck in Hell for so long, his troops itched to break free, and their anger at their lot only made them that much more violent.

Hell was a barren wasteland. Food was next to impossible to grow here. Happiness, joy, those were things that Abaddon couldn't recall ever experiencing here.

And yet it was joy and happiness that had first drawn him to the humans. He'd wanted to see why they had such joy in their lives even though they seemed to have so very little. It took him time, but eventually he realized it was the connection with other people. Two people could be as poor as the wretches in his city, and yet at their baby's laugh, giant smiles would appear across their faces as if there was nowhere else they wanted to be.

Abaddon hadn't understood that. And he wanted to.

He also wanted the riches that the world could provide. He'd grown jealous. He could admit that. Jealous of all humanity had while angels, whose life was all about duty, had nothing.

But instead of arriving in paradise, he'd ended up in Hell. His days here were numbered now though. It was down to hours before they would finally begin climbing out of this pit.

Footsteps sounded from the hall. Abaddon turned as Brock appeared in the doorway. Abaddon took another sip of his drink as he studied the man. He would kill him as soon as the battle was over. And he would make sure he stayed down in Hell.

But he'd need him for the battle. That much was true. He was a good fighter. In fact, he was among his best.

The ambition he saw in his eyes was something that Abaddon had identified from the first day. And Abaddon knew that as soon as he got his chance, Brock would stab him in the back, quite literally. He couldn't allow that to happen. He wouldn't allow that to happen. After all he'd done to arrive at this moment, he certainly wasn't going to let some upstart take it away from him.

For now, though, the man had his uses. He waved him in. "Come."

Brock bowed his head as close to subservience as the man was capable of. "I've returned from Sterling Peak."

His tone of voice caused Abaddon to spear him with a look. "What happened?"

For the first time Abaddon could remember, Brock looked uncertain. "I was discovered at D'Angelo's home. They know that he's been feeding us information."

Placing his glass on the side table, Abaddon crossed his arms over his chest. "Who discovered you?"

"My brother, two members of the Seven, and Lucifer's daughter."

Abaddon grunted as he stood and started to pace, his mind whirling. So Lucifer's daughter knew that Abaddon had a spy amongst their ranks. "Your man, will he stand up to interrogation?"

Brock shook his head. "No. D'Angelo is an opportunist. And he will see that the opportunity now lies in him sharing as much information as possible. It's the only way he will be able to get a more comfortable punishment."

Abaddon grunted. Comfortable. What he wouldn't give to be comfortable.

"Should we postpone the invasion? They will know we're

coming. Or should we switch the timetable? Arrive sooner than they planned?" Brock asked.

Abaddon thought over his suggestions but discarded each one. He shook his head. "There will be no change in plans."

"But they know we're coming."

Abaddon nodded. "Yes, they do. But they're only humans. They have Addison, it's true, but our numbers will overwhelm them. They won't be able to stand against us, not for long. Our victory will be decisive. They will no doubt move most of their forces to counter us. We will go through them like a hot knife through butter. It is better this way. They won't be able to stand against us, and then the rest of the world will fall that much faster at our feet."

Picking up his glass, Abaddon smiled and raised it in salute to Brock. "Soon, victory will be ours."

CHAPTER 66

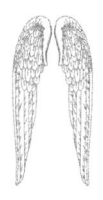

GRAHAM

It all came down to this battle. Graham walked through the lines of Rangers as he made his way to the small stage that had been set up in the field at the edge of Sterling Peak. On his right, slightly behind him, was Addie walking straight ahead, her eyes focused. On his other side was Donovan, his expression just as grim.

The three of them made their way through the throngs of soldiers. Slowly, the talk amongst the crowd dwindled. As Graham strode up the three short steps to the top of the stage, it was utterly silent. Addie and Donovan took their place on the ground below him, their backs to him, facing out to the crowd.

Graham took a moment to stare out over the sea of faces. Many of them were known to him, but many of them, he would never know their names. He may not even know their names if they passed from this world in the fight to come. They would have fought together on the same ground, but he would never have known of their existence.

It was not an easy thought.

Scattered amongst the Rangers were the civilians. Some of them had picked up a weapon for the first time in the last few days.

It gnawed at him. The fact that people would die tonight or in the next few days and Graham would have no awareness of their passing beyond the fact that they were part of a large number.

But he stowed those feelings away. They weren't helping. They only made his job harder.

His gaze drifted down to Donovan. The bruises from the previous attacks were still there. But Donovan would not stay out of this fight. He was back in fighting shape, or at least close enough.

And after what had happened in the refugee center, he was looking for some payback. Graham just hoped he would keep it in check until the right time and then unleash all of that anger on the demons.

His gaze slid over to Addie. Addie, who'd blown his world apart in all the best possible ways. Addie, who'd shown him and the rest of the world what true courage was. Addie, whose greatest gifts most people thought were her fighting skills and her flaming wings. But Graham knew that wasn't true. Her biggest gift was her heart. She truly cared for the innocent, whether she knew them or not.

In this fight, though, he was counting on her being as formidable as he'd seen her in the past. No, actually, he was counting on her being even more formidable. Because as much as he had faith in the abilities of the soldiers under him, he knew that there was a very good chance that they would lose the battle ahead.

And this was a battle they simply could not lose.

Taking a breath, he began. "Rangers and fellow citizens, the time is upon us. We have all been raised on the stories of the Angel Wars. We have all been raised on the exploits and bravery of those soldiers during that dark time.

"Make no mistake, future Rangers will be raised on the stories of your actions here today. You will be the ones written down in the history books. You will be the ones that Rangers wonder about and aim to emulate. You will be the ones who will be in the stories and the songs."

He took a breath. "The battle ahead will not be easy. Some of us will fall. But we must be victorious. It is not just Sterling Peak and Blue Forks that will suffer if we lose. We must hold the line against this demon threat or all of us are lost."

Casting a glance over her shoulder, Addie looked into his eyes. A small smile crossed her face before her wings unfolded. Turning back to the throng of soldiers, she let the flames shoot out wide. A murmur stirred amongst the Rangers. For many, this was their first time seeing her wings, although they had heard the stories.

"We are not alone in this fight. We have some individuals with us who bring with them special abilities."

Grunt materialized on the stage next to him. He'd been there all along, just waiting. On the other side of him, Torr appeared.

The murmurs of the crowd grew louder.

"These are some of the ones who will fight amongst us. Know their faces. Know they are on our side."

Grunt let out a roar. The soldiers let out a cheer at it. Graham placed a hand on Grunt's back and ran it through his fur as he nodded at Torr before turning his focus back to his troops.

"I know the odds seem daunting. I know the fear that you feel. I feel it too. But fear has no place in this fight. What will happen, will happen. Fear will only get in the way. So send it away. Focus on the now. You are warriors. You have been bred for this moment. You have been trained for this moment. And make no mistake we will succeed in this moment."

The crowd let out a roar of agreement. Grunt added his roar to the cacophony.

Raising his fist in the air, Graham stared out over the faces looking to him to set the tone. His voice echoed through the air. "We fight for the world and the people we love. We *will* repel this force. We *will* protect our people. We *will* be victorious!"

The Rangers screamed and hollered, shouting their agreement. And for the first time, Graham noticed the civilians in the back adding their yells.

Graham looked out over them, nodding even as deep inside he prayed that his words proved true.

CHAPTER 67

ADDIE

The yells of the warriors rang out through the night air. I looked out over the group of men and women in front of me, my chest feeling tight. Not all of these soldiers would still be alive when this battle ended. It was entirely possible that I wouldn't be alive either.

Straightening my back, I let my wings flame higher. Whatever happened, I would take as many demons with me as I could.

My gaze shifted to the side of the stage where Noel stood. We locked gazes for a long moment. So much was said between the two of us without words. She'd been my family these last long years.

We'd fought over whether or not she would be allowed to be part of this fight. I had wanted to keep her away, along with Torr and Micah. But the truth was, she would be part of it no matter what. Either today or down the road, this fight was hers too.

I couldn't order her to stay back. And even if I could, she was determined to do her part. She could fight. She promised to stay with Torr and Grunt. The three of them working together could take down demons. I'd seen them do it before. It didn't make it any easier to see her here.

But she would stay at the back of the fight, hopefully out of reach of the biggest groupings. It was a small solace.

Micah had wanted to come as well, but that was where I put my foot down. He was staying with Sheila, who promised to keep him in the house. Sheila had also promised that if the battle turned, she would flee with Micah.

I wasn't sure where they would go, but I promised I would find them—if I survived. That last part, I didn't say out loud, but I could tell that Sheila heard it nonetheless. She had given me a long hug and promised that she would keep him safe.

Franklin and Mary were with her as well. They would all head over to Blue Forks tonight and stay with Mary's relatives, or at least at their house. The relatives had already fled. They were older and would not be of much use in a fight.

Graham had tried to get Mary and Franklin to leave, but they had been adamant that they would not leave him unless it became absolutely necessary.

Blue Forks still had about half of its population. The younger, more able-bodied individuals had stayed behind to fight. Some of them had crossed the bridge and were now in the lower levels of Sterling Peak, waiting to do their part.

Four hundred soldiers would be the first line of defense. The other eight hundred were told that they needed to go and rest. In four hours, they would switch, and another four hundred would take their spot, and so on and so on until the demons finally arrived.

Despite Graham's orders, I didn't think any of us would be getting any sleep, although I understood Graham's reasoning. The last thing we needed was the demons not showing up for three days and everyone too exhausted to even raise a sword.

But I didn't think it would take that long. In my gut, I knew that Abaddon would be here before the night was out. He'd been waiting for this moment for too long. He wouldn't let time stretch out before he claimed the victory that he was so sure he could achieve.

Even as the worries and fears danced through my mind, I held my head high, my expression confident. I didn't want any of the soldiers seeing my doubts. I had become a symbol. People would look to me for courage.

So I needed to project the same look of fierce determination that I saw on both Graham and Donovan's faces. I needed to project confidence in the battle to come. Even though inside, I feared that it would be of no use. That when the battle ended, the humans left standing would only be slaves for the demons.

Lucifer hadn't returned yet. I hoped that everything was all right. With the demons no doubt massing on the other side of the portal, I worried that he had been grabbed. At the same time, I knew the risk he was taking was the right choice: the addition of Grunt's herd could make all the difference in the battle to come.

I flicked a gaze up at the sky, but there were no streaks of light, no sign that Vera was returning either. Part of me prayed that she got back in time, and another part of me hoped that she stayed away for her own safety.

Anyone who was part of this battle was fair game. And my father, Vera, and I would be prime targets. If they could take us out, it would demoralize the other soldiers and make the victory happen that much faster.

Because if even we three with all our abilities couldn't stand up to the demons, what chance did the rest of them have?

CHAPTER 68

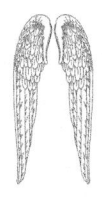

ABADDON

Dust swirled in the air as Abaddon walked along the field. His soldiers were lined up in rows, two thousand strong.

He grunted as he looked them over. The front lines consisted of the newer demons, the ones less well trained. They would be the cannon fodder, to be sent through the portal first. He had no doubt that the portal was being covered, that the humans would be waiting to take down the first of his soldiers as they crossed over.

Which was why Abaddon was going to send them through in such numbers that they would overwhelm anyone on the other side. That first wave was responsible for identifying any countermeasures that the humans had set up.

Once that was done, the rest of his legion would march through. And that's when the battle would really begin.

Excitement raced along his skin. After longing for so many

years for this moment, it was hard to believe that it was truly here.

Part of him marveled that this side of him had not faded away. Hope was not a thing that he thought existed within him anymore. But he hoped with everything that he was worth that they were victorious.

The only reason he had any doubt about his victory was the half-breed. Without her, they would mow through the humans in moments.

But she'd added her strength to this battle. And more than that, she'd pulled in Lucifer and Gabriel as well. He would not underestimate any of them. He couldn't. Their success depended on taking those three out at the first possible chance. Once they were gone, the humans would be nothing.

He smiled in anticipation of the battle to come.

His gaze locked on Brock's as he walked amongst the demons, making comments, critiquing individuals' fighting prowess. Giving them tips for where to aim and what to do.

Abaddon had considered putting Brock in the front line, but Brock had already amassed a following of sorts amongst the demons. They would rebel against Abaddon if Brock were killed in the first few moments of battle.

So he'd have to wait until the battle was underway and then find his moment to take Brock out of the equation. He had no doubt that moment would come.

Battle was a chaotic endeavor. People liked to think that they could plan and organize and arrange for a battle, but it was a dynamic creature. The plans would become null and void almost from the moment of first contact. And then it was a constant shifting of objectives and plans if you had any hope of success.

Abaddon welcomed that chaos. He reveled in that chaos.

He stretched out a clawed hand, staring at the talons at his fingertips. He remembered a time when his skin was a pale pink. When his fingers had been long and sinewy. It had been so long since he'd seen that form. He could barely bring it up in his memory.

When he'd shifted over to this form, he'd walled away certain aspects of himself. Every once in a while, though, he caught a glimpse behind those walls.

When he'd heard the name Gabriel mentioned, that had opened the door to an old memory. He remembered Gabriel. He'd liked Gabriel, even though Gabriel hadn't understood his dissatisfaction with his role in his life. During the civil war, Gabriel had a chance to end him and had shown pity.

He rolled his claw into a fist. Weakness. She should have finished him when she'd had the chance. All of this could have been avoided then. But she'd shown him mercy, and now the world would pay for that failure.

He hoped that Gabriel was at the battle. He hoped that he was able to cross swords with her again because *he* would not show any weakness. He would end her as she should have ended him.

And he would continue on, cutting a bloody swath through the humans that stood up against him until all that were left cowered in fear.

Then he would stand upon the corpses of those that had been slaughtered and rule the world as he should have been able to do eons ago.

It was his destiny.

It was his birthright.

And it was his time to claim it.

Brock walked over to him and gave him a nod. "They're ready, sir."

Abaddon looked out over his troops. The humans knew they

were coming. He could wait, stretch it out, make it so that they were more nervous, more tired.

But he didn't want to wait. He'd waited long enough. He nodded. "Then let it begin."

CHAPTER 69

ADDIE

Like many of the Rangers, I'd been adamant that I would not sleep that first night. But at the same time, I wanted Noel and Torr to get some rest. I didn't want them in the battle to begin with. I certainly didn't want them going into it tired.

But the only way that they would rest was if I did as well, so the three of us unrolled some bedrolls under one of the trees. Grunt plopped down next to us as we all lay staring up at the night.

It was quiet for a long moment, each of us lost in our own thoughts before Noel spoke. "Are you scared?" she asked.

I didn't answer right away. Part of me thought I should say something soothing, something that would gloss over the fears racing through me. But Noel deserved better than that. "I suppose I am. I think it would be crazy not to be scared. But I know when the fight begins that all that fear will go away. You just live in the moment. And sometimes those moments can last a lifetime."

Noel nodded, looking up at the leaves.

On her other side, Torr already had his eyes closed, although I knew he was not yet asleep. It was on the tip of my tongue to try and get them to step away from the fight yet again. To go join Micah over in Blue Forks and hopefully be safe from any of the violence.

But I knew it wouldn't do any good. And I did not want our last moments together to be filled with anger and frustration. So instead, I reached out and took Noel's hand giving it a squeeze. "Thank you for making me a part of your family."

"You made Micah and me a family. These last few years have been the best of my life."

"Mine too... I think," I said.

Noel gave a small chuckle. "Well, being you only remember the last few years of your life, I would hope that they were good."

I wondered at all of that. Would my memories ever return? Not that I was complaining. What I had now was so much more than I ever imagined. But I would like to remember my mother. I had these senses of her but no true memories.

A soft snore rumbled out of Grunt as he rolled onto his side. He was such a loving soul. And yet when called upon, more ferocious than ten demons. He would protect Noel to the best of his ability.

I hoped that would be enough and that he would be able to keep himself and Torr safe as well. Although that seemed like an awfully tall order for one creature. And yet that's what I was doing, placing all of my hope on him.

Next to me, Noel had closed her eyes. The camp had gone quiet. Soldiers were spread out. Some lay straight on the flat ground. Others had found bedrolls like us. A few sat up, talking softly around the fire.

Everywhere I looked were Rangers and civilians, trying to give themselves a moment of peace before the battle began.

Knowing that whatever would happen would happen, I let my eyes close. There was no changing it now. Now there was just the waiting.

My eyes flickered open one last time. Looking around, I hoped I would catch sight of Graham, but there was no sign of him. No doubt he was in the thick of things.

Two familiar figures walked out of the darkness and headed toward us. Watching them approach, I smiled. Placing her bedroll next to me, Tess sat down giving me a nod, as Laura unrolled a bedroll on the other side of Noel. Then two of them lay back without a word and closed their eyes.

These were probably amongst my last moments, but I was also surrounded by friends and those I loved. I smiled. There were worse ways to go.

CHAPTER 70

GRAHAM

The night was quiet. Graham had instructed the soldiers not on watch to get some rest before the change of guard in four hours. He himself had no plans on sleeping tonight. If they made it through the night, he would get some sleep early tomorrow. But he wanted his soldiers to be resting.

He climbed down from the lookout tower. Donovan stood waiting for him below. "All good?"

"They're wide awake and focused." He paused, eyeing his second. "How are you?"

"Fresh as a daisy," Donovan said, falling in step next to him.

Graham grunted in response. He knew that Donovan wasn't at a hundred percent, but he needed him here.

He could trust Donovan. Donovan would tell it to him straight, which not all of his Rangers would. His second would pull no punches, and Graham was going to need that in the battle ahead.

Together, they walked toward the portal. Graham met the gaze of the Rangers standing, or sitting in some cases, waiting for the demons to come through.

He hated that they were at this point. He hated that these Rangers that he walked by would be the first ones in the thick of things. But that was the lot of the soldier. You were placed in dangerous situations.

So he shut down those feelings and pushed them away. Now he had to think like a commander, not like their brother or their friend.

Donovan spoke quietly next to him. "They're ready. They know what the plan is, and the captain of each regiment is well trained. And they've passed that training down to their Rangers."

Graham believed him. The Rangers he was staring at now were battle hardened. He wasn't worried about them, or at least not as much as the newer Rangers, the ones who, in some cases, had never fought a demon. They were who he was concerned about.

He had them teamed up with more seasoned warriors to make sure that they didn't fight any demons alone. But sometimes the young could be cocky. He would lose many of them to that arrogance in the fight ahead.

He and Donovan stopped six feet away from the marker of where the portal opened. He couldn't see it. Donovan couldn't see it. None of the humans could. Only Addie, Lucifer, Gabriel, Torr, and probably Grunt could.

But for the rest of them, they'd had to place markers so that they knew exactly where to look.

Looking up into the trees, Graham made sure that the lookouts had a clear view.

"Commander?" a Ranger asked as he held up a flaming torch.

Graham turned back to the portal and nodded. "Light it."

The Ranger thrust the torch into the pot on one side of the

portal. A massive flame erupted, wrapping around the wood that had been piled up inside. Then he walked to the other side and did the same.

They would feed the fire all throughout the night to make sure that they were able to see the demons when they finally emerged.

Graham nodded and then walked back through the lines of his Rangers. He stopped and spoke with the few of them that he knew, trading old jokes and stories. To the Rangers whom he locked gazes with, he gave a confident nod or exchanged a few short words. By the time he and Donovan had finished walking through the men, it was almost time for the next watch.

Donovan stepped next to him as they reached the main street of Sterling Peak. "This isn't on you, you know."

"What do you mean?" Graham asked.

"The deaths that we know are coming. It's not on you. You didn't choose this fight. It was coming no matter what. But with you in charge, with the resources we have, we've got a chance of surviving this."

"Do we?"

"We do. We've got Addie, Lucifer, and Vera."

"Those last two aren't back yet."

"But they will be. They won't leave us in the lurch."

Graham wished he could share Donovan's conviction. But Lucifer had returned to Hell. It was entirely possible that Abaddon had been waiting for him and that he was out of this fight.

And as for Vera, he liked Vera. But she was wanted by the angels. She'd been chased down and captured by them before. It was entirely possible that as soon as she'd shown her face, they'd locked her up or worse.

So he wasn't counting on either of them returning. He couldn't. He had to deal with the resources he had now.

His gaze drifted over the group of soldiers that slept. Scattered amongst them were some Rangers talking quietly. Others walked around, looking like they were trying to lose some excess energy.

He didn't spy Addie amongst the group, although he knew she was out there somewhere. It was better that he didn't see her right now. They both needed to get their game faces on. And the two of them knew each other too well to believe the game face.

Donovan nudged his chin toward the tent that had been set up for Graham and his officers. It was where they would strategize. "I don't suppose you're planning on getting any sleep?"

"Eventually. But you can go if you want to take a moment."

Donovan shook his head. "My place is by your side." He nodded toward the soldiers who were starting to head back toward the front. "The watch is changing."

"Well, let's go make sure that everybody's got their positions down," Graham said.

Graham and Donovan went through the same procedure except for the lighting of the torches. But they did go make sure that the urns were still well stocked with wood and that the Rangers in charge of them knew to keep them well lit.

Darkness had truly fallen by the time Graham started to climb the second lookout tower. The new shift had gone up just moments before. Graham stared out over the trees as he climbed. He'd had some of the trees taken down in the area outside the portal to make sure that his soldiers could fight and had room to maneuver.

As he crested the platform, he grabbed onto the railing and looked toward the portal. The flames on either side cast an eerie glow into the clearing.

It looked dangerous. There was nothing welcoming about those fires.

Corey, one of the Rangers from Sterling Peak, stood with

Emily, another Ranger who Graham was familiar with. He nodded at both of them. "You know what to do."

Emily pointed to the gong next to her. "I start banging on this as soon as we see anybody stepping through that portal."

"And I set off the flares," Corey said.

"Correct." He turned back to look at the portal, but the space in between the twin fires was empty.

"Do you really think they'll come tonight?" Corey asked.

"Yes," Graham said without hesitation. "They've been waiting too long for this. They're not going to put it off."

"We're ready for them," Emily said.

"Damn straight," Donovan agreed.

Graham was about to add his agreement when movement from the corner of his eye pulled his attention. His head jerked back toward the portal as six demons rushed through.

"The alarm!" Graham yelled as he dove for the ladder and slid most of the way down to the ground. Donovan was right behind him as the gong rang out into the night air. Screams and yells followed it, all coming from the direction of the portal.

The Rangers all stirred into action but held their places, not pressing forward. The last thing they needed was for everyone to crush forward.

But Graham sprinted through all of them. "Make way! Make way!" he yelled.

The Rangers shifted to the side as he and Donovan barreled through.

Despite the din, he could hear the calls of the archer brigade as they sent arrow after arrow at the invading horde. Pulling his sword, Graham spotted the fight that had begun up ahead.

Already he could see a few bodies of Rangers on the ground. But there would be time to mourn later. Now was the time to make sure that no more Rangers joined them. With a yell, he dove into battle, cutting off the thrust of one demon who was aiming for the neck of another Ranger already embroiled in battle with a second demon.

His sword clashed with the demon's as Donovan slid along the ground behind him, slicing his own sword along the back of the creature's knees.

The demon's hesitated for just a moment. It was all Graham needed. He swiped the demon's sword to the side and then slid his sword along the creature's chest.

Behind him, Donovan plunged his sword into the creature's back and twisted.

Sensing the encroaching threat, Graham turned to meet the blade of yet another demon. As their blades crashed, he kicked the creature between his legs. The creature's eyes widened. Graham shifted to the side and slammed the hilt of his sword into the creature's face before running it along the creature's neck. Blood spurted in a rush and he kicked the demon away.

After that, he lost count of the moves and demons that he fought as he whirled and sliced, fighting to protect everything he held dear.

CHAPTER 71

ADDIE

The demons struck in the dead of night. The alarm rose as the sky was dotted with stars. Calls to arms rang out, jolting me from sleep.

Despite my intentions, I'd fallen in deep. It took me precious seconds to remember where I was and what was happening.

Next to me, Tess shook my arm. "It's beginning, Addie," she said before taking off.

Laura met my gaze. I nodded back at her. "I'll be right behind you." Without a word, she took off into the night, following Tess.

Torr and Grunt were already on their feet, both of their bodies tense.

Noel cinched the belt that held her swords around her waist. She tapped her thighs to double-check and make sure her extra knives were there. She grabbed the bow and arrow, slipping the carrier over her shoulder as she clutched the bow.

This was it.

I turned to the three of them. "You stay at the back. You

protect one another," I said, my gaze shifting over the three of them. "And if you need to run, you run. Don't take chances."

Each of them nodded back at me. My heart clutched at the fear I saw on their faces.

Once again, it was on the tip of my tongue to talk them out of being involved. But to do it at this moment would suggest I didn't have faith in them. And I could not allow them to go into the battle ahead doubting themselves.

"You can do this. Look out for one another, that is the most important thing. But if the battle is not going well, know when to retreat. Get to Micah, get to Sheila, and get them out. Live to fight another day. I *will* find you."

Hugging them all quickly, I sprinted away, swallowing down my fear and my heartache while wiping the one tear that crawled down my cheek. There was no time for any of that now.

I burst into the air without my flames on my wings and soared over the heads of the soldiers racing forward. As I approached the portal, I slowed, hovering above the battle to assess the situation.

Demons poured out of the portal, stepping on their brethren who'd been downed with arrows. But even as I watched, those who'd been killed disappeared from view.

Behind me, the first lookout tower had been destroyed. And down below it, demon and humans met in battle with cries ringing out and blood being spilled on both sides.

Taking a breath, I inflamed my wings and dove down low. I pulled my sword from its sheath, gripping it in my hand as flames encircled the blade. And then I went down a long line of the demons, slicing along their backs. They cried out, arching their backs.

Six dropped to the ground, and the Rangers were on them. A seventh turned around and lunged at me, but I dove out of the way, my wings hitting another demon and setting him aflame.

He screamed, running out into the trees, setting the trees on fire as well.

"The half-breed!" the call went out amongst the demons.

A group of eight demons charged toward me.

Bursting into the air to keep out of their reach, I felt power well up in my chest. I flung a ball of light into their center. It exploded, sending each of them flying. I stayed aloft, sending out ball after ball, careful to keep it away from the Rangers.

From the corner of my eye, I saw a Ranger surrounded by three demons. Before I could reach him, the demon behind him had grabbed him by the head and twisted.

The man dropped to his knees and went face first into the ground.

My heart plunged. But that was only going to be the beginning of the dying, so I shoved it away. Fine-tuning my throws, I offered whatever I could to the battle unfolding in front of me.

CHAPTER 72

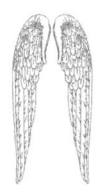

The fireball engulfed a demon who'd crashed to the ground. A Ranger crushed his sword through the creature's back. My fireballs had been relentless, but now the fighting was too thick for me to use them safely.

Wasting no time, I dove down. Flipping over, I aimed myself feet first toward a towering demon. My feet crushed into its face as I dropped into a group of six of them.

Whirling, slashing, and lunging, I didn't think but simply reacted to the threats around me without any conscious plan.

When I was done, the six lay in pieces at my feet. I didn't stop to focus on them. There was no time. To my left, four more advanced on a group of Rangers already taking on two demons. I moved to intercept them, cutting two of them at the back of the knees as I entered the fray.

And that's how it went. I moved from fight to fight, no thoughts, no fears, just a whirlwind of death. My only conscious thought was that I needed to take down as many demons as I could, as fast as I could manage.

As Rangers become overwhelmed, I rushed to their aid.

Often, I felt the bloom of loss when I arrived too late. If a demon tried to creep up behind me, I'd flame them with my wings brought high, leaving them as charred stumps.

On and on I fought, never stopping, never letting myself think beyond the next fight. The sounds of battle, the dying and fighting, blended together around me, creating a horrific symphony.

Then a sound different from the others cut through the haze. My head jerked up, turning to the sound of crashing wood that came from behind me. Whirling around to face the new threat, pain slammed into my chest as heavy wires wrapped around me. A heavy ball at the end of the wires pressed tightly against my rib cage, cutting into my skin with each breath.

My knees buckled. For a moment it seemed impossible to even take a breath. The moment passed, and air rushed into my lungs. But my side and chest ached, letting me know my ribs were bruised if not broken.

Squirming against the wires, I struggled to break free. But each movement was harder than the last. My strength felt like it was draining away.

In the flickering light, my gaze locked on the metal ball at my chest. There was something familiar about it. Shock slammed into me as I realized where I had seen the dark material before. It was a hellstone. The material that had drained the strength from Vera and was now leeching me of mine.

No. I couldn't let this happen. I struggled against the bonds, but I could barely move. The material didn't even give a little.

As I fought to break free, the fighting continued unabated around me. A Ranger caught sight of me, his eyes widened. He stepped forward as if to help, but a demon slashed the man across the neck. Blood sprayed the ground and soldiers around him. As he crashed to the ground, his gaze locked on me. I was the sole witness to the light draining from his eyes.

Then ahead, I noted one demon making his through the crowd, ignoring the fighting around him, his attention locked on me, a smile upon his face.

As he approached, my blood ran cold. Brock stared down at me and smiled. "You're mine."

He raised his sword into the air. Trapped and barely able to move, I knew there was nothing I could do to stop him.

CHAPTER 73

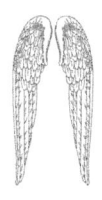

GRAHAM

Graham knew the moment that Addie joined the fight. From the corner of his eye, he'd seen the flashes of her fire as she soared over the troops. Part of him had wanted to call out to her, to tell her to get away, but he tamped that protective instinct down.

And then for the next thirty minutes, he'd only caught glimpses of her, as he'd been engaged in his own battles.

She'd stayed in the air for a while, sending bolts of fire into the demons below. He'd been happy to see her keeping herself above, out of the fray.

But once the fighting became too packed, she'd stopped, no doubt to make sure that she didn't harm the Rangers in the close quarters fighting.

Then she dove down, and he lost sight of her in the fighting masses. But every now and then he'd see flashes of her light and know she was still fighting. She was still alive.

Her flaming wings acted as a beacon pulling demons toward

her. Graham found himself fighting his way toward her as well and caught sight of Donovan doing the same.

Now Graham ducked under the swipe of a demon's claw and cut the demon along the thigh. Blood sprayed, gushing down his leg. He'd hit an artery. He brought the sword back and sliced the demon along the back before another Ranger plunged his knife into the demon's throat.

That was how it was the entire fight. He'd taught his Rangers how to fight in teams, so they worked together, taking down the demons two at a time.

But they hadn't been the only ones who'd been successful. Even now, he could see the Rangers that had lost their fights, their blood soaking into the ground beneath them.

In his mind, he shut that horror away, tamping down his emotions. There would be time for all of that later. In the thick of the battle though was definitely not that time.

For a split second, his attention was pulled as Addie's wings flamed high. Then, just as quickly, they blinked out. No trail of fire, no lingering glow. They were extinguished.

His heart jumped into his throat.

"Donovan! We need to get to Addie!" he yelled as he slipped to the side of a demon that overextended his lunge. As he passed, he sliced at the back of the demon's thighs, opening two huge cuts on each leg. He left the finishing to the other Rangers. His heart raced as he craned his neck, trying to see Addie. But there was no sign of her, no flicker of her fire.

Why couldn't he see her?

Then ahead, through the battle, he saw the demons parting to allow another demon to get through.

With horror, Graham watched as Brock appeared through the fray. The flames threw shadows across his face, making the horns that had started to appear on his skull appear larger.

And Graham knew that he had something to do with Addie's light disappearing.

Cold fear took root in his chest. He slammed his foot into the torso of a rushing demon and brought his sword across the demon's neck as he fell.

A demon thrust a sword toward him from the side. Distracted by his brother, he didn't get out of the way in time. A shallow cut bloomed along his ribs. Blood seeped into his shirt as he whirled around and impaled his sword into the demon's chest. He tugged the sword up and pierced the creature's heart.

Donovan reached his side as Graham yanked his sword from the demon's chest. Alarm flashed in his second's eyes as he took in the cut along Graham's ribs. "You okay?"

"It's just a scratch," he said, waving him off. And even if it wasn't, there was no time for Graham to run and get it seen to. Everyone needed to stay in this fight as long as they could.

"Move!" Donovan yelled, shoving Graham aside as a demon jumped off a fallen Ranger, bringing his sword down with two hands.

Catching the demon in mid-jump, Donovan sliced his sword across the creature's chest. As the creature landed, Graham twirled and brought his sword down on the back of the creature's neck.

Then Graham was moving again. The fight had thinned out, and he could see Brock, but more importantly, he could see Addie. She was on the ground, some sort of metal wiring wrapped around her.

Brock stood up above her, his sword raised to bring down the killing blow.

CHAPTER 74

ADDIE

On my back, I struggled to roll onto my side. I needed to *move*. I needed to get out of the way. But the wires were wrapped all the way down to my hips. I couldn't get any purchase.

And there wasn't time as Brock raised his sword.

Fear lanced through me, followed by a strange sense of calm. *This is it. This is the end.* I tensed as Brock smiled. Time seemed to slow as the sword started its arc toward me. The flames of the fires flickered off its blade.

In my mind, I saw Noel, Torr, Micah, and Graham. I pictured the life that I had hoped we would one day have. And I hoped that somehow they escaped my fate.

Movement to my side pulled my attention as Graham burst out of the fighting around us. He tackled Brock around the waist. The two crashed to the ground. I rolled to the side as Brock's sword sliced down, catching me in a shallow cut along the cheek. I rolled away, trying to stay out of the fight between brothers.

By the time I stopped, they'd been swallowed up by the battle surging around them. I couldn't see what was happening or even where they had gone.

And I still couldn't move much. I was helpless here. And as soon as one of the demons realized it...

A roar sounded to my right. My head jerked up trying to pinpoint its source as demons cried out. A path appeared through the fight as demons were thrown aside.

Then Grunt was in front of me. Grabbing onto the hellstone, he pulled on it with his teeth.

"Addie!" Torr appeared at my side. Using his sword, he started to saw through the metal cabling.

Grunt continued to pull at the stone. Even the small space that Grunt was giving me from the stone helped. I felt less light-headed, as if some of my strength was returning.

A demon charged at us. Before I could let out a yell, a small figure slid in from the side, catching the demon on the back of the legs before bringing her sword up in between them.

Noel jumped to her feet, leapt onto the demon's back, and plunged her sword into the creature's neck before leaping off and turning to dispatch a second demon that had attempted to attack her from the side.

Sweat beaded on Torr's brow as he tried to cut the cable. "This isn't working. I can't get through."

"Help Noel," I said as two demons started for her.

With a last worried glance at me, Torr leapt to his feet and jumped to Noel's aid. I turned to Grunt, who held the ball in his mouth. "Can you break off that ball?"

I wasn't sure if he understood. But then his teeth clamped down hard. He twisted his head from side to side, working his way through the metal.

And then he jolted back.

My power swirled back through me. I looked down. The ball was gone.

Grunt spit it away. He looked at me for a moment before leaping over my head. His jaws latched onto the neck of a demon who'd been attempting to sneak up behind me.

Lying on the ground, I let my power soar through me. Making sure none of my people were nearby, I closed my eyes and let the fire burn through my wings and through the wire.

It melted, falling off me in pieces as I stood.

Noel and Torr stood with Grunt, the three of them back to back as demons moved in.

"Rangers, get down!" I yelled.

Torr, Noel, and Grunt hit the ground, as did all of the Rangers near me. My wings burst out with energy, sending fire ten feet into the air around me.

The demons caught fire, smoldering and dropping to their knees. Noel dove out of the way as one dropped right where she'd been crouched. She quickly patted out a flame that appeared on her sleeve.

I hustled over to them, helping Noel up. "What are you doing here? You're supposed to be at the back!"

Noel shook her head. "The demons made their way through. There *is* no back. They're everywhere."

Over at the portal, the demons were still pouring through. And then I looked around for Graham. I couldn't see him anywhere. *Graham, where are you?*

CHAPTER 75

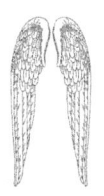

GRAHAM

Arms wrapped around Brock, Graham hit the ground and pulled Brock away from Addie. He managed to get them six feet away before the crowd swallowed them up. Then he rolled to his feet, pulling out his knife as his brother yanked himself away.

Brock chuckled, his voice unnaturally deep. "You think you can take me, little brother? You think now that I have all of this"—he gestured down to his body—"you can defeat me?"

"I guess we're about to find out."

"Yes, we are," Brock said before he lunged forward.

The move was classic Brock. He always fought the same way. His extra muscles and green skin didn't change any of that.

Darting to the side, Graham stabbed Brock quickly in the ribs as he passed. With a bellow, Brock lashed out with a backfist that Graham just barely dodged and then danced away.

Brock narrowed his gaze as he turned. "I'll make you pay for that."

All of the cruelty that Brock had inflicted upon Graham over his life rolled through his mind. The anger that he'd had to swallow down through his childhood and as a Ranger under Brock's command flared bright. The anger burned through his blood, strengthening him as his gaze narrowed.

His brother had been a demon long before he'd gone to Hell. And Graham wasn't going to hold anything back.

Once again, Brock darted forward, coming across with a large swing aimed at Graham's neck. Instead of moving out of the way, Graham twirled into Brock, zipping three quick jabs to his chest before slipping around to his back.

With another bellow, Brock turned and shot a side kick out at Graham that caught him right in the ribs. He stumbled back. Pressing his advantage, Brock brought his knife up over his head.

Graham slipped slightly to the side, grabbed onto Brock's hand, and helped him bring the knife down in an arc, except he directed it into straight into Brock's own chest.

A puff of air whooshed out of Brock's mouth as his knife pierced his skin.

Adding his other hand, Graham yanked it up, creating a cut from his navel up through his chest. He stopped right below his heart. Then Graham pulled another knife from the back of his belt and plunged it under his brother's chin.

Brock's eyes widened as Graham shoved him away.

There would be no confusion this time. No wondering what had happened to Brock. No, this time he was truly dead.

CHAPTER 76

ADDIE

Fighting side by side, I stayed with Grunt, Noel, and Torr. Time seemed to speed up and slow down at the same time. In my own fights, it was as if my opponents were moving in slow motion. And yet my heart was in my throat when a demon lunged at one of the others so incredibly fast.

But no matter what they did, no matter how many demons they sent back to Hell, the demons kept coming. *We need to shut down that portal.* An idea flickered through my mind, but before I could follow through on it, light streamed down from the heavens. *Please*, I begged as I watched it approach with both hope and fear.

Then in a burst of dust, Vera leapt into the middle of the fighting about twenty feet away. Cries rang out as demons fell in a whirl of Vera's blades.

Keeping Noel and Torr in sight, I made my way toward her. A demon tried to run around her, and I released a small fireball into his chest before I slammed a side kick into the creature's head, breaking its neck.

My breaths came out in pants as I looked around. Vera was only a few feet away. "Vera!"

She met my gaze. I raised my eyebrows to ask the question, but Vera was already shaking her head. "They haven't decided!" she yelled before she brought her sword up in a backhand move that took off a demon's arm.

The hopes that had risen so fast at Vera's appearance plummeted just as quickly. The angels weren't coming to help us. It was up to us.

The fighting had brought me closer to the portal. The demons coming through hadn't slowed.

From the corner of my eye, I noticed movement in the lookout tower. Flicking a glance toward it to assess the threat, I did a double take. A man stood leaning against the railing, watching the devastation below, looking entertained.

I narrowed my eyes at Uriel. I hadn't seen him arrive. Catching me gaze, he gave me a long, slow smile.

Anger, dark and deep, surged through me. More than anything, I wanted to slice that smile off his face. But right now, he was not the priority. But if I survived this, I would track him down and make him one.

Commotion by the portal drew my attention. Three demons rushed through the portal. But instead of entering with a bloodthirsty scream, they all cast fearful looks over their shoulder.

Then two ganta, beautiful in their terrifying presence, stepped through, and standing between them was Lucifer.

CHAPTER 77

Grunt let out a roar as the members of his herd appeared with deafening bellows of their own. Lucifer looked around, taking the fight in with a single glance.

My gaze quickly ran over him, but he looked unharmed, although I could see the blood dripping from his sword. With a battle cry, he rushed forward, the ganta at his side. Six more ganta poured through the portal behind him.

The creatures wasted no time, spreading out, seemingly able to make the distinction between demon and Ranger with ease.

Both Rangers and demons started to run from the creatures. But then the Rangers began to cheer as they realized that the ganta were on their side.

The fighting began with a renewed spirit, and my hope bloomed anew. Maybe we had a chance after all.

A cold blade pressed against my throat. A hand gripped the back of my neck. Uriel leaned down close to my ear to be heard. "I think you've caused enough trouble, half-breed."

CHAPTER 78

There was nothing I could do. If I moved even slightly, Uriel's blade would cut open my neck.

Slowly, he pulled me back from the fighting.

"Addie!" Noel yelled, darting for me. But a demon stepped in her path, blocking her way.

"So much trouble from one little half-breed. Abaddon wants to kill you himself, but things happen in battle," he seethed, his hand tightening around the handle of his blade.

Then Uriel cried out. Gripping his arm, I thrust it away from me. Diving for the ground, I rolled out of his reach.

Behind me, Uriel thrust out a kick at Vera. With a laugh, she shoved the kick down, launching her own and catching him on his chin. His head snapped back.

He growled, his eyes slits as they focused on Vera. "You're a traitor. Michael should have killed you."

Her own look was no less menacing. "I'm not the traitor, Uriel. You and Michael have lost your way. It's not too late to stop this."

Uriel laughed. "Why would I want to stop this?"

Vera flicked me a quick glance before her focus returned to Uriel. "Get out of here, Addie. I've got this."

I didn't want to leave Vera. I didn't trust Uriel.

But then Torr let out a cry behind me, followed by a scream from Grunt. It wasn't a scream of victory but one of pain.

"Go," Vera ordered before she darted forward, her sword clashing with Uriel's.

Turning, I took off into the air. A quick scan of the masses below me showed Grunt on the ground, a demon above him. Emitting my own roar, I came down, slamming my boots into the chest of a demon raising to strike at Grunt again. The demon fell back, crashing into three others. Two ganta let out roars behind them before clasping the four amongst their jaws.

Grunt stumbled to his feet and then fell back heavily on his legs. A bloody gash ran along his rib cage. I dropped down next to him. "You okay, boy?"

He licked my hand in response and shook his head. I ducked away to avoid getting covered in slobber. The gash was long but not too deep.

A growl erupted from Grunt. He darted past me, grabbing a demon by the calf and pulling him away.

The demon dropped to the ground so fast that his neck broke with the impact of his chin on the ground.

I jumped back into the fray.

CHAPTER 79

The fighting seemed to have no end. My heart broke at the bodies littering the ground. Even with the addition of Vera, Lucifer, and the ganta, it was clear we were losing. Graham worked his way toward me. Donovan was by his side. Both had cuts and gashes along their arms, legs, and necks.

Graham met my gaze. "We have to retreat."

"To where?" I asked.

"We'll make our stand at the bridge."

I nodded, even as my hope went into free-fall. The bridge was the backup plan, the last resort in holding the tide back. If we didn't hold the bridge, then this was over.

"I've already sent out the call. I told the people of Sterling Peak to evacuate whoever's left. We need to buy them some time."

My heart in my throat, my gaze searched for Torr and Noel. I caught sight of them still fighting, one of the ganta at their back. Lu was nearby. My breath came out shaky, adrenaline from the fight still coursing through me.

This was it. This would truly be the last stand. I met

Graham's gaze. A thousand emotions and words flew through the air between us. But neither of us said a word. We both had jobs to do. And each second we were out of the fight, lives were lost.

I bolted up into the air. Power built up in my chest. Taking a deep breath, I scanned the ground below me, marking my targets. I sent fireball after fireball at the demons as they crowded together.

But even with that, I could feel my strength waning. I had been fighting nonstop for what felt like hours. So had all the others. We couldn't keep up this pace for much longer.

To my right, Uriel and Vera were still locked in battle. They burst into the air, taking the fight up above.

Uriel threw something at Vera. I couldn't make out what it was. It looked like a dust of some sort. She stopped in mid-flight and plunged to the ground.

A gasp escaped me even as I darted toward her. Putting on a burst of speed, I caught her right before she hit. Crashing into the ground, I kept my arms around her as we rolled. We came to a stop, and I lay Vera gently on her back, noting the dark dust along her face.

"Hellstone dust," Vera whispered.

Cringing at the thought of it, I already felt myself weakening just being near it. I moved to wipe it from Vera's face, but she grabbed my hand. "No. Don't get it on you."

But it was too late. Dark smudges were along my arms from where I had grabbed Vera. It was already seeping into my skin. I could feel my energy draining away.

Uriel landed lightly on the ground only a few feet from us. He smiled as he walked toward us. "Look at this, the two of you just waiting for the kill."

CHAPTER 80

We were a dozen feet from the nearest fighters, and even if I called out to them, all they would do was die if they interfered. I held my tongue.

"You did good, Addie. You fought well," Vera whispered.

"It wasn't enough."

"But it was a good fight, a righteous one. There's no honor in Uriel's actions or Abbadon's."

Uriel smiled as he pulled a knife from his belt. "Maybe not, but there is victory."

Light burst across the sky. Uriel faltered, squinting as he looked skyward. The rest of the battle seemed to stop for a moment as well, as everyone turned their gaze at this new interruption. Shooting stars burst across the dark sky and aimed for the ground.

"Angels," I whispered. Cradling Vera tighter, knowing I wouldn't be able to protect her in my weakened state, I begged silently, *Please be here to help.*

As each light hit the ground, an angel in glorious armor stood straight and tall. In a heartbreaking moment, everyone held their breath, waiting to see whose side the angels would fight on.

Then an angel took a sword and rammed it into the stomach of the nearest demon. Her action broke the spell. Angels, dozens of them, continued to drop to the ground. And in each place they landed, demons died.

Uriel looked up in shock.

But before he could move, two angels dropped to the ground on either side of him. They latched onto his arms and put cuffs around his wrists. His sword dropped from his hand as he dropped to his knees.

"Hellstone cuffs," Vera whispered.

Another angel dropped lightly to the ground and walked over to us.

She pulled a pouch off her belt and stuck her hand in before coming up with a white powder. She blew it gently toward us. A light coating fell over both Vera and myself. As it sank into my skin, I felt my strength start to return.

"What is that?" I asked.

"It's an antidote to hellstone." She extended a hand and pulled Vera to her feet. I scrambled to my feet behind them. Turning to the fight, it was clear that the angels' arrival had turned the tide. Some of the demons were actually running back to the portal to escape.

But there was one standing at the edge of all the action. I met his gaze: Abaddon. Without a word, I burst into the air and flew over the heads of those still fighting. Abaddon stood waiting for me, his eyes lighting up at the sight of me coming near.

But I didn't reach him before Noel snuck up behind him and slammed a metal baton into the back of his knees, causing him to wobble. She dropped him to the ground and then slammed the baton into his face.

Blood burst from his nose as I dropped down and yanked the

amulet off his neck. Tossing it at Noel, I slammed my open hand down onto his chest, sending all of my power into him. "You will never hurt anyone again."

Electricity rolled from out of my hand, bursting into Abaddon, who screamed in pain. Noel fell back as Abaddon started to glow.

Energy pulsed out of my hand and into him over and over again. Slowly, his skin began to change. The dark green shifted paler and paler until it was the same color as a human's. At the same time, his body began to shrink, his horns crumbling to dust.

Falling back from him, my mouth dropped open and my eyes went wide. He lay on the ground now, in all ways appearing like a human man. His cheeks were gaunt, as if he was starving.

"Addie?" Noel asked, a tremor in her voice.

I held up a hand to keep her back as I inched forward.

Abaddon's eyes opened, and pale brown eyes met my gaze. Tears swam in them. A smile crossed his face. "Thank you," he whispered before his chest went still.

Noel moved to my side, leaning against me as she stared down at Abaddon. "What just happened?"

"I don't know." Had I somehow turned him human? Had he actually just died? Was that possible?

But the proof was right in front me. He didn't disappear like the other demons. He lay on the ground, fully human now, freed from his demon state.

Noel held up the amulet. "What do we do with this?"

Lucifer cut through the crowd, coming toward us he looked down at Abaddon, his eyes widening. Then he saw the amulet we held. "I'll take that," he said softly.

Without question, I handed it over to him. He dropped it on the ground and then took his sword and slammed it into the amulet.

A burst of energy exploded from it. The wave rolled over everyone on the battlefield. I stumbled back, holding on to Noel to keep her upright.

The wave of energy seemed to stop everyone in their tracks. Then, one by one, the demons started to disappear.

Stepping next to my father, I watched a seven-foot demon with massive horns simply vanish. A glance around showed no demons in the immediate area. "What just happened?"

He smiled. "Purgatory just reopened. All the souls that were supposed to have gone there rather than Hell have slipped into Purgatory. All that's left are the original demons."

"How'd you know that would work?" Noel asked.

"Just a sense. I could feel Michael's grace around it. And whatever it was doing, destroying it seemed the best option."

My gaze shifted from my father to Abbadon's body to the portal. The crazy idea that slipped through my mind earlier reemerged. I started toward it.

"Addie? What are you doing?" Noel asked as she jogged to catch up to me.

"I want to try something." Reaching the portal, two ganta stepped next to me as if to keep guard. I smiled my thanks up at them. Lucifer, who'd followed us, gently pulled Noel back and out of the way.

Closing my eyes, I raised my hands, staring at the portal. I pictured all the damage the demons had done, not just today but over the years. Then I pictured the portal shrinking and shrinking until it was gone.

A loud pop sounded, cutting through the air. My eyes flew open, and my jaw dropped. The portal was gone. The ganta sauntered away, but I stayed rooted in spot. "Did I just do what I think I did?"

"It's gone. The portal's gone," Lu said as he stared at me.

"You closed it?" Noel asked.

"I guess so." My mind raced as I pictured the other portals in Hell. "If that really worked, we could go back to Hell, close all of them."

Vera dropped down to the ground next to me, nodding at the spot where the portal had formerly been. "The angels and I will round up the last of the demons and send them back through. You did good, kid," she said, throwing an arm around me.

I looked up at her in shock and then looked around the battlefield. "Did we actually win?" I asked.

My father nodded before he took to the air. "I'm going to help."

Wrapping an arm around my waist, Noel stared up after them. "It's over?"

"I think so." Scanning the area around us, I frowned. "Have you seen Torr or Grunt?"

"I think I saw them back that way." She gestured back behind us.

As we turned, my legs felt wobbly. After all the energy we'd exerted, I was finally feeling the effects. Next to me, Noel tripped over nothing. I reached out and caught her before she hit the ground.

"Thanks," she said.

Together we stumbled back through the crowd. Even though I knew I should still be on guard, I simply wasn't capable of it. I'd turned Abaddon human. I'd closed the portal to Hell, and Purgatory was now open. My brain was simply fried at this point.

But I needn't have worried. There were no demons left. It was just the Rangers and the civilians. Most were walking wounded. People were walking amongst them, giving first aid. I caught sight of Dr. Jade setting up a triage center.

I promised I'd go help, but first I needed to find our family. And as if I'd conjured him, the crowd parted, and I caught sight of Torr. He carried a young woman over to Dr. Jade and placed her gently on the ground.

Then he turned, and his gaze caught mine. A relieved smile crossed his face as he started to make his way toward us, holding his side.

Scanning him as I hurried over, I didn't see any life-threatening injuries, although he had nicks and cuts all over the place. Grunt limped behind him and then dropped to the ground in front of us.

"You two okay?" I asked.

Torr nodded looking around. "Did we win?"

A smile began to spread across my face as I grabbed both Torr and Noel and hugged them tight. "Believe it or not, I think we did."

CHAPTER 81

ONE WEEK LATER

My father was right. Vera confirmed that Purgatory had indeed been empty. With the portal closed, no more demons could come through, at least at that location. But there were still some trapped on our side.

It took three days of working with the angels to roust them all. And then Vera and I went and closed all the other portals in the country. More portals across the globe were still open, but there were no reported incursions. Without Abaddon, Hell was no doubt in a state of turmoil.

Now I stood on the back lawn of Graham's estate. He stood next to me with his hand wrapped in mine. Despite our plans to finally get some time alone, there had simply been too much for both of us to do. Graham was overseeing the new government that would be formed across the country.

The first election would be held in two years' time for not only a prime minister, but for an advisory council. The positions were open to all, with certain age restrictions. But before he did that, he sent out a new policy that took place immediately: the distinction between Angel Blessed and Demon Cursed was no longer allowed.

He'd also taken D'Angelo's home and turned it into a halfway house for those who'd been displaced by the fighting. Right now, he was supposed to be reviewing the destruction that the demons had caused and the plans for how to fairly allocate rebuilding sources. Then he had another three funerals to attend. He'd been at multiples each day. All of the Seven had. There'd been simply too many for Graham to attend them all in person.

I knew it was the toughest part of his day. And I wanted to be there for him, but unfortunately, just like him, there were some duties only I could perform.

Graham's gaze was warm but worried as he gazed down at me. "Be careful. And if there are any problems, or anything doesn't feel right..."

"Trust my instincts," I said with a smile.

"Have I told you that before?" he asked.

"No, but I've said it a time or two." I glanced over at where Noel, Torr, and Micah stood. Behind them was Grunt and two ganta. Lu and I had transported a few of them back to Hell, but these two seemed to want to stay. They were a little younger than the others and seemed fond of my gang. So it looked like I now had three giant pets.

I probably should find a house for all of us to live.

Turning away, I simply added that to the giant list of to-dos I already had drummed up. Graham kissed my cheek. The warmth spread from there down to my toes. "Be careful," he whispered again into my ear before stepping back.

"Are you ready?" Lucifer asked as he stepped to my side.

Vera took my other side, and Callista, the angel who'd given us the antidote to the hellstone dust, stood next to her.

"I'm ready." Focusing my attention on the space in front of

us, I closed my eyes, picturing a portal and the destination I had in mind. Wind pushed my hair back, and I opened my eyes, unsurprised to see the portal. For the last few days, I'd been regularly making portals. Unlike the other portals, these were only temporary and would simply vanish as soon as we went through them.

It turned out it wasn't just Hell that I could portal to. I could make a portal to just about anywhere I thought about.

But this time, I wasn't taking us somewhere fun. No, this time, we were heading back into Hell.

CHAPTER 82

The portal emptied us out right outside the camp where we'd first freed the refugees. The camp was empty, not a soul in sight. We didn't waste any time. We simply headed to the location of the portal, and I closed it, just like I'd been doing for the last week.

For the next few hours, that was all we did—traveled from portal to portal, closing them. In that time, we only saw three demons, and they each kept their distance. The last portal we closed was just outside Jabal City. Once it was closed, I turned and looked back at the city. It was eerily quiet. I didn't see or hear a single person, demon or otherwise.

"They're really all gone," Lu said, looking around.

I nodded. We'd expected as much. All of the refugees had simply disappeared, including all the members of my father's camp.

Even Cornelius was gone. Tess had been with him. She had watched as he slowly disappeared from view.

"I still don't understand how all this happened," Callista said.

"Me either," I replied. "But I'm glad. I just wish we could be sure that everyone was in a better place."

"We are," a voice said from behind me.

Heart pounding, I whirled around. Then a smile burst across my face. "Cornelius."

He looked so healthy, so happy. He'd gained weight, and there was a peacefulness about him he hadn't had before.

The smile on my own face dimmed as I realized what his presence meant. My smile dropped and despair tore through me. "No. You were sent back to Hell?"

Cornelius shook his head. "No. I went to Purgatory."

Ver a frowned. "How are you here, then?"

Cornelius shrugged. "Apparently I've been chosen to deliver a message."

"From who?" I asked.

"I think you know," Cornelius said. "You've reopened Purgatory. Hell has been emptied of all but the original demons."

"What will happen to them now?" Lu asked.

"They'll spend their time here, and when, if, they start to see the error of their ways, they'll have a chance at Purgatory themselves."

"What about Abaddon?" Lu asked.

Glancing around, Cornelius said, "He's around here somewhere. I have a feeling he'll be here for a while. But there are hopes that even he is on his way to change."

It should have been good news, but fear took root in my chest. "But if that's the case, what does that mean for my father?"

"Lucifer has been a good and faithful servant. He gets to choose his next steps. He may return to on high, or if he wishes, he may spend time somewhere else." Cornelius gave me a knowing look.

My father took my hand. "That's an easy choice."

"I thought it might be," Cornelius said. "You have done well, Addie. More than was expected. You can return home knowing that the world is a better, safer place because of your part in it."

Staring across at the man from me, I knew something was off. "You're not Cornelius, are you?"

He smiled. "Not exactly."

A gasp sounded from either side of me, and then all three angels lowered to their knees, their heads bowed. The peace and love coming from the being across from me rolled through me. "Are you—"

"A friend," he said. "And a fan. I'm proud of you, daughter of Lucifer. And now I'd like to give you a gift." He stepped forward, gently touching the side of my temple.

Memories rushed through my mind. I stumbled under the onslaught of them. My father jumped to his feet, holding me steady. Looking into his eyes, I felt all the love he had for me. Countless memories of the two of us together flashed through my mind. Tears pressed against the back of my eyes.

"Dad."

Tears appeared in his own eyes before he hugged me tight. "You remember."

I held onto him as tears rolled down my cheeks. How could I have forgotten him? And my mother, I saw her. I felt in my heart all the love she had for me as well. "Mom," I whispered, and my dad held me tighter.

The two of us stood there, clinging to one another for a long time before finally I stepped back and looked around in confusion.

Vera, who'd gotten to her feet, smiled as she wrapped her arm around me. "He's gone. But he's never too far away."

CHAPTER 83

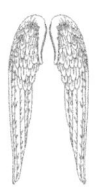

It was strange stepping through the portal back into Sterling Peak. So much had happened. I felt like I'd just gotten a huge chunk of my life back.

And yet, even with the memories, I knew that those times were in the past. My future was waiting for me here.

Speaking of which, Graham sat on the back veranda. He was the only one there. He jumped to his feet as we appeared. Vera and Calista took to the sky without a word. I frowned as I watched them leave.

"I'll keep an eye on the kids. Graham looks like he needs to talk." My father kissed my cheek before his wings unfurled, and he took off as well.

A glance at Graham's face made it apparent that my father was right. Worry rolled through me. "What's wrong? Did something happen?"

"What? No, no. Everything's fine." His words were right, but I could hear an undercurrent of nerves. Before I could ask again what was going on, he took my hand. "I need you to come with me. Can you do that?"

"Of course."

He smiled and drew me around the side of the house. As we stepped off the estate, we headed down toward the bridge. He slipped his arm around my waist and pulled me tight. Before we reached the bridge, he turned down Tess's street.

"Are we visiting Tess?"

"Nope, we're going to the house next to hers."

I frowned. "Who lives there?"

"You'll see," he teased.

Bursting with curiosity but also liking this playful side of Graham, I let him lead me to a cute little two-story home. It was a little bigger than Tess's but not by much. Without knocking, Graham opened the front door and stepped inside.

"Won't the owner be upset that we're just wandering in?"

"Well, I guess we should ask them. Addie, are you upset we're here?"

"What?"

He took a step back, throwing his arms wide. "This is yours. For you, Micah, Noel, and Torr. There's even a giant yard where I think the ganta will fit. They might wander over to Tess's sometimes, but I'm sure she'll be okay with that."

"This is mine?" I asked.

He nodded. "The residents of Sterling Peak and Blue Forks, along with the Rangers, bought it for you. After everything you did, we all agreed this was the least you deserve."

I stared around in shock. There were thick wooden floors covered in deep plush rugs. A comfortable sectional was placed in front of what I was sure was a working fireplace. There was a dining room to the right, and down the hall, I could make out a kitchen. Stairs in front of me led to a second floor.

I had a home. I turned in a circle, trying to take it all in. When I turned back to Graham, he was kneeling on one knee. A ring was in his hand. "And I'm hoping that there might be room here for me too."

I stared at him and then the ring. "You want . . . Are you asking . . ." I couldn't seem to get the words out.

"Addie Baker, will you marry me?"

Joy burst through my chest as I threw my arms around his neck. "Yes, yes, a thousand times yes."

Graham laughed, twirling me around. Then he placed me on the ground and stared deep into my eyes before his lips found mine.

"She said yes!" Noel called out just before the front door opened and people spilled in. Donovan and Tess carried in trays of food, along with the rest of the Seven. Noel and Micah sprinted over to both of us, hugging us tight. Lucifer, Vera, and Grunt carried drinks. Beth and Nigel from next door hurried in as well, both of them with their arms ladened down with trays.

With Micah's arms wrapped around me, I smiled at Graham over his head. "What about your house?"

"I'm turning it into apartments for the people from Blue Forks."

"What about Mary and Franklin?"

"I was hoping they could live here. There's an apartment along the back that would be perfect for them."

"Absolutely." And those were the last words I was able to say to him before I was pulled away by my father to give me a hug and wish us both congratulations.

For the next thirty minutes, it seemed like everyone I had ever known, even in passing, wished me congratulations. The party spilled out into the yard and even into Tess's yard. Everywhere I looked, there were people talking, laughing, and having a good time. A band even appeared on Tess's back porch, and people cleared space for dancing.

After two hours, Graham pulled me into a quiet corner of the yard. Hidden under a willow tree, he pushed my hair back behind my ear. "Are you happy?"

I looked up at him and at all the people celebrating with us. I never imagined this was what my life could look like. The traces of the demon war were still evident in the damage to Sterling Peak and the fear in people's eyes. It would still be a long road back from that. And yet right at this moment, all that worry, fear, and horror seemed so far away.

Wrapping my arms around Graham's waist, I smiled up at him. "I'm better than happy. I'm home."

Also by Sadie Hobbes

The Demon Cursed Series

Demon Cursed

Demon Revealed

Demon Heir

Demon War

The Four Kingdoms Series

Order of the Goddess

BOOKS BY R.D. BRADY:

Hominid

The Belial Series (in order)

The Belial Stone

The Belial Library

The Belial Ring

Recruit: A Belial Series Novella

The Belial Children

The Belial Origins

The Belial Search

The Belial Guard

The Belial Warrior

The Belial Plan

The Belial Witches

The Belial War

The Belial Fall

The Belial Sacrifice

The Belial Rebirth Series

The Belial Rebirth

The Belial Spear

The Belial Restored

The Belial Blood

The Belial Angel

The Belial Templar

The A.L.I.V.E. Series

B.E.G.I.N.

A.L.I.V.E.

D.E.A.D.

R.I.S.E.

S.A.V.E.

The H.A.L.T. Series

Into the Cage

Into the Dark

The Steve Kane Series

Runs Deep

Runs Deeper

The Unwelcome Series

Protect

Seek

Proxy

The Nola James Series

Surrender the Fear

Escape the Fear

Tackle the Fear

Return the Fear

The Gates of Artemis Series

The Key of Apollo

The Curse of Hecate

The Return of the Gods

Be sure to sign up for R.D.'s mailing list to be the first to hear when she has a new release!

About the Author

Sadie Hobbes is a dog lover, martial artist, avid runner, mother, wife, and Amazon best selling thriller writer under the name RD Brady. She can often be found before dawn wandering her yard with her dogs, dictating her latest novel. If anyone were to see her, they would seriously question her sanity as well as her fashion choices. (Think rain boots over pajamas plus a bulky cardigan). But it works for her!

If you'd like to hear about her upcoming releases, sign up for her newsletter through her facebook page.

She can be reached at sadiehobbesauthor@gmail.com or on her Facebook page.

Copyright © 2022 by Sadie Hobbes

Demon War

Published by Scottish Seoul Publishing, LLC, Dewitt, NY

All Rights Reserved. No part of this book may be reproduced or transmitted in any form or by any means, electronic or mechanical, including photocopying, recording, or by any information storage and retrieval system without the written permission of the author, except where permitted by law.

Printed in the United States of America.

Printed in Great Britain
by Amazon